Danny King was born in the wacky ██████████ celebrated throughout the land for its ██████████ ers. In 1979 he moved to the marginally less wacky town of Yateley in Hampshire where the townsfolk passed up dancing in favour of smashing bottles over each other's heads and kicking in the kebab van on Friday nights. He has worked as a shelf-stacker, a hod carrier, a postman, a sub-editor and a magazine editor, but now works from home for himself. And you don't win a bun for guessing which one he prefers. *Milo's Run* is his sixth book and the sequel to *Milo's Marauders*, but don't worry if you haven't read *Marauders* yet because he gives you a bit of the old catch-up schtick in the prologue. He is currently working on his seventh and eighth books, *School for Scumbags* and *White Collar* respectively, but still hasn't made up his mind which to pump out next. For details of past, present and forthcoming books, including film, TV and stage developments, check out his website at dannyking-books.com. He now lives in Stoke Newington, north London with his girlfriend Jeannie, where again nobody dances, but that's just because they're far too busy towing away his car every five minutes.

Praise for Danny King's *Milo's Marauders*

'Enjoyable, unpretentious stuff, and King knows his onions – he's done porridge more than once' *FHM*

'Anyone with a pulse will find themselves pulled into this novel and be engrossed and amused by its heart-racing antics and wit . . . These cockney jokers had me literally laughing out loud on many occasions' *The Crack*

'A snappy, slangy novel that morphs heist caper with black comedy and crawls inside the criminal mindset' *Buzz*

Praise for Danny King's *Diaries*

The Burglar Diaries

'One of the few writers to make me laugh out loud. Danny King's brilliant at making you love characters who essentially are quite bad people' David Baddiel

'Occasionally hilarious, if morally dubious, *The Burglar Diaries* is well worth buying – and definitely worth half-inching' *GQ*

'This is the sweet-as-a-nut, hilariously un-PC account of the jobs [Bex] has known and loved – the line-ups, the lock-ups and the cock-ups. If ever there was an antidote to *Bridget Jones's Diary* this is it. *The Burglar Diaries* is the first in a series. Long may it run' *Mirror*

The Bank Robber Diaries

'It's low on morals but big on laughs, so if you can thieve one, by all means go for it!' *BBM*

'Danny looks set for a long and healthy career going straight . . . to the top of the best-sellers list' *Penthouse*

'The best (and funniest) British Crime novel since *The Burglar Diaries*' *Ice*

The Hitman Diaries

'Once again the comic genius and hilarious one-liners have you warming to the anti-social protagonists of Chris, Sid and Vince; more cock-ups than hold ups . . . a thoroughly un-pc but rewarding novel' *BBM*

'The action flows as thick as the blood and the jet-black humour will leave you wondering whether to laugh, cry or vomit' *Jack*

The Pornographer Diaries

'Danny King's filthiest and funniest novel yet' *Buzz*

'A wonderfully funny book for any bloke who's ever perused the top shelf; and for any woman whose boyfriend keeps a porn stash under the stairs' *Desire*

MILO'S RUN

Danny
King

A complete catalogue record for this book can
be obtained from the British Library on request

The right of Danny King to be identified as the author of this
work has been asserted by him in accordance with the
Copyright, Designs and Patents Act 1988

First published in 2006 by Serpent's Tail,
4 Blackstock Mews, London N4 2BT
website: www.serpentstail.com

Printed by Mackays of Chatham, plc

10 9 8 7 6 5 4 3 2 1

Acknowledgements

Once again I'd like to dust off the usual suspects and line them up for a big thank you. First up, my editor John Williams, a consummate pro and a stand-up guy, at least until the pubs open; next, the big boss himself, Pete Ayrton, and the rest of the chaps at Serpent's Tail, without whose tireless work and continued support I'd have to get a real job; to my best mate Brian McCann for running the best wedding/portraiture photography business in and around Sandhurst at unbelievably competitive rates (I don't know how he does it) and for posting all the details on his website www.brianmccann.co.uk; to Clive Andrews (and wife Jo) and all the chaps and chicks at the *Mirror*, thanks for all the subbing shifts and how about tapping that star key on my reviews a few more times?; to Dan Coleman for giving me an advertising speak tutorial for a forthcoming book in exchange for looking at print-offs of the view he'll have from his seat in Arsenal's new stadium; to Nat Saunders for the photographs on my website that I keep forgetting to credit him for; to my fabulous foreign rights agent Emma White for telling me that she's never been thanked in a book and for flogging all of mine to a load of bewildered Belgians; to Céline Rivere for passing her translation exam translating extracts from *The Hitman Diaries* into foreign; to

Kate Finnigan and Jolyon Green for inviting me to their wedding and for agreeing to let Jeannie tie a piece of elastic to the bouquet; to Andrew Crockett and Petra Kolarikova for pretty much the same deal only out in the Czech Republic, which means I'm going to have to get on a plane when I hate flying; to the late dearly departed Ronnie, for all the love, dead birds and fur balls he brought into Sam Sidaway's life; and finally to you guys out there, the fans, for continuing to buy my books when it really should be obvious by now that I'm just a big foul-mouthed illiterate dimbo. I can't thank you all enough.

This book is dedicated to my wonderful, beautiful, funky girlfriend, Jeannie Crockett, who I met while writing it, for teaching me the true meaning of happiness and the proper use of exclamation marks! With all my love!!

Prologue: A brief recap

Right, then, where were we? Oh yes, that was it, we were wondering where Parky had got to . . .

'We can't sit here waiting for him so put your fucking foot down!' I shouted at Patsy, prompting him to spin us out into the road just as half a dozen angry coppers sprinted around the corner after us.

I stared at them through the back window with a mixture of horror and relief as they shrank down to the size (if not shape) of ants then disappeared altogether after we went round a couple of twists and turns. Goody, in the front, looked back at me and puffed out his cheeks as if to say, 'Phew, that was close'. Unfortunately, as far as I was aware, the Old Bill didn't work along the lines of 'out of sight, out of mind' so I knew all we'd done was bought ourselves half a mile and a few precious seconds while every copper in the pay of the county of Hampshire frantically searched their pockets for their car keys to get on after us.

'Where are we going?' Patsy asked, as he wrestled the steering wheel this way and that. Patsy was almost breathless with panic and I didn't blame him, the shit we'd just pulled.

'As far away from here as possible,' I fervently hoped.

I think, for the benefit of those of you who've just come

in, I should perhaps take a moment to backtrack a little and explain what it was we were running from.

There'd been eight of us originally: myself (Darren Miles, or Milo to my friends); Goody and Patsy, who were in the car with me; Parky, who had made it as far as the car but then had just kept on going (fuck knows where he was now – the back of a police van, I'd stick a tenner on); Jimbo and Bob (Jimbo was tackled and brought down by the Old Bill as we were making our break for it, but the last time I saw Bob was when we were still inside the supermarket); Jacko, who I also saw stopped in his tracks by half a dozen uniforms; and Norris, who I'd deliberately sent off in the wrong direction just to fuck him up. You may think badly of me doing this to a colleague – honour among thieves and all that old guff – but it was Norris's fault we'd found ourselves in tramp's padding in the first place, so lots of luck with lollipops sticking out of it to that bastard.

'Always someone else's fault, isn't it, Milo, never your own?'

This is what my brother Terry, or more likely my former girlfriend, Alice, would say if they could've heard me recount all this.

Girlfriend? Actually, I take that back. Girlfriend's not a big enough word for what Alice meant to me. She was everything to me. Absolutely everything. My love, my decent side, my smile, my . . . Alice. That's what she was. She was my Alice.

Unfortunately, I'd royally fucked that one up just as I seemed to fuck up just about everything else so that she was no longer my Alice, she was now just a dull ache, a nagging regret and an emptiness in the pit of my stomach. I would've loved her to have been more to me once again but she'd just as soon smash a plate over my head or more likely turn me into the Old Bill as look at me these days. Why, you might ask? Well, I'll tell you, I'd committed the cardinal sin. No, I didn't knock her about or shag her sister for a joke, I did something much worse — I made a promise to her which I failed to keep. Actually, come to think of it, I'd made hundreds of promises to her during the course of our time together which I'd failed to keep, but this one was the big one; I'd promised her that I wouldn't go back to prison again, and see if you can guess what I did.

Yes, that's right, five years I got (well, three and a half if you knock off my early release).

Unfortunately it wasn't early enough for Alice's liking. They say that in the scheme of things five years is barely a tick of the clock, but in this tick Alice managed to boot me out of her life, find someone called Brian who didn't knock her about, shag her sister for a joke or, most import-antly of all, go to prison for five years at a time, marry him, have a child with him and get on with the business of moving on with her life — which isn't bad going when you think about it. By the time I got out again (just a few months ago) all that was left of our once wonderful relationship was a frosty stare and the refusal to believe, or care, that I'd changed my criminal ways.

Well, she was half right, I guess, for it wasn't my old tricks that I got up to but a whole load of new ones this time around. Boy, what a mess.

The biggest robbery this county, and certainly this town, had ever seen — probably. A supermarket — a big, out-of-town megastore. The one up by where the old gas works used to be, you know, just past the ring road. We'd tried to knock it off.

God, it makes me shake my head in disbelief just remem-bering how optimistic we'd been. I mean, what the fuck were we thinking about trying to hold up a supermarket? Oh, don't worry, we'd had a plan alright; hit the place on a Sunday night (1 a.m. Monday morning actually) when only a few shelf-stackers and a couple of minimum-wage security guards stood between us and what we thought was £120,000 (it actually turned out to be more like £350,000 but we didn't find this out until the morning).

You see Norris – he was the fucking criminal genius mastermind behind the plan – reckoned he had all the inside knowledge to pull this job off and assured us he'd thought of everything. Well, he'd been a shelf-stacker there in the past so of course he'd known all about the safes and alarms and security provisions and all the rest of it because the supermarket liked to keep their lowly can monkeys in the loop about these sorts of things, didn't they (I still can't believe I believed him about this)?

Unfortunately, the one thing he didn't know about was the time lock on the safe. We'd had the codes, the keys, the staff and the night manager at our disposal but there was nothing we could do about any of it until eight the next morning because that was when the time lock deactivated. Unbelievable.

So now you know why I was so pissed off with Norris. Also, he's a full-time wanker and has been his whole life, way too many things to go into now and none of them particularly relevant so you'll just have to take my word for it. No bad thing could come out of Norris doing a serious stretch.

And a serious stretch was what the eight of us were suddenly facing the next day when, with just a quarter of an hour to go until eight o'clock, the police suddenly rolled up in numbers and told us to pack it in.

Twenty years, that's what I reckoned we'd all get. Well, me certainly. Some of the lads had a little bit of form for petty thievery and so on but I was the one with time already on my card, so I'd be the one they'd throw the book at. Twenty years. That's like a quarter of an average man's life (or a third for blokes from Glasgow). And not just a quarter, but the best quarter. Those few short years in between childhood and middle age when a man was meant to nail it all down and make his mark in life. The only things I'd get to mark down if Patsy didn't get us out of here would be notches on my cell wall — 7,305 of them in all.

What had I got myself into?

Armed robbery, that was what. Not only that, conspiracy, false imprisonment and wounding with intent, perhaps even attempted murder, you never know. I've always thought of myself as a bit of a slippery customer but you'd be amazed what the Old Bill can make stick once they put their minds to it. See, we'd had a bit of a mishap in the canteen during the night, which was where we'd held all the shelf-stackers and so on. A few of the lads had got a bit careless and let their guns off by accident and a ricochet had nicked one of the shop girls in the arm. It was nothing serious and we'd patched her up and turned her over to the Old Bill as soon as they'd arrived but none of this would count for much once the courts got to hear about it. These wankers didn't have a sense of humour when it came to gunning down innocent young shop girls during the course of robberies, no matter how flukey a shot it had been.

Not only this, one of the lads had taken a couple of pot shots at the Old Bill from the supermarket when they'd first shown up. They'd only been warning shots, to stop them from storming the place before we knew what was going on, but even so, that doubled the sentence for all eight of us right there. It didn't matter who pulled the trigger, we'd fired on the Old Bill, and that was big-boy territory. Christ only knows how bad things would've got if the silly fucker had actually killed one of them by mistake. They would probably have sent in the SAS or somebody to blow all our heads off. Well, perhaps not, but I doubt we would've found ourselves in one piece come the end of proceedings.

So there we were, trapped in a supermarket with cops on all sides, £350,000 in used notes, about a hundred hostages and no way out. And, worst of all, Alice giving me a right fucking hard time about it through a megaphone the other side of the police lines. Just what I needed. Weasel (that's Detective Sergeant Haynes to his friends, or at least it would be if he had any) had brought her down the moment he'd sussed out I was the man behind the mask. I don't know why he'd had to involve her, he knew as well as anyone that it was over between me and Alice. I think he just went and got her to be a cunt about things. Insult to ugliness and that whole crate of bananas. One final humiliation in front of the world for luckless old Milo and his prison-bound buddies.

Well, we'd shown them. Or at least three of us had. As for the rest of the lads, the poor fuckers, what could I do? It had been every man for himself when we'd made our break for it and it could just as well have been me who'd been nabbed today instead of them (it might still be, in fact) so what could anyone do about it? There'd been no guarantees, no bullshit promises that I'd lead them out of the supermarket and into the promised land of freedom, hallelujah, but we'd all signed up for it nevertheless. Slim to fuck-all chance, that's what odds I'd given us of still being loose this evening, but slim to fuck-all looked worth a punt from where we'd been sitting. I mean, what did we have to lose?

So, how had we managed to get away?

It was a combination of ideas really. We knew we couldn't shoot our way out and we seriously doubted we could tunnel our way out. We certainly couldn't drive, fly, beam or flush our way out of there, unfortunately, so this really only left us with one option – we ran.

Patsy had been posted as lookout when the robbery had started (and a fine fucking job he'd made of it too) so that he'd been well out of it when the police had turned up. So well out of it, in fact, that the lanky bastard had stretched those beanpole legs of his and scarpered home to leave the rest of us to it. Well, I soon saw about that. With a few well-aimed threats and half-baked promises (mostly about the rest of us agreeing to testify that he hadn't been there from the start so that he'd escape with a much lighter sentence if our laughable escape plan didn't quite come off) I'd managed to lure him back and get him to park up just beyond the police lines with the motor running.

Unfortunately, only four of us tops could probably have found seats in the waiting transport, but I really didn't see this as a problem – this was how slim I thought our chances were. Still, just to be on the safe side, I'd sent Norris off in the wrong direction just before we set off and that thinned us down a little.

Yes, yes, yes, we understand all this, but how did you get past the police lines? I hear you skim-reading.

Well, it was simple really, I started a stampede. We had a hundred or so shelf-stackers at our disposal so we bunched them all up together by the exit, told them we'd made a bomb, then hid among them as they fled for their lives. Bit of an irresponsible thing to do really and I'm sure a few people were hurt in the resulting mêlée but, you know, I was all out of PC ideas at the time. The Old Bill outnumbered us on all sides so I figured we needed to find a way to somehow outnumber them. This idea was as good as any. No, actually that's not true – this idea was the best of the bunch.

We'd made a bomb too, not a real genuine bomb, just something that looked like a bomb to whip the shelf-stackers into one. A load of Calor gas bottles connected with wires to a sandwich box full of Battenberg cake that was about as likely to explode as my socks. Still, it did the trick and everyone fought to get as far away from it as possible.

Me and the lads had, of course, changed our duds and were now dressed as shelf-stackers on the outside and walking cash dispensers on the in, what with all the cash we'd taped to our bodies. We'd originally estimated that we'd each see around £15,000 from this job, not a lot when you think about it, but then we didn't realise it was going to take all fucking night and a re-enactment of the end of *Escape to Victory* to get us out of there, did we? In the event, we'd actually bagged closer to £38,000 each (or in me and Goody's case £60,000, as there'd only been the two of us there when we'd finally got the safe open), though Patsy knew none of this. Like I said, he'd been outside the whole time, so as far as he was concerned he was still expecting just £15,000.

Of course, to the lads I'd insisted on bringing out his full share of £38,000 with me under my clothes but now I was here, sitting in the back seat of the car counting it all up in my head, I was in two minds as to whether or not to do the right thing by him.

I mean, the bastard did leave us there to stew, didn't he. Also, I needed every last penny to get as far away from Britain as possible (and stay there) so it would be a bit naive of me to hand over £23,000 unnecessarily, money that I might very well need just a few short years down the line if I wanted to stay this side of the Scrubs gate.

Also, I might add, my sentence was likely to be a hell of a lot longer than Patsy's should we both get caught. If I was to ask Patsy which he'd rather have, ten years less or £23,000 more, I knew which he'd plump for, so why bother actually asking him?

Put like that, I was actually doing Patsy a favour (perhaps I should take another grand for my troubles?).

This is the true beauty of having a criminal mind, you can justify just about anything to yourself if you try hard enough.

'Where are we going?' I think was the last thing Patsy had asked before I went off into one.

'As far away from here as possible,' I replied.

'Thailand?' Patsy suggested. He'd had a thing about Thailand ever since he'd read that book, *The Beach*. He reckoned it was all true and that there were actually sun-drenched beaches like the one in the book, magical, mystical places where modern man had yet to tread, where there was nothing to do all day but swing about in hammocks, eat coconuts and read shit books like *The Beach*. I mean, yeah, sounds nice, doesn't it, particularly if, like Patsy, you'd spent most of your life selling Biros and fags in RG News six days a week, but I'd bet the reality of it would be a lot more boring. I bet, after three days of looking at parrots and building sandcastles, you'd get bored out of your fucking mind. I know I would. Get a nice tan, yeah, sure, lovely, everyone likes that, but then who could go more than a week without going down the pub? That was the thing I'd missed most of all when I was inside (other than Alice, of course), being able to just stroll down the road and get myself a pint of lager and, if I was feeling flush, a packet of cashews.

In fact, I was making myself thirsty just thinking about it. Not that there was much chance of us stopping off for a quick one just yet.

'Thailand? Possibly,' I told Patsy as we skidded into Coombe Lane. I caught Goody's eye and gave him a wink to get him on board then added, 'Though I'll be fucked if I know how we're meant to get there with no money, Pats.'

Patsy looked a little crestfallen at this, although that could've just been relief at not burying us halfway up the front of the 485 bus to Winchester.

Goody rearranged his jutted-out eyebrows in confusion and thought about what I'd just said.

'What?' he finally asked.

'Listen, lads, don't worry about the money, I've got some money,' Patsy shouted back to us as he overtook a long line of traffic and ran a yellow light. 'I did as you suggested, I emptied the safe at work and had about five grand away. That should give us a little bit of a chance. Also, if we can stop at a cashpoint, I've still got a few quid in the bank. It's not much but it's better than nothing,' he told me, making me feel like the biggest cunt in the world.

I thought about this for a moment then let my conscience get the better of me.

'Actually, Pats, I was only joking, we did get the money,' I reluctantly confessed.

Patsy swerved from side to side in surprise and we suddenly picked up an extra 10 mph from somewhere.

'You did? Fucking hell! How much?'

'Let's just concentrate on getting out of here first, we can think about that later,' I quickly said before Goody managed to stick his big fat size-nines in it.

'You're the boss, Milo,' Patsy said, getting his head down. 'Right, where to?'

Part One
RUNNING

Losing the Old Bill

'Keep going this way, up to the high street and get to the multi-storey next to the Metcalfe Centre.'

'Why? What's there?' Goody asked.

'A roof,' I told him.

'What?'

See, it was like this – no matter how much distance we put between us and the Old Bill on the ground, the flash bastards had a police helicopter motoring around overhead the last time I'd looked and those things were harder to shake off than a rumour in a playground (especially if you were the drama teacher). There's no traffic up in the air, they can travel at 150 mph and they're equipped with the latest *You've Been Framed* technology. The only way to lose them is to duck out of sight and switch motors before they can converge every flatfoot in the area on your position. If we'd been in London we could probably have jumped out and onto the Underground and lost them that way, but the only underground things around here were the twice-monthly all-male parties that Trevor and Mitch in number 28 thought nobody knew about and a fat lot of good they were going to do us. No, we had to put something solid between us and the eyes in the sky and find a new set of wheels. And we had to be quick about it.

'Just get under cover. I don't care if you have to bomb the wrong way up the exit, just get us out of sight,' I ordered Patsy.

I looked at the speedo. We were doing between 60 and 75 mph up some pretty suburban streets and I didn't like it one bit. Luckily, most of the midday traffic, which wasn't actually that much, to be honest, was still tied up around the supermarket. The police had the whole place sealed off in all directions and cars heading that way were backed up a couple of miles on either side of the store. Coming away from the place was another matter. These roads were relatively clear because nobody particularly wanted to come away (except us). Half the town had taken the day off work to go up there and see all the local scumbags get their comeuppance and they weren't about to leave without seeing something they could tell their mates about.

As it happened, this worked out very nicely for us.

'There! There! That left, down there!' I shouted in Patsy's ear as he flung the car into Pemberton Avenue.

I looked through the back window. There was still no sign of the Old Bill. A lot of them must've either been a bit slow off the mark, penned in or a bit of both. I doubt they expected to have to use their motors. The element of surprise had been with us. But that surprise wouldn't last long thanks to those nosey cunts in the clouds.

'Right here! This one. It's alright, it's a short cut.'

Patsy yanked up the handbrake and spun the car the full 180 degrees, slamming me around in the back seat like a pea in a whistle and making Goody somehow scream and suck in a breath at the same time. The back of the Orion came to rest against the front of a Mondeo and we lost precious seconds wearing out a bit of tarmac before Patsy had us pointing in the right direction again.

'Just keep it nice and steady, you're doing fine,' I reassured him. 'But just fucking hurry up about it as well, alright?'

There couldn't have been more than half a mile of side streets between us and the main road but Patsy somehow managed to lose himself twice and clobber six more cars along the way before we burst out onto the main London road.

'Right, that's it, now put your foot down and use your horn, that's what it's there for.'

Most of the other cars on the road got out of our way a bit sharpish when we loomed large in their rear-view mirrors tooting our horn and flying like a judge out of a whorehouse, but there was the odd Rover or traffic island that thought they had right of way, though neither was there for very long.

'Slow down, for fuck's sake, Pats!' Goody screamed at him, white faced, white knuckled and green gilled.

'Don't you dare, Pats, fucking go for it, almost there,' I countered.

We skimmed the side of a bus, broke every window in the Orion and ran over a pigeon before we finally had the Metcalfe Centre in sight, and when we did I checked out of where the back window had been and was amazed at the distinct lack of blue flashing lights.

Unbelievable. Somebody up there must've had money on us.

'SHIT!' Patsy shrieked with terror, avoiding a cyclist by the skin of his cagoule and driving over a bin instead.

'Just a little bit farther, Pats, keep it together,' I urged him, and looked up ahead to where we wanted to be.

There was a little bit of a tailback heading towards the turning for the car park so I told Patsy to get up onto the pavement and drive around them. People dived into shop doorways and over walls to get out of ours and death's way as we mounted the kerb and drove at them as if they weren't there. Surprisingly, no one comically fell off a ladder, ended up swinging from a banner or pushed a pie into anyone else's face that I saw, though one bloke did accidentally stumble through a plate-glass window, but I wouldn't have said that was all that funny. Strangely amusing, perhaps, but not funny.

We screeched around the last bend to the multi-storey and found three cars and a ticket machine barring our entrance. Patsy was so petrified that he was working on pure instinct and started queuing up to take a ticket. However, next to the Way In there was the Way Out, so I smacked Patsy on the back of the head and told him to shift our arses up there.

'What the fuck are you waiting for, Pats?'

Unfortunately, a big yellow barrier barred our entry up the exit and unfortunately those cunts in NCP had decided to make theirs out of steel and not balsa wood, which was what I'd been given to believe, through years of watching cop movies, was industry standard for car park barriers.

We smacked into it once and smashed what was left of the windscreen into our faces at a hundred miles an hour. I thought we were going to be stuck there but a moment later some shopping-laden housewife stuck her ticket in the machine and the barrier lifted off our bonnet and we had our way in. Patsy got straight on to it and drove at her Audi with all the menace he could muster, forcing her into a quick reverse and out of our way.

'All change,' I told the lads, kicking open the crinkled back passenger door and thanking the Orion for all it had done for us.

Patsy and Goody climbed out along with me. All three of us looked a little bit wobbly on our pins. My heart was going like Minnie the Moocher and it felt like I didn't have a single hair on my body that was touching another. I sucked in a great lungful of air and immediately looked around for a second set of wheels.

'Which car?' Patsy asked, almost doubled up with exhaustion.

'Hers will do,' I told them, pointing at our new friend in the Audi. 'I'll do the driving this time if you don't mind, Pats, you just get her in the back and keep her quiet,' I said, and we surrounded her motor on all sides and yanked open the doors.

'What, are we taking her with us or something?'

'No time to explain, just do as I say,' I shouted, and pointed my gun in her face. The housewife stared down the barrel of my gun and stretched all the holes in her face.

We had to take her with us, unfortunately, we didn't have a choice. I wasn't taking her to use as a hostage or anything like that (believe me, I'd had enough of hostages to last me a life sentence), we just couldn't leave her behind to go blabbing to the Old Bill as to what car the tall, fat and wiry e-fits had changed into because this would've defeated the whole purpose of changing cars. All I wanted to do was get the helicopter's eyes off us long enough so that we could carjack our way out of town, put a few miles between us and Weasel, then find somewhere to hole up and have a cup of tea until this all blew over, but we couldn't very well do this if we left behind a witness every time we made a move. You could argue that there were plenty of other witnesses all around, but despite our unauthorised entrance, none of the multi-storey's other customers seemed to be paying us much attention. As long as we didn't make too big a scene of this we could get out of here and clear off before anyone started taking an interest.

'Open your gob and I'll fucking kill you. Do as I tell you and you'll live,' I growled at the housewife, pulling her from the driver's seat and handing her to Patsy. Patsy stuffed her into the back and dived in on top of her and her shopping bags while me and Goody climbed in the front. I scanned all around the car park but no one seemed to be gawping at us in open-mouthed horror (or even slowing down for a butcher's).

'Help, no, help . . .' she tried yelling, but Patsy pushed his hand over her cakehole and his gun under her chin and we drove through the still-open barrier.

'Get down in front, Goody. You too, Pats, they're looking for three of us, so keep your loaves out of sight.'

Goody and Patsy did as they were told and I pulled out of the car park and back onto the high street. Up the far end of the street (about half a mile away), in the direction we'd just come from, the Old Bill Roadshow suddenly skidded into view, sending people jumping for their lives all over again. Somehow I resisted the temptation to whack my foot down and get us out of there on the double, and managed to keep it together enough to calmly cruise out of there at a steady pace, around the mini-roundabout, off to the right, then up the nearest side street before the Old Bill closed the place down.

I realised that the pie in the sky had directed them to the car park and reckoned that as long as I drove carefully and sensibly enough we could put a maze of houses between us and them before they'd figured out we'd swapped motors.

'Stay down, everyone,' I kept telling them as I steered us nice and gently over a dozen speed bumps then up a hill, around a school, through an underpass and down a couple more side streets, zigzagging us as far away from all that commotion as possible.

The suburbs were quiet but this was just because we'd temporarily shaken off our pursuers. I gave this Audi's anonymity about five minutes tops but these five minutes, at a steady 30 mph, were enough to put a couple of miles between us and those brave wankers in blue.

As we went along, I kept my eyes open for possibilities. I could feel time ticking down and wanted to swap the Audi for something else as soon as possible, this time somewhere

where there weren't so many CCTV cameras to record us doing it.

I drove around for perhaps another mile or so before admitting to myself that we'd probably used up our luck quota for the day already and that any further breaks we'd almost certainly have to make for ourselves.

Beechbrook Avenue, the road we were travelling up at the moment, was a bit of a posh old neighbourhood, but one I'd deliberately targeted. See, an avenue has trees on it, and Beechbrook Avenue was so resplendent (an appropriate word for this street and one I've been using ever since Porno Paddy dropped it on the Scrabble board in Brixton and walked away with all our fags) that the main drag was practically overgrown with a canopy of leaves. If we managed to swap cars here, the helicopter would have a job spotting the abandoned Audi from the sky. Unfortunately, there were no conveniently open garage doors or further female shoppers to kidnap, everything was frustratingly quiet.

I drove around a couple more roads before finally passing another car. A Metro – what the fuck were we meant to do with that? I let the lucky bastard go about her business and felt my insides start to tighten.

Only twelve minutes earlier me and Goody had been standing in a supermarket surrounded on all sides by armed Old Bill. We'd done so unbelievably amazingly well to get out of there and this far – farther than I'd ever imagined possible – that we couldn't let it slip now. And by the way, I do seriously mean that. At the time, despite my bullshit bravado, I was convinced we were all caught. I know I said we'd had a chance, a slim to fuck-all chance, yeah, but that wasn't why I'd made this break. The reason I'd made the break was simply this – I knew that if I didn't I'd regret it for the rest of my life. Getting caught is one thing, but giving yourself up is something else altogether. I mean, can you imagine how torturous it would be to spend all that time lying in a cell, looking at the ceiling and thinking 'What if'?

I had twenty years coming to me, for fuck's sake, that was going to be hard enough as it was without that particular headache keeping me awake for the next 7,305 nights.

However, we *had* managed to get away. At least, we'd bought ourselves some breathing space. Now every move was about capitalising on that space. A move here to widen it there, or a small gamble there to widen it here, until eventually we'd made enough moves and taken enough gambles to widen our breathing space up so much that we were clear for the rest of our lives. Perhaps if we all started smoking a hundred a day we wouldn't have to move and gamble so much, but we were still a little way off that yet.

We passed two more economy vehicles (our next motor would have to be big enough to carry three robbers and two hostages and keep four-fifths of us out of sight) before eventually a suitable opportunity presented itself.

A BT van. It was parked up by the side of the road and next to it was its driver, sitting on a little stool in front of a green junction box examining a big knotted rope of tiny wires. I pulled up beside him and Goody saw what the move was before I even opened my mouth. He climbed out of the passenger side, tiptoed up behind the bloke and clobbered him over the head with a swing of his pistol. The bloke went down like a sack of King Edwards and Goody caught him before his head had a chance to do itself any more damage on the pavement – which was surprisingly considerate of Goody, when you think about it.

I jumped out of the driver's seat and tried the doors on the van. Matey had thoughtfully left them unlocked so we had him and his stool out of sight and in the back after half an anxious minute once we'd made room for him.

'Anyone see that?' Goody asked, looking this way and that.

The street was unbelievably quiet and there didn't seem to be anyone telephoning the Old Bill from behind twitching curtains but I gave the wires sticking out of the junction box a real hard yank just in case there was, then closed the doors again.

'Don't worry, he'll be okay. A bastard of a headache but I got him just right,' Goody reassured me. 'Training,' he added, giving me a little wink. This was no doubt a reference to his army days, but now wasn't the time to press him further, no matter how much he looked like he wanted me to ask him about the ins and outs of smacking BT engineers over the nut.

'Okay, Pats, stick her in the van,' I told Patsy, opening the door for him and his charge. 'Lady, I don't know what your name is but if you give us any more fucking trouble I'll have my mate lay you out the same as he laid out matey. Alright? Do as we say and no harm will come to you. Have you got all that?'

I whispered all this to her as we dragged her out of her motor and meant every word of it, though I hoped we wouldn't have to resort to that sort of rough treatment with a woman. They tell birds these days who take these anti-abduction classes that they should never allow themselves to be taken from one place to another by an abductor; that they should kick out, stamp, scream and scratch, even if it means getting stabbed in the process, but never allow themselves to be taken somewhere that it isn't public. Once they have been, suddenly the abductor is in complete control and it's basically game over at that point. Not that we had anything like that planned for her. Personally I would've loved to have left her behind with all her shopping but we simply couldn't do that. Not until we were clear of trouble.

I just hoped she'd opted for evening classes in pottery over self-preservation.

Very carefully, Patsy climbed off her and pulled her out

of the car keeping his gun to her back at all times. It was then I remembered that – other than myself – Patsy was the only one of us who still had bullets in his gun. He'd been outside and far away when I'd collected all the ammo off all the others in order to prevent them from trying to *Wild Bunch* their way out the supermarket, earning us all some lead in the head, so this was an even more tricky situation than I first realised. But what could I do? Not a lot, unfortunately. Sometimes these things are just out of your hands.

The woman struggled to break free once she was clear of her motor but we had a couple of good firm handfuls and we held onto her fast. It wasn't much of an attempt, to be honest, more a reflex desperation not to be driven off in a van by three no-nonsense strangers rather than a serious bid for freedom, but in the struggle I accidentally grabbed one of her tits. I let go of it as soon as I did it and even instinctively apologised to her but our housewife went through the fucking roof and it took all of mine, Patsy and Goody's strength to load her in the back of the van. When I finally let go of her, the bitch caught me a good one right across the chops with her heels and we had to bundle Patsy's lanky frame on top of her before we could get the doors closed.

'Why does everything have to be such hard work?' I asked Goody, rubbing my poor old face. Goody didn't seem to know, or if he did, he wasn't letting on. He simply went round to the front and climbed in the passenger seat.

I closed the doors up on the Audi and the junction box and made one last sweep of the street. Still no signs of life. Way off in the distance I could hear the sound of a helicopter's rotor blade, though I couldn't see it. This suited me just fine.

I got behind the wheel of the van and twisted the keys. The diesel motor choked to life instantly and a moment after that we were on the go again.

The whole change-over had probably taken only two

minutes, though two minutes is a lot of time to be spent doing anything in a situation like ours. Luckily, the time had been a wise investment because now we had a clean set of wheels, a blind police force and an open road.

By the skin of our teeth we'd lost the Old Bill. Now it was time to go and get ourselves well and truly lost.

Roads to nowhere

We motored along at a steady pace and kept our eyes peeled (which is a horrible expression when you think about it). Goody told me to slow down because we were doing 40 mph in a 30 mph zone but I ignored him because everyone knows that only OAPs and people who are out to abduct kids drive at 30 mph through a 30 mph zone, so I decided to use my own judgement and risk it. Besides, I really wanted to put a couple of hundred miles between us and them before they had the chance to set up police road-blocks all over the place, and an extra 10 mph might just have been the difference between us making it out of the county or finding ourselves trapped in the cordon.

I'd almost let myself relax when just around the next bend my heart leapt into my mouth at the sight of a police motor as it appeared at a turning just up ahead and sat there staring at us.

'Put your foot down,' Goody shouted in panic, but I told him to stay calm, act natural and see which way the wind was blowing before we threw our kites into the air. The cops had spotted us, yeah, of course, but seeing as we were both driving half a ton of metal, glass and petrol this was not necessarily a bad thing. The question was, had they spotted us as a BT van or as a bunch of criminals on the run in a stolen BT van?

In situations like these, there's only one thing you can do – stare straight ahead, say a short prayer and whistle as tunefully as you can manage. Animals, cavemen and miserable fucking neighbours have been honing these skills for millenniums, but evolution eventually peaks and in me this not-drawing-attention-to-myself technique had been perfected. I like to think that nowadays I can stare straight ahead and keep on walking so well that I'm practically invisible to the rest of the outside world. You could be loaded down with shopping, sitting in the pub with an empty glass or selling raffle tickets outside Woolworths. It wouldn't matter. To you, I'd be little more than a gust of wind and a strange nagging feeling that you'd missed an opportunity. I'm that good.

However, that's on foot.

I couldn't tell you what I was like in a motor.

I took my foot off the accelerator just a little to drop us down to 35 mph and kept tabs on the rozzers out of the corner of my eye as we sailed past them. My eyes went straight to the mirror and Goody and I watched them for a few agonising seconds before they pulled out of the avenue and showed us their rear end.

'Fucking hell, I thought that was it,' Goody said, clutching his heart and puffing his fat cheeks out. That had been the closest we'd been to the Old Bill since we made it to Patsy's waiting motor and it hadn't been something I'd enjoyed. My heart was thumping like a drummer on a solo and my throat was as dry as an Arab's Sketchley's.

'Anything to drink back there, Patsy?' I asked.

'Like what?' he replied pointlessly.

'Here, do you think perhaps I should hide under the dash?' Goody asked me.

'Any excuse to get your head in my lap, huh?' I joked.

'No!' he replied indignantly, as if I was serious, a sure sign he was stressed. 'Just in case there's any more Old Bill up the road, best if they don't see the both of us.'

I didn't have an opinion on the matter and told him to do whatever made him happy, so he scrunched down onto the floor in front of the passenger seat for about three minutes before complaining he had cramp in his legs and scrunching back up again. That was all the scrunching that went on for the rest of the journey.

I'd grown up around this town so I knew its streets and those of the neighbouring towns like the back of my gloves. I used this knowledge to steer us clear of all the major roads until we were in the arse end of a lot of woods somewhere between the outlying villages, then I made a play for the motorway. It would mean leaving the relative sanctuary of all these housing estates and country lanes for a couple of long straight A-roads, but if we could just get onto the motorway we could be a hundred miles from here in less than two hours. It had to be worth it.

Shit or bust, I believe the French call it.

I pulled the van out into some light traffic and we followed the flow for a few miles. Two police cars came wailing towards us from up ahead and passed us without so much as a sideways glance. Goody and me made like statues each time they passed and Patsy asked us where we were going every few seconds until I was ready to turn us into the oncoming traffic just to shut the bastard up once and for ever.

'I don't know, it doesn't matter. Just away,' I kept telling him, though this wasn't good enough for Patsy, who demanded a street-by-street commentary every time I turned the wheel.

'Patsy, you do your job and let me do mine,' I finally told him, referring to our unwilling and extremely uncooperative female passenger.

'Yeah, Patsy, she's going to give us away if she keeps banging away on those fucking doors like that. Now shut her up,' Goody agreed.

Patsy tried sweet-talking her, he tried reassuring her and he even tried bargaining with her. He tried just about everything in the pacifist's handbook to try to get her to play ball but she was determined to leave this world how she'd entered it and kicked, struggled and screamed every time his hand slipped off of her face.

'It's okay, it's alright, we're not going to hurt you,' Patsy would reassure her in his best *Play Away* voice, only to get one in the plums and his fingers bitten by way of a response.

'Help! . . . se hel . . . get the . . . fucking . . . bas . . .' she'd squawk as Patsy braved some other part of his anatomy to quieten her down.

'Please, please, be quiet, we promise, honestly, we're not going to do nothing. Just be quiet,' he'd plead, and eventually she'd run out of steam and it would all die down for a couple of minutes, then we'd pass a police car with its horns blowing and she'd be at it again.

See, the trouble was, Patsy was being too nice to her. Not a heroic thing to admit but it was true. How can you expect someone you've taken against their will to cooperate with you if you've removed the threat of violence? There has to be some sort of incentive to keep their traps shut and let you drive them out into a nice lonely spot in the woods, otherwise why else would they let you? Our female hostage wasn't going to play ball out of the goodness of her heart, and telling her if she didn't pipe down she was going to get us nicked and herself rescued probably wasn't the most convincing of arguments.

'Patsy, if she doesn't start behaving right away, you're just going to have to kill her,' I shouted back at him, and gave Goody a little wink to reassure him that I didn't mean it.

Goody passed the wink onto Patsy, who promptly told her that I didn't mean it. What a cunt!

'No, Patsy, I mean it,' I repeated, then communicated my wink again, this time a little more forcefully.

Once again, unbelievably, Patsy told her I didn't mean it and that I'd just winked.

'It's alright, don't worry, no one's really going to kill you. We just need you to be quiet for a little bit longer so that we can . . . ARGH, fucking GET OFF!'

This time I repeated my threat but left all winking at home. When Patsy finally extracted his fingers from her jaws he looked up to see Goody pointing his gun at her head and telling Patsy to get out of the way.

'No, wait, don't,' Patsy said, shielding her body with his. Patsy turned to her and suddenly implored her to be quiet. 'Please, please, be quiet, they mean it, they really do,' he told her, and finally this shut her up.

'One more fucking peep out of her and I'll fucking do her. Even if I have to shoot you to get through to her, I'll do it,' Goody promised them both, waving his empty gun in their faces for dramatic impact before facing front and rolling his eyes at me.

You said it, mate.

We were going to have problems with Patsy before this whole palaver was over, I realised at that point. The sooner I got those bullets off him the better.

Up ahead, the traffic was gradually thickening the closer we got to the motorway. To all intents and purposes it looked like a plain old ordinary day, but it felt to me like anything but. You know how sometimes the world just looks different sometimes? I always felt it the first day out of nick, and usually on Christmas Eve. Everything around you looks more like a picture of itself than how it would look normally. I'm not sure how to describe it properly but it's kind of like you're looking at something and seeing everything about it, not just a shopfront here or a litter bin there or whatever your eyes are focusing in on at any given moment, but everything as a whole. It's like you're sucking in every piece of information and your brain is doing its damnedest to take it all in.

The light's different, the day's different and somehow even the concrete's different. Everything looks the same, but it feels different. Know what I mean?

Well, anyway, that's how the world looked to me at that moment in time and I couldn't understand how everyone else was just going about their business without noticing it.

It made me feel unbelievably self-conscious; not a great way to be when you're desperately trying to blend into general anonymity. Every little thing I did felt laboured and false, as if all the other drivers were looking at me and thinking, 'See how he just indicated to go around that corner? He did that deliberately because he knows that's what normal people do when they go around corners, but I could tell when he did it he was just doing it so that we would think he was a normal driver, and not a criminal on the run. Blimey, how obvious can a person be? Look, he's at it again, slowing down for those traffic lights. What's he think he's doing? He's standing out like a whole sore hand.'

It got so bad that the wheel slipped in my fingers a couple of times and my wobbly foot fell off the accelerator, making me veer and stutter around a few of the corners. Each time I did it Goody would look at me accusingly as if I'd done it deliberately, but I was all butterflies and twenty thumbs – hands and feet.

After a few more turnings we heard a groaning coming from somewhere in the back. I looked over my shoulder and saw the BT engineer waking up and not enjoying his Monday one little bit. He was rubbing his head and starting to stir and Goody asked me if he should clobber him again.

'No, better just leave him, we don't want to kill the poor cunt,' I told him, and shouted back at the engineer to lie still and to try not to move.

'Where am I? Oh, what's going on?' he asked, choking on the pain of a killer headache.

'You've had an accident, mate, you've banged your head really badly and we're taking you to the hospital,' I told him, making Goody stick out his bottom lip and nod approvingly.

'An accident? What happened?' he asked, all worried, so I made up some old flannel about him smacking his head on the van door when he stood up and hitting it on the way down again. 'How did I do that?' he grunted, starting to stir.

'No, mate, don't move, seriously, stay where you are,' I urged him, worried that he'd clock Patsy and Naggy in the back there with him and work out a few things for himself. 'Listen, I don't want to alarm you, but we think you've broken your neck, mate. Don't move, just stay as you are and let the doctors take a look before you go doing anything, otherwise that could be it, mate, game over for you.'

'What? Oh my God. Oh my God, no . . .' He started to panic, so I told him to calm down and concentrate on not moving. 'Please, I'm married . . .' he pleaded with us as if he were trying to strike a bargain.

'Well, that ain't my fault,' Goody replied less than sympathetically.

Our engineer friend bought our story about him being injured and we didn't get another peep out of him for the rest of the journey except for a bit of desperate whimpering. Our female passenger, though, that little cunt, started playing up all the more to try to rope matey into matters and Patsy had to try to smother the bitch before she gave the whole game away.

'It's a trick . . .' she'd blurt out. 'Don't listen . . . You're okay . . . you're not hurt . . .' and so on, but matey was having none of it and remained perfectly still. What must've been going on in his head I have no idea, but the whole journey must've seemed like one gigantic nightmare come horribly real and he was taking no chances.

'Patsy!' Goody yelled, suddenly losing all semblance of patience.

'I know, I know, I'm trying,' Patsy replied, wrestling with her all over the back of the van.

'Ah, Father, which aren't in heaven. Hello be thy name . . .' old BT started to recite as Patsy and Lara Croft started rolling over him, knocking each other in the face as they went.

'Man, we've really got to get some new wheels,' Goody pointed out helpfully.

I was about to agree with him when something way up ahead caught my eye. The traffic was thickening up and slowing down, and suddenly there, way off in the distance, something was twinkling by the side of the road. No, it wasn't twinkling, it was flashing. Yes, that was it, something – or several things actually – were flashing about half a mile in front of us and the traffic was slowing down.

'Oh, fuck, roadblock!' I yelled, stamping on the brakes so that Patsy, BT and Pain-in-the-tits slid across the floor and concertinaed up into the front seats. I heard some urgent braking behind our back doors and waited for a crunch but luckily one never came, just an angry horn and the words 'you stupid cunt'.

Beyond those flashing lights was the junction to the motorway. The bastards had somehow managed to leapfrog us and had a couple of cars up there vetting the traffic.

We'd been too slow.

'Argh, my neck,' someone in the back was yelping but I didn't have time to listen.

'What do we do?' Goody gasped, pushing himself back into the passenger seat.

I looked around us; fields, woods and fist-waving drivers overtaking us on the inside and out.

'Fuck . . . I . . .' I babbled, dazzled by the approaching headlights with my fluffy ears in the air.

'Turn us around, get this thing going, get us out of here!' Goody was shouting in my ear, while the others disengaged in the back. It didn't sound like much of a plan but it was the best we had so I stuck the van in reverse and rolled us backwards and forwards across two lanes then a grassy central reservation, much to the indignation of my fellow motorists, until I was pointing 180 degrees away from all that flashing unpleasantness, then floored it.

Goody kept an eye on the mirror to see if the orchestra of horns that had struck up around our unlawful manoeuvre had caught the attention of the Old Bill, but they seemed to be staying put for the moment.

'One of these cunts will grass us up,' Goody told us, referring to the line of traffic now stretching back the way we'd just come.

'Maybe. Maybe not,' I said. The odds were fifty-fifty. We had just braked and run from a police roadblock, but then again so had half a dozen other drivers and we couldn't all have robbed supermarkets this morning. Drink-driving, no insurance, no licence, impatience or any number of other reasons could explain a person's reluctance to stop for the Old Bill.

Once again, I was just trying to blend in.

'Shit!' Goody said, staring at the side mirror intently.

'What?' I asked, not liking the sound of this one bit. 'Shit!' rarely precedes good news.

'Fuck,' Goody elaborated.

'What?'

'I . . . hang on. Bollocks! Shit, go,' he said, looking over his shoulder.

'What is it?'

'What d'you think? One of them Old Bill has just pulled out and is coming this way.'

'Shit,' I agreed, and moved the accelerator two inches closer to the road.

'Move it, Milo, we've been rumbled.'

'Not yet we ain't,' I told him, which was true. Like I said, at least a good half-a-dozen other motorists were taking evasive action, so how could that nosey bastard know who was who or why any of us were dodging his checkpoint. He was probably just getting after us on the off-chance and to make sure no one else legged it out of the line.

I took the van quickly up to eighty and threw it through some light traffic before spotting a little dirt trail leading up into the woods.

'Hang onto your hats, this is going to get a bit bumpy,' I warned everyone, though they were already crashing around in the back like a load of slam-dancers on double-bubble.

'But I've got a broken neck,' matey objected.

'Well, hang onto your neck, then,' Goody told him as I hit the brake and flung the wheel left, taking us off the road and into the Great British countryside.

I checked the mirror as soon as we were through the gap and hoped that the long sweeping curve had hidden our move from the oncoming Old Bill.

'Arghh, ha ha!' someone was crying in the back, and I bounced us over every pothole and rut I could find, smacking the side of the van against a tree at one point and staving the front lights in on a gatepost that no longer exists.

'Did he see us? Is he coming?' Goody was shouting at me through the clatter of stones and revs, but I couldn't fix my eyes on any of the mirrors as we were jumping about too much.

'I can't see,' I shouted back. 'Take a look.'

Up until this point Goody had been using all his limbs to wedge himself into his seat, but the moment he let go of the ceiling to take a look he went flying about in the cabin, knocking into me and making me veer off the trail and into the woods. I managed to keep us going for about another five seconds before a big old oak had the final say.

Air bags exploded in mine and Goody's faces, disorienting me momentarily so that I thought I was still driving. I wrestled the bag out of the way and tried reaching around it to grab hold of the wheel again before realising there was no longer any need.

'Fuck!' I coughed when I looked through the shattered windscreen and saw the big old cunt that had stopped us in our tracks. I gave my arms and legs a quick shake to make sure it was just BT's van I'd smashed to bits and was a bit disturbed to discover my little finger on my right hand no longer bent in a way it was supposed to.

'Shit.'

I stared at my misshapen finger in horror, lost to all other concerns, so Goody took it upon himself to jump from the van and turn his eyes on the trail behind us.

'Milo! Milo!' he called urgently, and it took me a moment to snap out of it and join him on the track.

'I'm hurt,' I had to tell him, rushing over to him to show him my finger.

Goody looked at my injury, then at me, then told me not to worry about it.

'Look,' he said, turning my attention to the way we'd just come. He'd pulled his gun out of his coat so I pulled out mine, but the only sign of movement behind us was a long winding cloud of dust that was swirling about in the breeze as it settled back down to earth.

We stood like statues for a moment, straining our ears to listen out for anything unwelcome racing up to meet us, but the only sounds were the normal sounds of the country accompanied by the ticking of the van's engine as it cooled down, probably for the last time.

'What d'you reckon?' Goody asked.

'I don't know. I think maybe we shook him off at that last turn,' I said optimistically. 'That's if it was us he was coming after in the first place. If he was after one of the other motors then we should be okay, but if he starts wondering where we got to it won't take him long to double back and call up on the radio for a bit of help.'

I figured at worst we'd probably bought ourselves about ten minutes. There were plenty of other trails around this neck of the woods and even the one I'd thrown us down had half a dozen other little paths branching off of it, so they weren't going to find us in the next minute, even if they started looking now.

Ten minutes. That's what I gave us. It wasn't long, but it was a big improvement on the thirty-second head start we'd had only a short while ago.

All at once a terrific banging started against the back doors so we pulled them open and stood back as we let the rest of our crew tumble out. The woman jumped out first, snarling, hissing and biting at us like a particularly fucked-off rabid dog, but she stayed her distance when we threatened her with our shooters.

Next out was Patsy, looking slightly worse than the front of the van. He went to grab hold of the woman's arm but she sidestepped him and lashed out as he struggled to get a grip.

'Get the fuck off of me!' She slapped him and I saw that most of Patsy's cuts and bruises had probably been sustained long before our crash.

'Alright, alright, Pats, don't worry about her, leave her alone,' I told him, then pointed my gun at her. 'You, you just behave yourself otherwise we'll be forced to take you with us.'

This was a complete and nonsensical bluff, but it got her attention and gave her a carrot she was keen to crunch – the belief that her little adventure was almost over. She stopped the worst of the fighting after that but she didn't drop the antagonism, demanding to be let go now and calling us cowardly fucks who hid behind guns and all sorts of names that had the three of us almost blushing.

Weird, isn't it, when you hear a woman shout the word 'cunt'?

'Oi, give that fucking jaw of yours a rest for half a second, won't you? Blimey, I feel sorry for her poor old man.'

'My old man would soon sort you out, you streaky piece of . . .' she started up again, prompting Goody to ask if it wouldn't be easier just to shoot her and be done with it.

'Surely it's got to be worth it, hasn't it?'

'What about matey?' Patsy asked.

I told old naggy-tits not to go wandering off and the three of us looked in the back of the van for Mr BT. We could hear some gentle groaning going on under boxes of tools and rolls of cables so Patsy and Goody cleared the worst of it and asked him how he was doing.

'What do you mean, how am I doing? I've got a broken neck,' he replied, hardly daring to move his lips.

Me and Goody looked at each other and told him he hadn't really.

'I wouldn't put any fucking money on that,' Patsy told us, rubbing his own Gregory.

'Go on, get your arse out of there, you're fine,' I ordered BT, and the three of us dragged him out and to his feet and stood him over next to naggy.

'What's going on?' he asked, still holding his head. When none of us answered, he turned his whole body around to naggy so as not to move his neck and asked her the same question. 'What's happening here?'

'What do you think's happening, we've been kidnapped,' she told him, angry defiance still etched all over her face. I saw BT man think about this for a few moments, and I could almost hear him wondering how much we were going to ask for him.

'I wouldn't go that far, we just needed your van to get us away from . . . er, well, that's not important right now.' And it really wasn't. They'd read about it soon enough. No point wasting time just to keep them in the loop. 'What is important is that we're a bit fucked right now so we're letting you go . . .' At this naggy started walking off and I had to grab her by the arm and stick my gun in her face before her feet got the message. 'Just hold your fucking horses, will you.'

'You said you were letting us go so I was going. You did say that.'

'Yeah, but when I said we were letting you go, I didn't mean we were letting you go as in letting you go. I meant we were tying you to a tree and leaving you out here in the woods.'

'You're not tying me to anything, you bastard fucking son of a bitch,' she spat. She'd certainly grown in confidence since we'd met her. I had to give her that. What had happened to that frightened, pliant bundle of hysteria we'd hijacked in the multi-storey? I'd really liked her. See, there you go, that was Patsy's baby talk for you. He'd reassured all her fears away so effectively that now all that was left was anger, resentment and the will to fuck us up in everything we did. That's women for you. Mind you, all these fires were probably doubly stoked every time she thought about her shopping. Given the choice, next time perhaps I'll try to nab someone who's just been to Safeway rather than Iceland.

'Here, here's some tape,' Goody said, finding a big roll of electrical tape in the back of the van.

'No!' she shouted, and tried to leg it, but she didn't get

more than a couple of steps before me, Goody and Patsy had grabbed a handful of her each and started taping her to the tree next to where the van had come to rest. She was yelling, screaming, kicking out at us and all sorts so I stuffed some tape over her mouth to end that particular earache and spun her in a shiny black cocoon until we all had one less thing to worry about.

'You going to give us a problem too?' I asked BT, and he shook his head gingerly, and dropped down next to her. He complained about feeling slightly nauseous, what with the whack on the head and everything, so I said we'd leave his gag off if he promised not to go shouting his mouth off until we had a decent head start. He agreed, much to the dismay of his fellow tree hugger, so I granted him his request. Well, it wasn't going to do anyone any favours if he choked to death on his own puke the moment we were out of sight, was it now?

'Look, don't worry, you ain't going to have to spend all night here. If no one's found you in the next couple of hours I'll give the Old Bill a ring myself and let them know where you are. Okay?'

'Okay. Thanks,' he said, making me feel really bad about everything we'd put him through.

Naggy just scowled at me, and I wondered if I had time to go and find a few ants.

At this point Goody stepped up and spoke to BT man too.

'One question; are you a benny tied to a tree?' he said, and giggled to himself. 'Well, how often am I going to get a chance to ask it for real?' he said, and wandered off, not waiting for an answer.

You can say what you like about Goody but he's never been one to waste an opportunity.

Jack's in his box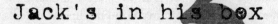

The first thing I had to do before I went anywhere was get the money off my body. Time was at a premium, I knew it, but I couldn't take another step taped up the way I was. My skin was sweaty and sore from all the running I'd done and the day was blisteringly hot (definitely not ditch-digging weather) and this had all combined to leave me feeling red raw and deeply uncomfortable.

Not what I would've expected from such an expensive suit.

Also, little bits of grit had somehow got themselves in between the money and my skin and they were driving me mental to the point where I would happily have swapped the entire hundred grand for a nice soft, fluffy towel. Goody agreed with me on everything, so the two of us slipped down to our grots and started the painful process of removing the money.

A lot of it had come loose already what with all the sweat and jumping about, but the sweat had only unstuck it from my skin, all the hairs remained firmly attached. Even the jumping about hadn't dislodged these bastards, though it had certainly dislodged a few tears. No, this was suddenly Patsy's job, though for the agony it brought my already red-raw skin I'm sure old naggy would much rather have done it.

'Look, just do it quick, Pats, give it a good tug, just get the stuff off,' I told him, my eyes already swimming after only two bundles. I looked down at my body and counted at least another twenty to be removed, and my lips wobbled at the prospect.

Patsy peeled the next bit of tape off my long hairy legs marginally faster than he'd peeled the last two bundles but the squeamish bastard kept stopping every time I hollered, which was all the time.

'Urgh, I don't know if I can do this,' he quavered, tugging at the tape rhythmically so that I enjoyed all the benefits of the pain without actually having any of the stuff removed.

'Just fucking do it,' I told him. It had to be Patsy, I'd already tried it myself and had almost passed out on the first attempt. I wasn't one who could inflict pain on myself, though I could happily dish it out to other people, as Patsy would find out if he didn't stop torturing me, but it never came to that. Goody – who had a freakishly flabby and hairless body – had untaped himself already and interceded for Patsy.

'Let me have a go,' he said, shoving Patsy aside and tearing into me without pausing for breath.

I don't know if I screamed or not, but Christ I did inwardly. Goody wasn't listening, though; he ripped, tore, gouged and snatched great handfuls of me as he relieved me of my cash in less than ten seconds, and when he was done I shivered, hugged myself and almost blubbed before I was able to pull myself together again. I got dressed (minus the supermarket overalls, of course) and patted down my poor aching body.

Never again will I take for granted a neatly sculpted bikini line.

On top of all this, I caught my injured little finger a

couple of times pulling my arms into my sleeves and this sent shock waves throughout my body, almost propelling me over the edge. I thought about trying to turn it back myself but just touching it gave me the big wobbly one and my legs almost buckled from underneath me. Now was neither the time nor the place to go passing out like a virgin on her honeymoon.

'Come on, then, we'd better get moving,' Goody said, pulling me back to earth. We'd been there almost ten minutes now. That was about as much lingering as we could afford. I wrapped my little finger up to its neighbour with a short length of electrical tape, just to keep it out of further harm's way, and tried to put it out of my mind. Unfortunately, I had a feeling of dread in the pit of my stomach that told me there was a horrible painful experience waiting for me somewhere down the line, but there was nothing I could do about that now. I'd sob like a little girl over that bridge when I came to it. All I could do now was keep on running.

'Which way?' asked Patsy.

'That way, across the field and towards that church spire in the distance, I reckon,' Goody said, indicating the path with his hand.

'Oh, well done, you fucking doughnut,' I said, pointing back at BT and naggy, who caught the whole briefing.

'Oh.' Goody shrugged. 'We'll have to go another way, then, won't we?'

'Twat.'

I emptied BT's knapsack of his sandwiches and flask and packed up my cash. Goody made similar use of a canvas toolbag he found in the van, and finally we were ready to go.

'All the best, folks, sorry about all this and everything. Mind how you go,' I told BT and naggy-tits, and me, Goody and Patsy set off into the trees.

It felt good to be moving again and I let out a sigh of relief as we left the van behind. My clothes felt incredibly soft and loose on me once again and I couldn't help but feel optimistic about our chances all of a sudden. Here we were, on foot, in the middle of the sticks, no roads, houses or cops anywhere in sight, with our destiny in our own hands. Things were definitely looking up.

'Where are we going?' Patsy asked.

'I haven't got a fucking clue,' I replied.

But then again, I wasn't really thinking of where I wanted to be. At this moment in time all I was thinking about was where I didn't want to be – i.e. down the cop shop. Anywhere else we found ourselves was just fine and dandy with me.

That said, it was a good question. I mean, where were we going?

What did people do in this situation?

Stick to the woods for now and try to get as far away from the scene of the crime, that was pretty much the extent of my thinking for now, but perhaps it was time to start working out a slightly longer-term strategy than just this.

Where could we go?

Abroad would seem like the obvious choice but wasn't going to happen today, which was a pity really because today was probably the last chance we'd have of making it abroad. If we'd thought of it, we could probably have had false-bottom suitcases, passports and tickets already in our possession so that we could've gone directly to Gatwick or wherever and flown out straight after the job. Even with all the hullabaloo that was going on and the stand-off and everything, even with being clocked by Weasel, we could still probably have made it onto a plane and into a different time zone before they'd a chance to throw a security blanket around all the airports and ports and so on. We could've got to Spain, bunked a coach and disappeared off into the Brava with all the other faceless Brits and simply vanished into Europe after that. France, Germany, Italy, even Hungary, for fuck's sake. It wouldn't have mattered to me, just anywhere where we didn't have our pictures in the papers and a load of nosey bastards to go grassing us up to *Crimewatch*.

Still, like I said, it was a bit too late to go worrying about all that now. Spilt milk under the bridge and that old chestnut. We just had to concentrate on the here and now and worry about the later when we found it.

So, okay, say for the sake of argument that we did have a ten-minute head start over the Old Bill. How were we going to go turning those ten minutes into a day? Then a week? Then a fortnight? And so on and so forth.

I didn't know.

It must've been a lot easier to disappear back in the olden days, when no one had tellies, no one had computers, no one had telephones, motors or newspapers. Well, there were newspapers, I suppose, but no cunt could read. Even as recently as pre-war days, the ordinary working men and women of this country, who made up the bulk of the population when all's said and done, could no more afford a telephone or a motor car than I could a gold hat. Everything was simpler back then. Your friends were your neighbours (for no other reason than the fact that they happened to live next door to you) and everyone heard news and gossip down the pub or over the back fence on wash day and so on. If I'd pulled this supermarket job at the turn of the century (hang on, that was only a couple of years ago. Alright, the century before that) and legged it off up to Ipswich or somewhere with all the proceeds, barring any silly future run-ins with the Old Bill that would be that, I would've been in the clear. They might have had a crude Etch-A-Sketch of me up in Ipswich police station and all that but, like I say, as long as I didn't go knocking off any policeman's hats or shooting my mouth off down my new Suffolk local, I could lead a normal life among the general population and no one would have any reason to bat an eyelid at me.

That said, plenty of villains *were* caught back then so I suppose it wasn't as easy as all that. I guess the trouble was that they didn't know to scarper off to Ipswich or somewhere else. For back then, their street and their pubs and their family and all the rest of it were their whole world.

Why go to Ipswich where nobody knows you, when you can sleep under your nan's stairs in Fleet and still knock around with your mates under the cover of darkness?

It's a basic flaw in all villains; as true today as it was all those years ago and probably one of the reasons Her Majesty's holiday camps do such great business. Don't get me wrong, I'm sure I'm just as stricken as the next bloke. I mean, look where I came straight back to when I got out of the shovel. In my experience, though, criminals suffer from homesickness ten times more than your average normal law-abiding types and I'll explain why.

See, everyone gets misty eyed for the familiar from time to time, and I don't care how much you say you hated it where you grew up, or how rusty the slide was down your local park, or who painted over your cricket stumps when you were ten, most people retain a place in their heart for that shit-hole they call home. They might not actually ever want to visit it this side of everlasting death, but just knowing they can is usually good enough for most people. Take that away, however, and see what it does to a person.

There's a weird reaction, like I said, in criminals in particular, where they can't get back there fast enough. So many of the blokes I met inside were picked up around their girlfriends' houses, their mates', their parents', or even their locals, for fuck sake. All places they should never have been a million miles anywhere near if they wanted to stay clear of the pokey and carry on seeing the sky whenever they fancied, but these silly fucks just couldn't help themselves. Like moths to flames they were.

So, and this is getting back to the olden days, supposing you did make it away with your horse, your musket and your pillowcase full of your Lordship's candelabras, where would you go? You don't know anything about the world outside your parish boundaries, so where do you – an ill-educated, toothless, illiterate silver collector with low morals and even lower IQ – run in times of trouble? Nine times out of ten it'll be your nan's stairs. And the one time you won't will be when your old man's hiding under there already.

I'm serious about this too. I read something about this famous thief of the eighteenth century (it says eighteenth but it's actually the ones that start with a seventeen though. Confusing, isn't it?) called Jack Sheppard who was sentenced to hang by the neck until dead but kept on escaping all the time.

Now, Jack wasn't a Dick Turpin or a Captain Pugwash or anything like that, he was just a skinny little geezer who nicked a couple of plates and a few candlesticks off his employer and who was sentenced to kick for it. The reason he became so well known, however, was that he kept on getting locked up and kept on doing a bunk. He even made it out of his escape-proof cell in Newgate when he was loaded down with shackles, chained to the floor and checked up on every half hour or so. He still managed to get away. He became a major celebrity in his day, simply because of his exploits, and he was in the papers all the time back then. People paid good money to see him in his cell and the King even commissioned to have a portrait of him done so that he could hang it in his bog. When Jack was finally driven from Newgate that last lonely mile to do the

Tyburn jig, 200,000 people turned out in the hope of seeing him pull off his greatest escape yet. Unfortunately, for them and for Jack, they all went home disappointed.

Now I mention all this for a reason, and not just because it's well interesting, which it is, but for this. After four successful escapes from the hangman's noose, see if you can guess where Jack Sheppard was arrested that fifth and final time.

Yes, that's right, on a pub crawl around the West End with a couple of prostitutes.

Naturally.

He was born, raised and nicked (on four previous occasions) in Covent Garden, and it was here that he returned to every single time, despite once making it as far north as the then green and pleasant fields of Tottenham. The silly bastard could've just kept on going and made it to Ipswich and freedom but he didn't know anyone there so he just turned back, came home and got hanged.

What a mug.

He was nineteen.

What I would've given to have been on the run in Jack's day. I wouldn't have come back for anything, especially with a noose waiting for me, and I certainly wouldn't have gone on the piss around where I lived with a couple of tarts. I mean, they did have prostitutes in Ipswich too, Jack.

Not that this was getting me anywhere. I didn't live in Jack's day and my problems weren't going to be solved by simply riding over the parish border. People did have tellies. They did have computers, phones, motors, and there was even the odd occasional bit of news in the newspapers these days. Everyone knows everything about everyone else (everyone of interest, that is) and the world turns around on gossip. Tara Palmer-Tomkinson's only got to scratch her arse in public and ten million mobiles up and down the country beep with the breaking news, so what chance did me,

Goody and Patsy have of leading a happy and normal life in Ipswich? Mind you, what chance did anyone have?

No, we just had to keep on going. Keep our heads down. Stay out of sight and, most importantly of all . . .

We had to keep running.

A walk in the woods

4

'Stick to the trees,' Goody told us, as we skirted along next to some field. 'In case any of those helicopters fly over.'

Patsy suddenly disappeared from our left and me and Goody bounded on another two dozen yards before we looked over our shoulders and saw him pointing his ears at the sky.

'I can't hear nothing,' he told us.

'Come on, Pats, keep on moving,' I told him, breathless and shaky after only a mile of progress.

Patsy got himself going in our direction again and I managed to restart the perpetual forward fall that was my run as the three of us bounded on.

'I couldn't hear no helicopters,' Patsy told us again when he caught up.

'They'll see us long before we hear them,' Goody replied, and I wondered if that was true. It didn't sound true, but then Goody had more experience of helicopters than I did, so who was I to argue?

'How will they know it's us?' Patsy gasped in time with my grunts. 'I mean, you both ditched your overalls so how will they know we're not just three normal blokes . . .'

'. . . out for a run in the woods in the middle of summer in our clothes on the day of the biggest robbery this town has ever seen,' Goody said, finishing Patsy's sentence for him. 'I don't know, I expect they'll give Sherlock Holmes a bell and ask him what he reckons.'

We stumbled on for another hundred yards or so before Patsy asked him about heat cameras on helicopters.

'Not in the day. Especially not on this fucking day. It's a hundred degrees, for fuck's sake, Patsy,' Goody exaggerated, though probably not by much.

We crashed on through more bushes, branches, bracken and scrub for another twenty minutes before my feet demanded I laid off them for a bit.

'Oh, fucking hell, let's stop. Just hold up a second,' I pleaded, grabbing hold of a branch in an effort to dodge the floor. 'Hang on.'

Patsy and Goody checked their strides and came to a halt a short way in front. Goody looked back to see what the problem was and figured it out once he clocked me.

I was fucked.

In fact, I was really, really fucked.

I hadn't done this much running in a single day since we'd all done cross-country at school, and I hadn't exactly done a lot then either. All the fags, the booze, greasy food and lack of exercise in the intervening years since that last sneaky bus ride had caught up with me with a vengeance, and no matter how closely the Old Bill were behind me, I simply couldn't manage another wobbly step.

'What?' Goody asked impatiently.

'I just need five minutes,' I told him, and dropped down to my arse. What sheer bliss!

Goody grabbed me by the arm, cutting my rest break rather shorter than I would've liked.

'Guess again, Milo, we haven't got five minutes. The Old Bill could be right behind us for all we know,' he said, yanking me to my throbbing feet.

I knew he was right, and if I had a breath in my body and

one of the others had fallen on their arses, I would've said exactly the same thing to them. But the problem was that I didn't have a breath in my body. In fact, my heart was smashing against my ribcage so hard that I could hardly hang onto a gasp and my lungs were ballooning like a pub accordionist who'd just heard the shout for last orders.

'We can walk for five minutes, just to catch our wind, then we'll take to our toes again, but we have to keep moving,' Goody told us, dragging me in the direction of Patsy.

The three of us ducked and dodged our way through the trees and jumped the occasional ditch where we saw fit, but we didn't let up again throughout all of it. The route we'd chosen was hard going and the ground was rough, overgrown, slippery and muddy in places, but we seemed to be making progress.

The three of us had decided, once we were out of earshot, to go roughly in the direction of the church spire after all, as hopefully this would be the last direction the police would look once they knew that we knew that they knew that we knew and all the other 'knews and knows' that resulted from Goody opening his fucking mouth in front of BT and naggy-tits. Patsy wasn't sure about this; his argument being basically one 'but they'd know' on top of all the others, but me and Goody had overruled him with a 'but we'd know' of our own, cancelling his argument out and confusing the lot of us.

At the end of the day, none of us really knew, not even Goody, who you would've thought would've known about this sort of thing. It just seemed like as good a direction as any and one with more greenery than tarmac, so that was the way for us.

Unfortunately, the thing about greenery is that it's actually a lot less hospitable up close and personal than it looks from far away.

'I'm really thirsty,' I croaked after a bit. 'Has anyone got anything to drink?'

'Like what?' Patsy replied for the second time that day.

'We should've brought old Matey's flask if we'd thought about it,' Goody said. 'And his sandwiches too. We might've needed them before the end of the day.'

'What flavour were they?' Patsy asked.

It occurred to me that Goody had a point. I had a hundred grand in my rucksack but I didn't fancy my chances of buying a Cornish pasty and a can of Coke around here any time soon. What were we going to do about grub?

'You can find food, can't you, Goody? You were in the army.'

'Yeah, I suppose, if I was still in Aldershot and I still had my mess pass I could probably rustle us up three plate-loads of grub, but other than that I reckon we're fucked. I know about as much about finding grub in the open and that sort of thing as I know about wearing skirts.'

'But survival skills and all that. Surviving behind enemy lines.'

'Yeah, you know, *The Bush Tucker Man*,' Patsy joined in, but Goody just shook his head.

'I spent most of my time driving a lorry. Why the fuck would anyone parachute me and my lorry behind enemy lines?'

'This can't be as bad as it looks. We're in the country, for fuck's sake, we're bound to pass a tree with apples or nuts on it or something. Just keep your eyes peeled for them and we'll fill our bags,' I told the lads, though the only things around here worth eating were us.

And we'd only been in the woods forty-five minutes.

My stomach gurgled as soon as the subject of food was brought up and the last drops of moisture evaporated from my tongue. Patsy went on and on about how we should've brought some grub with us from the supermarket when we made a break for it but neither me nor Goody were really listening. Instead, I spent the next five minutes working out exactly what I'd had to eat in the last twenty-four hours and it didn't add up to enough to keep a sparrow alive. I'd been a bit nervous prior to, and during, the job so that other than the odd chocolate biscuit here and there I'd not really eaten very much at all.

The more I thought about it, the more the dent in my guts grew.

'Come on, Milo, keep up,' Goody ordered, storming ahead through the undergrowth.

I didn't know how far we'd done but it felt like a good five miles, so that meant it was probably closer to one. Splitting the difference, I decided to call it three and asked Goody if he knew which way the church was and why we weren't there yet. We'd lost sight of the spire once we'd made it across to the other side of the field and now we were just weaving our way through the undergrowth in a random, path-of-least-resistance sort of direction.

'Yeah, I think it's over this way,' he told me, pointing straight ahead.

'How can you tell?' I asked, thinking he was going to say something about the sun or moss on the side of trees or something, but Goody just said:

'Well, I don't know, it's the way we've been walking, isn't it? It's bound to be up here somewhere.'

It was incredible to think that this bloke had spent nearly ten years in the army. Unbelievable.

'What about dogs? Aren't we supposed to run through a river or something to throw them off the scent?' Patsy asked.

'You find us a river, Pats, and I'll run through it,' Goody replied.

'No, I think he's right, Goody,' I added, after thinking

about this for a moment. 'I mean, it won't matter how far we run if they get dogs on our case, will it, now?'

'Well, yeah, I know, but what d'you want me to do about it? Cry you a river? We're in the middle of the fucking woods. There aren't any rivers around here. We passed a puddle back there if you want to have a quick splash about in it but I'm all out of rivers, bananas, crisps and Fanta. Sorry.'

'If we found a river, we could have a drink as well,' Patsy said, and that was the last thing any of us said for twenty minutes.

We carried on further and further, clambering over fallen trees and picking our way through rusty barbed-wire fences, but all of a sudden it didn't feel like we were making progress any more. I tried stupidly touching less and less leaves to try to minimalise the amount of scent I left behind but I wasn't even fooling myself. The way we were stinking, the Old Bill weren't even going to need dogs to catch us — some young constable with hay fever and a bunged-up nose could probably have tracked us down.

We went on for another half an hour, stumbling across paths, fences, trails, electrical pylons and the odd country road to remind ourselves that no matter how far we disappeared into the sticks, people were still around us on all sides.

By ten to four even Goody had shot his bolt, so we dumped ourselves on the ground for a quick rest and stayed there for the next ten minutes. We'd been on the hoof now for something like three hours, though we hadn't managed anything over walking speed for the last two.

'God, I'm fucked,' Goody told us, wiping his face with his sleeve. I mustered up enough energy to murmur in agreement but Patsy said nothing.

We were still in the woods, and it felt like we were on a

bit of a hill, but other than that I couldn't have told you where we were or even where we were near.

The three of us sat in silence with only our thoughts for company for a time before Goody finally spoke.

'I'm fucking starving too,' he said. Me and Patsy looked at him, then we went back to sitting in silence.

'Shouldn't we have reached that church by now?' Patsy asked.

'No, I reckon that was miles away,' Goody told him.

'But we've come miles.'

'Well, I don't know. Maybe we missed it, then.'

'Whereabouts are we?'

Goody thought for a bit then shrugged. 'I don't know. Around here somewhere. I think the motorway's this way, the way we're heading. If we keep going south we'll probably bump into something before long.'

'Are we going south, then?' I asked.

'Mostly. Walking into the sun, aren't we, so we're going south or south-south-west, something like that.'

As we were talking Patsy suddenly froze and told us to shut the fuck up.

'What? What is it?'

'I think I can hear . . . yes, listen. Hear it?'

I didn't hear anything for a few seconds but I kept my ears peeled and finally I isolated the sound. It was a helicopter. It sounded a long way off but that was changing fast. The beat of the blades grew louder and louder and the three of us ducked under bushes and bent foliage over to camouflage ourselves as best we could. The helicopter came no closer than half a mile or so but the simple fact that it flew over this way at all told us all we needed to know.

'You think they know where we are?' Patsy asked, as the chopper faded away.

'No, but if they found the van and they know we're on foot, then they'll probably have a good guess as to where to look,' Goody told us. 'I think we should get moving again. Get to the motorway, get a car and get out of here and as far away from this fucking place as possible.'

'Agreed,' I said, dragging myself out of my hiding place. As I did so I snagged my little finger on a branch and yelped out in pain. I clutched it tightly with my other hand and concentrated all my efforts on stopping my lip from wobbling, but it was no good. After a couple of seconds I coughed out a couple of recognisable sobs and had cause to wipe my eyes and nose.

Patsy and Goody stared at me as I whimpered like an injured dog, then all of a sudden the floodgates opened up and I booed my fucking eyes out.

'Er, are you alright, Milo?' Goody asked me, but I wasn't. I was hungry and thirsty and in pain and worried and miserable and lost. I was very, very, very unhappy. And if that wasn't enough, my little finger didn't bend the way it was supposed to any more and that frightened the shit out of me.

I spent about a minute letting it all go off before my eyes finally stopped raining and I was left with just a soggy nose and a somewhat tarnished reputation as a hard man. Patsy and Goody shifted awkwardly and waited for me to finish before Goody asked me what the matter was. It was the silliest fucking question I'd ever heard in all my life.

Everything was the matter.

Absolutely everything.

I was so unhappy about so many things that I really didn't know where to start: the long prison sentence awaiting me; the fact that I was never going to see Alice again; the cordon of angry coppers closing in all around us; the painful vacuum in my guts; and the absolute, all-encompassing hopelessness of our situation. I felt it from tip to top.

Everything was the matter.

I'd kept it all in until now because my mind had been

preoccupied with the immediate business of doing a runner, but one jaw-jarringly painful tweak of my little finger was enough to tear down my defences and leave me a blubbering wreck.

'You want me to take a look at your finger?' Goody asked, and I just nodded pathetically and handed it over. I'd regressed back to childhood and desperately wanted my finger kissed better and put right painlessly. Unfortunately, that wasn't going to happen. Especially now that Dr Goodman had taken over the case. This was going to hurt. A lot.

And I knew it.

Goody unwrapped the tape and wiggled my finger.

'Does that hurt?' he asked.

'A bit,' I told him, though it mostly just felt weird.

He examined it for a few seconds more and turned it this way and that before delivering his diagnosis.

'I don't think it's broken, I think it's just dislocated,' he told me.

'Are you sure?' I asked, though I trusted him to know what he was talking about. Goody had done all the basic first aid and field medical courses in the army, and while the rest of it had been one big long green waste of time for him, he seemed to remember this stuff okay.

'Seen this sort of thing before, ain't I? Blokes were always dislocating this or that on manoeuvres, it ain't nothing serious,' he told me, then uttered the words I'd been dreading hearing. 'I can pop it back in for you if you want,' he said, then pointlessly asked, 'Or would you rather do it?'

'No, you do it,' I told him.

'Okee-dokee, just keep your hand still and don't pull it away,' he said, holding my damaged finger in both hands.

'Ooh, I can't watch this,' Patsy said, turning his tail and scurrying off.

'Are you sure you know what you're doing?' I asked, a final uncertainty creeping into my mind.

'Yeah, don't worry about it. It's no problem,' he told me, then gave the tip of my painfully sensitive finger a quick sharp yank . . .

. . . Arhhha–ha–ha–hahah! . . . fuckin' . . . urgh . . . ******
*****

My pillow was really dirty.

It was also uncomfortable and lumpy.

Hang on a minute, I didn't have a pillow. My head was on the ground. Why was my head on the ground?

Come to that, where was my pillow?

Goody and Patsy looked down at me and asked me if I was alright.

I asked them where my pillow was. They didn't seem to think this was very important in the greater scheme of things and told me I should probably get up now. It was then that I noticed I wasn't at home at all. I was in the woods.

What? Why was I in the woods? Where the fuck was I?

It took a few seconds for the answers to slowly trickle back into my brain and when they did I half wished I was still out for the count.

Why had I been out? How long had I been out?

Shit, Goody was meant to be looking at my finger.

'. . . ngh fuckin' finger,' I slurred, offering Goody my hand again and apologising for taking a nap in the middle of him doing his stuff.

'I've done it already, it's alright, look,' he said, so I looked at my little finger and wiggled it a few times. It was swollen and sore and didn't bend as far as it once had but it was fixed and my spirits suddenly soared with relief and gratitude.

'Are you alright?' Patsy kept asking with concern.

I shook the grog from my head, wiped the dirt from my face and wiggled my little finger some more. Yes, I was alright. In fact, I was more than alright. I felt positively purged.

Goody hauled me to my feet and helped me brush some of the shit off my clothes.

'That's it, Milo, take it like a man,' Patsy chuckled, and after a few moments I began to chuckle too. I'd burst into tears, fainted and probably would've chucked my guts up if I'd had anything in my guts to chuck up, all within the space of five minutes, but none of that mattered now.

My finger worked again. That was all I cared about. My fucking finger worked again.

Yes! Yes! Yes! Yes! Yes! Yes! Yes!

Happy relief.

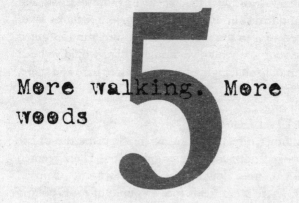

More walking. More woods

We got going again shortly after that. My head was still a bit woozy from my ten-second kip but the happiness I felt at having my finger back to normal gave me a much-needed spur.

Goody reckoned we should keep on heading south, so that was what we did, though his way took us over the hill we'd been camped on and it was tough going, especially considering the fact that none of us had had a bite all day long. As soon as my wooziness cleared my shakiness clocked back on and I was engulfed in a cold sweat that started on my newly acquired energy levels, so that after twenty minutes I was as fucked as ever again.

'I'm starving,' Goody told me and Patsy for the hundredth time.

Weren't we all.

I looked at every bush and tree we passed to see if there was anything to eat on them but there was nothing; at least, nothing a molly-coddled twenty-first-century consumer like me recognised as food. Surely you would've thought we would've passed a gooseberry bush or an acorn tree or something by now, wouldn't you, but no, there was nothing.

Not a sausage. How was that possible? How did bats and
squirrels and foxes survive out in the sticks, for fuck's sake?
They never went to the supermarket so surely, in this green
and fertile land you would've thought there would've been
a modicum of grub hanging off the odd tree here and there,
wouldn't you?

'I'm starving.'

'For fuck's sake, Goody!'

After another fifteen minutes we reached the top of the
hill and looked out across the woods below. There seemed
to be a lot of trees down there and they went off in all
directions. There were fields too; a couple of roofs poking
up among the greenery even and, way off in the distance, a
road. We could only see parts of it as trees obscured the
bulk, but it was all there. We couldn't even see the road
itself, to be honest, we only knew it was there because the
odd car, van or lorry, glinting in the late afternoon sun,
flashed past the gaps as they drove home for their dinners.
At one point Patsy thought he saw a police car and put a
tree between himself and the road, which was probably four
miles away. Me and Goody would've normally laughed at
this, but who had the energy?

We were about to carry on when something caught my
eye about half a mile away.

I didn't see what it was at first, just movement in the
trees, but it had definitely been there.

I stared at the point where I'd seen the movement for
about a minute but nothing happened, so I switched my
attention to another small gap in the trees about a hundred
yards ahead of the point I'd seen something and waited.

'Are we going or what?' Goody asked, but I wasn't
listening. I was staring, staring and staring some more at this
little clearing about 500 yards away, praying against prayer
that I hadn't seen anything more than the breeze in the
branches.

'Milo, what's up?' Patsy asked, and focused on where I was looking. 'What is it?'

'Oh fuck,' I muttered to myself, as three uniformed coppers broke from the trees and moved, in a line, across the clearing and in our direction. 'Oh, fucking fuck.' There'd be more down there, of course. A couple of cop shops' worth at least. All concealed by the green canopy but walking as a line through trees towards our position. After everything we'd gone through, the ground we'd covered, the hunger and the pain we'd endured, we were no further away from them than we were four hours ago.

'Let's move,' I panicked, bundling the lads off over the crest.

Way off in the distance I thought I heard a dog bark, but it could just have been my imagination. My refound, water-gripping fear playing tricks with my mind, possibly.

The three of us forgot our fatigue and went hell for leather through the trees. We skipped, jumped and thrashed our way through bushes as we tried to claw back some of that head start we'd so stupidly pissed away. We weren't able to go full pelt because the undergrowth tightened up on the southern slope but we picked, kicked and threw ourselves through the brush with hardly a thought for where we were going.

I scratched myself up something silly in a big thorny bush and Patsy gasped with pain when he opened his ankle up on some rusty barbed wire, but none of us stopped.

It made things slightly easier that we were now heading downhill. It also made things easier, as daft as this might sound, to know that there were actually a load of nosey coppers right on our arses. Up until we'd realised this, it had all been hypothetical (i.e. 'Let's keep moving in case there's a load of nosey coppers up our arse'). Hard to stay focused and motivated when it's all 'maybe', 'might be' and 'I wonder if', even when there was this much at stake. Much easier to dodge someone when you know they're coming and where they're coming from.

At least, that's the theory.

We crashed on further and put some real distance between us and the crest of the hill, when all of a sudden we dropped out of the woods and found ourselves on a wide dirt track. On the other side of the track were more trees, more nettles and millions more thorns.

'It's a fire-break, to stop forest fires spreading,' Goody told us to demonstrate his outdoor knowledge, though I didn't particularly care at that point. It was a clearing and we could run on it, that was all I wanted to know.

'What about the helicopter?' Patsy asked, but Goody and me were more concerned about the Old Bill behind us. It might not make much real sense, but it just felt better legging it for all we were worth along an open road while all those coppers were still hacking their way through the sticks.

After a mile or so the fire-break forked and we took the branch that seemed to be heading south. We ran along it for another 500 yards before Goody waved us into the forest and we jumped through the brambles and in amongst the trees, picking up from where we'd left off a mile or so down the road. Sorry, fire-break.

My heart was thumping in my chest and my throat was dry beyond thirst. I needed water. I needed food. I *needed* rest. Adrenalin had carried me this far but suddenly even this was all used up and my energy levels crashed to the point of collapse.

I trudged on regardless.

Well, what else was there to do?

Trees, branches, moss, bushes, bracken, potholes and thorns; it seemed like it was never ending. I had to remind myself that we were still in Britain, still in a place with roads, soft beds, big sofas, fish-and-chip shops and pubs. Oh

God, yes, pubs. What I would've given to be in the pub at this precise moment. To sit down in a lovely comfy seat with a lovely cold pint of Stella and a lovely hot basket of scampi and chips. How fantastic would that have been? I'd have had peanuts too, and bacon fries, and a big glass of Coke, just to quench my thirst, and obviously six or seven more beers, and I'd take my shoes off, and wash my face in the sink, and drink some of the water as I was washing, and . . . and . . . and . . . and . . . and . . .

. . . and I trudged on.

Sweat ran down my face, collecting in my eyebrows so that it could drip into my eyes. I tried to wipe the worst of it away with the back of my hand but all I succeeded in doing was wiping a big load of stingy grit into my already red-raw face. I used my sleeve next but this was caked in shit even worse than the back of my hand. Nothing about me was clean. Eventually I found a relatively dirt-free patch at the bottom of my shirt to mop my brow with and applied it to the back of my neck too. It wasn't exactly a cucumber facial but it did the trick and eased the stinging in my boat for a few precious minutes which, under the circumstances, was about all I had any right to ask for.

'You think they're still after us?' Patsy asked.

It was coming up to six. It had been over an hour since we'd stood at the top of that hill and spotted the Old Bill moving through the forest below us. I couldn't see any reason why they might've given up and gone home if they had our scent. They were probably back there right now, sniffing around the fire-break and coming on after us with fresh legs, full bellies, bottles of water and . . . and it wasn't fair. How the fuck were we meant to get away from them if they could just follow us to the ends of the earth and keep on resupplying on the way all they liked? It simply wasn't fair.

I wondered if there were more search parties up ahead too.

Were the cops behind us just herding us into a load more up front? I didn't know. I wouldn't have been surprised, but then this was such an enormous forest that they would've had to have been geniuses to know where to drop the other lot so as to intercept us. Ever since we'd spotted the thin blue line plodding our way Goody had taken us on a series of evasive manoeuvres (which in practice meant me and Patsy followed him whenever he changed direction). I wasn't sure about his tactics as it seemed to me that all this fucking about, going this way and that, was costing us more ground than it was making us, but Goody assured us that if there was more flatfoots up ahead, this would make it harder for the bastards behind to direct them towards us.

It seemed to make sense to Goody and I didn't have the strength to argue, so me and Patsy put our faith in the British army and went along with Private Goody's magical mystery tour until we were all well and truly lost.

'Haven't we been here before?' Goody asked me when we came out by a small clearing.

'Please don't tell me we've been going in circles.'

'No, we haven't. I ain't that daft, though it does all look the same, doesn't it?' he said, squinting at a load of trees.

'Fuck!' Patsy screeched, pointing across the field in wide-eyed shock.

Me and Goody panicked blindly and ran off in opposite directions but it turned out that it wasn't that sort of 'Fuck!'

'Look,' Patsy urged us. 'Look, blackberries.'

We skidded to a halt and turned to see where he was pointing. The bastard was only right as well. There were blackberries, tons and tons of them, covering a great bank of dark thorny bushes just the other side of the clearing.

The three of us broke cover and ran across the grass without a moment's thought as to who might see us. We snatched at the little squishy fruits and threw then into our mouths just as quickly as we could pull them off the bushes. Naturally, we also ended up scratching our hands to fuck and I had to suck a dozen tiny black thorns out of my thumb, but I didn't care, it was food.

Like most people who grew up in the sticks, I'd picked and eaten wild blackberries when I was a kid, but I couldn't remember them ever tasting this fantastic. I must've downed about a hundred or so when Goody told us he thought we should start making tracks again.

'We've been here five minutes, we can't waste any more time. Come on, we've got to go,' he said sternly.

'But I'm having my dinner,' Patsy objected with a big mouthful of blackberries.

'We have to keep on moving,' Goody demanded, so me and Patsy double-timed our fingers and stuffed a last half-dozen into our gobs before reluctantly agreeing.

'Fuck it, come on, then, let's get going,' I said, and the three of us stepped back into the trees.

The effects a little bit of food can have on you are incredible. Within just a few short seconds my legs had stopped shaking, my body felt stronger and the terrain seemed so much easier to walk on. In fact, if it hadn't been for the sudden crippling pain in my guts, I would've said I almost felt happy.

An hour later we heard a dog barking. We froze in our tracks and put our ears to the wind. There, up ahead, we heard it again. It couldn't have been more than a hundred yards away and we were blundering straight towards it. Along with the dog-bark there were human calls too. We couldn't make out what they were saying but it didn't really matter. Whatever it was, it wasn't going to be good news.

As one, the three of us turned on our tails and ran back the way we'd just come. After a couple of minutes Goody banked right and jumped through a load of bracken. We bounded after him and didn't stop until we hit another fire-break. Goody looked from left to right then dashed across. Me and Patsy followed suit, but halfway across I heard a cry for us to 'Stop!' and turned to see who'd made it.

Way off down the track, perhaps a hundred yards or so, two coppers were rushing towards us like Michael Owen onto a loose back pass. Half a dozen more suddenly emerged from the woods and joined in on the chase, and me and Patsy squealed in horror at the nightmarish vision approaching and charged into the woods after Goody.

'They've seen us, Goody,' I called after him.

'Oh, well done, Milo, nice one,' the cunt shouted over his shoulder without breaking stride.

The time for Goody's patented evasive action was over; we ran through the trees in one direction and we ran as fast as we could. Over my own trampling footsteps I could hear a dozen voices shouting this and that at each other as the forest around us came to life. Most of the voices seemed to be coming from behind us or over to the left of us, so we spun on our heels and darted off right. A few minutes later it was all going off behind us; air horns, whistles, shouting, running and some irresponsible cunt even shot a flare off up into the air. We were running through a tinder box, for fuck's sake, and he was shooting off flares?

Branches whizzed by and slapped us in the face and dead sticks and protruding roots did their best to try to trip us up, but we were way too determined for any of that old nonsense. Forget tiredness, forget pain, forget fatigue, I'd gone through too much in the last eighteen hours to end it sitting in the back of a police van with my hands in cuffs, having to listen to a load of wanker flatfoots outside con-gratulating themselves about what fantastic super-heroes they all were.

So I ran.

I ran so hard that my muscles burned and my sides screamed with stitches, but I didn't slow down. Not for a second, not for a step.

I ran.

I ran and ran and ran.

Goody threw himself down an enormous steep embankment and me and Patsy hurled ourselves on after him. We skidded down half of it on our arses and rolled the rest of the way on our heads. It wasn't exactly the most practical or comfortable way of negotiating the terrain but we seemed to be making good time so what complaints could we have?

At the bottom of the embankment, forty or so feet below the crest, there was a dried-up old river bed. Actually it was more like a stream, but seeing as it didn't have any water in it, whichever way you looked at it, it really didn't matter.

Goody seemed to think otherwise, however, and started off down the dusty trail without so much as a grunt of consultation. Patsy and me followed like lemmings playing at sheep and the three of us gave it everything we had as we attempted to lose ourselves again.

I quickly saw the genius of Goody's decision to follow the dried-up stream. The bed was at least a foot lower than the surrounding forest floor, it was free of the plants and debris we'd had to kick our way through up until now, and a tight canopy of branches and leaves had grown over it so that it was almost like running through a living tunnel. We had to stoop for most of the way but Goody had stumbled upon the perfect hidden short cut through a tangled sea of green.

Christ, I tell you, I truly did love that big dopey fuck sometimes.

'Where are they?'

'Which way did they go?'

'You go that way, to the far end, and I'll go this way!'

These were the shouts that broke out all around us as we

scurried through the undergrowth like frightened rabbits. I don't know how many coppers were out there but it sounded like a lot. There may well have been too many for their own good because they kept getting confused and going after each other in their mad rush to be the first to nick us.

'There they are.'

'No, wait, it's me, Barrie.'

'Not you, there.'

'Who, me?'

'Identify yourself.'

'Johnson, sir.'

'Who's that with you?'

'Wait, there they go. Over there!'

'What? No, it's just me.'

'Where's Barrie?'

'Over here.'

'Spread out! Spread yourselves out!'

'There they are!'

'No, it's me again.'

And so on.

They seemed to have abandoned the methodical approach that had worked so well for them up until now, right at the last moment. I guess they thought they had us the moment they spotted us and I couldn't really blame them for that. I mean, that's what I thought. But Goody and St Nicholas of Myra were working miracles for us and we cut through their lines as they stamped about the bush in their size elevens chasing Barrie around in circles and nicking each other.

The section of stream we were running down become more and more overgrown so that after a little while we were forced onto our bellies for a good long stretch. This slowed us down considerably but at least we were still hidden.

I was expecting a load of coppers to be coming after us down the stream but I guess they missed the turn. I was quite surprised by this but then I would probably have missed it too had it not been for Goody. Our luck couldn't hold out much longer, though. Surely the dogs would be on the scene soon and they'd pick up the trail right where we left it. That said, though, I wasn't sure I fancied their chances of getting through the stuff we were having to get through: thorns, stingers, smelly horrible green sludge that made me gag, and about six hundred torn and soggy porno mags.

After 500 yards of crawling along on our bellies like Action Man we came to the end of the stream and dropped down into a wider river. This was dry too.

'Don't any of these rivers have any fucking water in them?' I complained bitterly.

'Don't look like it,' Goody told me, snapping off a branch and thrashing it about in the dust behind us as we jogged twenty yards downstream, then stopped at a big old oak tree.

'What are we doing now?' I asked as Goody looked up among the branches.

'Climbing this tree.'

'What? Why, for fuck's sake?'

'Because I'm all out of ideas, alright? They might be looking for us on the ground, but if we can get fifty feet or so up in the air and hide among the branches they might just go straight past us.'

'But, but . . .' I started, but Goody wasn't listening. He asked us to give him a boost and grabbed hold of a low-hanging branch and pulled himself up. Patsy went next and made it to the branch, which was about eight feet above our heads, then there was just me.

'Don't touch the trunk otherwise the dogs'll sniff it,' Goody told me, lowering his hand. Patsy joined in and the two of them pulled me up without me having to lay a hand on the trunk.

Patsy started up the tree, climbing easily from branch to branch, but Goody leaned out with the branch he'd snapped off and thrashed its leaves over the spot on which we'd all been standing.

'We should've lost them in the undergrowth over there. They'll never get dogs through what we just crawled through. Hopefully they'll have trouble picking up the scent again if we mess up the trail for them,' he explained.

'Hopefully?'

'Yeah, hopefully. Well, I don't know, I ain't Barbara Woodhouse, am I?' he said, then started up the tree after Patsy.

This had all the makings of a terrible idea, but what else could we do? If we carried on going on foot it was only a matter of time before we got spotted again, and there were so many nosey coppers converging on this section of the woods that if that happened it would be game over for us. Goody figured our only hope was to disappear, to get our-selves out of eye level and hide in the densely packed canopy fifty feet up in the air. On the surface it was an okay plan. It would've been a great plan had it not been for all the dogs sniffing around down there and the fact that Patsy had his favourite red T-shirt on, but what could we do? Make like branches and work on a few pointless deals with God, that was about our lot.

We spread out around the tree top just about as high as we could safely go and hid amongst the branches. What we would've given for our combat jackets and ski masks now, but me and Goody had slung them back at the super-market when we'd made our break this morning – all those years ago.

After a few minutes the forest floor was flooded with boot steps and condescending voices. For ages I couldn't see anyone through the gaps in the leaves, then all of a sudden two coppers walked right underneath us. I squeezed my eyes closed in the childish hope that if I couldn't see them, they couldn't see me, and it seemed to work because when I opened them again the coppers were gone.

My heart pounded inside my chest and my ears rushed with fear. I really didn't like this one little bit. At least while we'd been running it had felt like our destiny was in our own feet. That may have been stretching it a bit but at least we'd been doing something. Lying here and doing nothing, waiting for one of our pursuers to come along and exercise their necks under our tree, I just felt helpless.

Not that I could do anything about that now. It was all in the lap of the Big Man upstairs, as they say.

For half an hour we hid and listened. I couldn't make out exactly what the Old Bill were saying but it seemed like they'd found the point at which we'd climbed out of the overgrown stream and were now fanning out in all directions. The dogs had probably sniffed out the entrance and then several flatfoots would've been sent through on their bellies only to find the same shitty sludge we'd crawled through ourselves. A few minutes later they would've wheeled the dogs around to the exit and given them a kick up the arse, but none of them seemed to be able to pick up our scent again. Perhaps Goody's magic brush had worked, or perhaps there were so many coppers down there that they'd trampled our odour right into the dust. I didn't know, I wasn't Barbara Woodhouse either. All I did know was that no dog came sniffing around our tree and me, Goody and Patsy went on lying among the tree tops undisturbed.

Things went on like this for some time and slowly the sky above our heads dimmed until I could no longer see the forest floor.

Torches swept through the woods all around us and it was only then that I realised the scale of the police operation – it was enormous. So much so that the whole forest seemed to flicker like magic. As far as the eye could see (which admittedly wasn't that far) there were tiny pinpricks of light dancing about in the trees. I felt flattered and deeply depressed all at the same time and wondered again just how the fuck we were meant to get out of the middle of all of this lot.

I guess someone up there must've been listening because a moment later whistles broke out all over the place and the Old Bill called their search off for the night. It took me a few minutes to work out what the whistles signified because when I first heard them I thought they were letting everyone know they'd found us, but I didn't feel particularly found at that moment so I squinted through the blackness to make sure that there weren't a load of coppers squinting back at me and breathed a sigh of relief when I saw that there weren't.

The significance of the whistles finally sank in when, one by one, the torches exited the woods, leaving us and the darkness behind.

'Where have they gone?' Patsy whispered to Goody.

'Didn't want to pay the overtime, did they, tight bastards,' Goody told him back.

'You mean that's it? We got away with it? We're free?' he asked excitedly.

'Yep, we're still free,' Goody replied. 'At least we are until sunrise tomorrow when it starts again.'

Getting away from nature

Climbing down a tree in pitch blackness is an experience I'll happily go the rest of my life without ever repeating. Three times I slipped, once when a twig I entrusted my twelve stone to broke off, once when that great clumsy cunt Goody stood on my fingers and once when I was on the very lowest branch, but didn't realise it, and woke up the whole forest with my screams as I fell eight inches to what I thought was my death.

'You alright?' asked Goody, jumping down onto my face.

'Argh! You fat cunt, get off me!'

I tell you, up until that moment I'd never realised just how dark the night could be. I'd wandered around after the hours of darkness plenty of times before, of course, as one does in my line of work, but I'd never known it like this. Sure, I knew that the night was meant to be dark but this was beyond a joke. The expression 'not being able to see your hand in front of your face' I'd always thought was just a euphemism. Surely you'd be able to see your fingers wriggling from two inches away no matter how dark it was? Guess again, it was true. I tried it. I couldn't.

See, I'd grown up knowing night-time to have a bit of an

orangey hue to it, especially around town. This was what I thought night-time looked like, and even when I'd day-dreamed about being Dick Turpin and riding off with Lord Fotherington-Smythe's wallet and mobile I'd always done so looking a bit black and white under local authority street lighting.

Well, let me tell you something, night-time is black. It's black, disorienting, scary and packed with stuff to trip over.

Me, Goody and Patsy tried feeling our way through the darkness to get out of it before the Old Bill showed up in the morning but it was absolutely hopeless. We walked into trees, slipped over shit, bashed our fingers on trunks and scratched our faces on low-hanging branches, and all that before we made it ten yards. We had no choice but to do as the Old Bill had done and called it a night. Besides, we really couldn't go on. All three of us were teetering with exhaustion and the onset of night just pushed us closer to the edge, so we found somewhere dry and relatively stinger free, then lay down . . .

. . . and plunged into a deep embracing sleep.

Tuesday started as it meant to go on and planted a boot up my arse by way of a good morning.

'Come on, then, get up. It's light,' Goody was saying as he laid into my back with his size nines. 'Wake up.'

'Wha . . . wha.. what . . . you fucking . . .'

Goody was right, it was light. It was also freezing. We'd lain out all night in just our trousers and T-shirts and suddenly we knew all about it. My arms felt like stone and I rubbed and hugged myself to try to kick-start the circulation as Goody warmed his boots up on Patsy.

'Je . . . Je . . . Jessussss . . . it'sssss f-f-fuckkkin c-c-cold,' I chattered, overcome with shivers and a sudden nausea. 'Wha . . . wha . . . what time is it?'

'Five. They'll be starting up again soon so we should get a move on.'

'Oh, fuck . . .' I retched, and puked up a thimble's worth of acrid bile.

'Have a drink,' Goody suggested.

'What? Have you g-g-got some?'

'No, but the leaves, they're covered in dew. Look,' he said, and once again he was right. Tiny moisture droplets clung to every leaf and I was able to suck up enough to soothe my burning throat, quench one per cent of my raging thirst and wet my face.

'Make the most of it while you can, it'll all be gone in an hour,' Goody told us, so me and Patsy drank some more until we could no longer stand the taste of leaves.

Not counting the ten-second sleep I'd enjoyed yesterday, this had been the first kip I'd had since Saturday night and a much-needed one it had been too. My mind was still woozy with sleep; it felt like it was stuffed with cotton wool and I was about as steady on my pins as Bambi's little sister after she'd been on the Scotch all night, but at least I felt better than I had at the end of the previous night.

Goody hauled me up to my feet and gave my arms and body a good rubbing all over, but it started to feel a bit bent, two blokes cuddling in the woods, so I told him to stop it. Patsy had no such objections, however, and Goody warmed him up until the pair of them could've passed for newly-weds. Then it was time to go.

'Which way?' I asked.

'Let's follow the river downstream. It's going away from the cops and it might even lead us to water, you never know,' Goody suggested, which sounded like a reasonable plan to me.

'You alright, Pats?'

'C-c-cold,' was all he could reply.

'Yeah, me too. Come on, then, let's get going.'

The three of us walked like rusty robots (who'd shat themselves) until our limbs loosened up, though even then we were hardly nimble. This simply wasn't our environment. I was hungry, thirsty, cold, sore, tired and I had cuts, scratches, bites and stings all over my body. We hadn't even been in the woods eighteen hours yet. What sort of a state would we be in after two days? I wondered. Dead probably. No, this settled it, we had to get the fuck out of here and take our chances back in the civilised world. Cars, houses, microwaves and tellies, I could handle all those things. Trees, bushes, flies and creepy-crawlies I clearly could not.

When I'd been in prison, I'd fantasised about strolling through the woods all the time. I'd always thought of them as comfortable, friendly places with butterflies and apples and saucy bits of stuff in see-through white dresses who went about their business stroking horses and wearing flowers in their hair. I'd even naively thought that if I was ever on the run I could just go and live in the woods like Grizzly Adams and survive on fruit and rabbits and fish and nature and all that other stuff until the heat cooled off and I was all forgotten about.

Hah, can you imagine that? What an idiot! No, if the last eighteen hours had done nothing else for me they had cured me of any sort of affection I felt towards nature. The woods were a horrible, nasty, spiteful, painful place that spun you around in all directions and tripped you up whenever it got the chance. They were places without reason, without hope and without mercy. Bulldoze the fucking lot of them if you like, you wouldn't hear a complaint from me. Stick a car park and a drive-thru McDonald's in place of Constable's *Hay Wain* and I'd punch out Sting's lights if he even looked like moaning about it. I didn't care any more. I'd had enough. Just get me back to the world I knew, with kettles and fridges and cafés, pubs, pavements and petrol stations.

I didn't want to be in the woods any more.

Goody dragged his stick broom behind us for about ten minutes before he got well and truly bored of doing so and convinced himself it wasn't doing any good anyhow, then slung it into the next thorny bush we came across.

'The dogs might smell it in there and maybe a few cops might scratch their hands getting it out,' he explained. 'Maybe not. But one can always hope.'

We kicked along for another twenty minutes or so and in that time the deafening dawn chorus slowly put a sock in it and settled down to a few background chirps. That's when we heard it.

It was a voice.

The three of us stopped and turned our ears back to where the voice was coming from. It sounded quite a long way away and we couldn't hear it too well, what with the breeze in the leaves and the rest of it, but it sounded like it was being shouted through a megaphone.

'Do you think that's for us?' Patsy asked.

'Probably,' I said. 'Or maybe some nature lover who likes talking to the trees, loads of them all at once.'

'Quiet, I'm trying to listen,' Goody snapped, angling his head the way people do when they can't quite hear something.

We let him listen for a while then Patsy asked him what it was all about.

'How the fuck should I know, I can't hear him,' Goody replied.

'I'll tell you what he's saying, he's saying, "Give yourselves up, you haven't got a chance, the place is surrounded and we've got bacon san'wiches and cups of tea waiting for you when you do".'

'You reckon they have?' Patsy asked.

'I don't know. Probably. Not exactly worth it, though, is it?'

'No. Still, bacon sandwiches. Imagine that. Fucking lovely, with red and brown sauce and a fried egg on top.'

'Yeah, cheers, Patsy, that's just what I need to think about right now.'

'You have red and brown sauce on yours, then, do you?' Goody asked.

'Yeah. Why, what do you have, just brown?'

'No, I don't like any sauces on mine, I just like to taste the bacon and the butter all melting together.'

'You can't have a bacon sandwich without sauce,' Patsy told him.

'Of course you can, sauce ruins it. You cover a bacon sandwich with sauce and all you can taste is the sauce. I eat bacon sandwiches because I like the taste of bacon. Fucking brown sauce,' he said dismissively.

'You're weird.'

'Yeah, and I'm starving,' I told them both. 'So put a fucking san'wich . . . I mean sock . . . in it, will ya.'

'You started it, talking about cups of tea and bacon sandwiches.'

'Look, it doesn't matter. Let's just get out of here. Come on. Let's find a road,' I told them, and we started walking again.

'He sounded like he was a long way away,' Goody said. 'Old matey on the mega-horn.'

'Good, let's hope he stays that way,' I replied, looking over my shoulder and picking up the pace.

Fifteen minutes later the miracle happened – we found water. The dried-up dusty tributary we'd been following for the last forty-five minutes led us to a long sloping bank then shot off down it and dumped itself in a river at the bottom. We heard the water before we saw it and the three of us ran down the trail in a frenzy of excitement, looking for the source.

The water itself was only about two feet deep, though by the looks of the river bank's sheer sides, it probably rose a bit further in the winter.

I dropped to my belly and scooped up a handful of delicious cold water and threw it into my mouth. It's not an exaggeration (but it is a lazy cliché) to say that it was the best thing I'd ever tasted. It tasted even better than my traditional post-prison beer and I couldn't down it fast enough. I scooped up more and more and washed the grit and shit from my arms, face and neck and didn't stop until I was freezing cold and half drowned. Goody and Patsy were on their bellies either side of me doing the same and when Goody was done he looked over and gave me a smile of utter contentment.

'Fucking lovely,' that was his verdict.

'Do you think this water's safe to drink?' Patsy asked.

'Doubt it. Probably full of fertiliser and fish hooks and shit but I'm ready to take a chance,' I said, washing my hair and cleaning the gunk out of my ears.

'It could be poisonous, though,' Patsy worried some more.

'It's not poisonous, Patsy, look, there's little fish in there. They'd all be floating upside down if it was poisonous,' Goody told him.

'I suppose,' he conceded, less than convinced.

I drank some more but Patsy's seed of doubt ruined the experience for me and made every subsequent mouthful taste like battery acid and the piss of a thousand ramblers, and then, when I looked closer, I saw thousands of tiny little creatures wriggling away just below the surface. A cold shiver came over me when I realised a few hundred of their mates were now probably wriggling away inside my guts and I just hoped I got them before they got me.

'Shall we get out of here?' Goody suggested, jumping in up to his waist.

'We walking in the river, then?'

'You wanted a river to walk in, well, here's a river. So come on in, the water's lovely.'

My nads disagreed with Goody's assessment and crawled up inside my body for warmth when I leapt in, but after a day of running around under the burning sun there was something quite refreshing about the cool flow on my tired sore legs, and the three of us started downstream.

'Let's go this way, we'll walk with the flow, it'll be easier,' Goody told us, and I was all in favour of anything easier.

'What time is it?'

'Almost nine o'clock.'

'Perhaps we should get out of the river now, I can't feel my legs any more.'

'Wherever we get out though, the dogs'll just pick up our scent at that point and have us again.'

'For fuck's sake, Goody, what are we supposed to do, then, walk all the way to Brazil? We can't stay in here for ever.'

And we certainly couldn't, especially not after that deep bit we'd encountered back a short way which had come up to our shoulders. Me and Goody had walked through it carrying our money over our heads, though I'd hit an underwater pothole and ended up saturating a hundred grand. Patsy had dived to my rescue and together we'd pulled the bag clear before it had got completely soaked through, but I was now desperate to get out and check its contents.

'What we need is a boat,' said Able Seaman Goody, as we hit another deep bit.

'You reckon?' I replied, as the water rose around my chest. 'Oh, fuck this, I'm getting out,' I said, chucking my bag up onto the bank and clambering up after it. Patsy followed me out and together we pulled up Goody, though he wasn't too happy about it.

'Well, you know, what do you want us to do? I'm sorry, mate, but we're not fucking mermaids. I mean, fuck me, come on, I thought I was having a hard enough time of it walking in the woods but you managed to find somewhere even worse. Jesus!'

'But they always do it on the telly.'

'Yeah, and on the telly they've usually only got a couple of rednecks and a couple of bloodhounds on their backs, not the whole of the Hampshire Constabulary scanning the woods for us. Walking around up to our necks in water isn't going to shake them off.'

'You think there are still that many, after all this time?' Goody asked.

'I don't know. Cost a lot of money, I'll tell you that, what with the helicopters and the manpower and everything else. That's a point, I haven't seen or heard any of them today either.'

'Fuck me, lads, look,' Patsy gasped, catching us on the hop twice in two days as me and Goody threw our wet bodies into the long grass.

'What? What? What is it?' Goody demanded, scanning the sky.

'A road,' he said, and pointed 200 yards downstream to a red-brick bridge that crossed the river. We would probably have blundered right up to it but a car went over and caught Patsy's attention. Goody dragged him down out of sight and we studied our route back to civilisation.

'It looks clear,' Goody whispered. It looked more than clear, it looked perfect. Next to the bridge (on the other side of the river, naturally) was a little stone cottage. I didn't know who lived there or if anyone was home. At that stage I didn't particularly care. All I knew was that inside that cottage there would be food, drink, warmth, a change of clothes and car keys (maybe).

And after the day and a half I'd just had, no one – and I do mean no one – was going to stop me knocking on that door.

Look who's coming to breakfast

I told Goody to circle around to the back door while me and Patsy hit the front. I wiped the water from my eyes, checked that the coast was clear and rang the bell.

'Police, sir. Open up, please!' I called through the letter box and clattered it urgently. A few seconds passed then a shadow approached the frosted glass and raised the latch. Before whoever it was had a chance to peer out I put my shoulder to the door and bundled some poor unsuspecting old lady over onto her arse. Patsy picked her up and dusted her off, while I demanded to know who else was home. Her eyes instinctively darted towards the kitchen out the back, but there was no need for her to say anything because at that moment some old fella in a vest stepped out and gawped at us in confusion.

I spun round and thrust my gun into his face, then asked him the question I'd just asked her. 'Who else is home? This is your only chance because if we find anyone else in here we'll kill them, and we mean it,' I warned him sternly.

'There's no one here, only us,' he promised, wiping the recently flicked river water out of his eyes.

'You sure?'

'Just me and my wife. Our daughters are long gone,' he explained.

'What, dead?' I asked.

'No, married.'

'Oh,' I said. 'Oh. Congratulations.'

Matey blinked a couple of times and said, 'Thank you.'

I lowered my gun and told Patsy to do the same, then we reunited him with his wife and marched them into the kitchen.

'You're the ones they're looking for?' the old fella said, as we sat them down at a big pine table in the middle of the kitchen.

'Yes, and this chap here too,' I told him, opening the back door for Goody.

'Hello,' Goody said breezily as he stepped inside.

'They've been round here, then, have they? The Old Bill?' I asked the old fella.

'Yes. Yesterday. And it was on the news too. They said you were in the woods.'

'They were right, we were,' I told him, then almost launched into one about what a hard time of it we'd had, but that would just have wasted time. If the police had been here, then chances were they'd be coming back. Particularly if the dogs found where we'd climbed out of the river. We didn't have long, an hour or so, maybe only half that, but that was long enough to get ourselves together.

'What do you want with us?' the guy finally asked.

'We're starving,' Patsy whined pathetically.

'Yes, we really need some food. And some water. And clothes. An old jumper, trousers, coat, anything like that,' I told him.

The old man and the old lady swapped stares, then the old lady got to her feet and asked if we wanted a cooked breakfast.

'Oh God, yes.' Patsy nodded, and melted into a seat.

Tensions between us thawed further as she clattered pots and pans about and filled the kitchen with wonderful smells. Me and Goody took the weight off our feet and sat down with Patsy and matey at the table.

Three cups of steaming hot tea appeared in front of us then, a moment later, all pandemonium broke out when the old lady dropped half a dozen heavily buttered doorstops in between us.

'Oh, thank you, thank you, thank you,' Patsy said over and over again, stuffing two slices at once into his face.

'You know, I wouldn't fire your guns if I was you, they're all wet. Likely to blow your fingers off as much as our heads,' the old fella told us, all matter-of-fact.

'No bullets anyway, Dad.' Goody showed him.

'Oh,' the old fella replied, somewhere between relief and disappointment.

'You two have still got some ammo, haven't you?' Goody said to me and Patsy.

'Yeah, but like the fella said, it's probably useless. I don't really want to go shooting anything if I can help it anyway,' I said, reassuring our hosts.

'Did you fall in the river?' the old fella then asked.

'No, we were walking through it, to shake off the dogs,' Goody told him.

'Oh.' He nodded. 'You should've got a boat,' he said, and Goody flashed me a look.

'That reminds me, have you got a tumble drier around here somewhere?' I asked.

'Yes, it's out in the garage. Do you want me to put your clothes in it for you?' the old woman asked.

'No, just our money,' I told her, unzipping my knapsack and feeling the mash of cash inside.

'Got wet too, did it?' the old boy asked. What was it with retired folks and obvious, dead-end questions?

'Yes,' I answered, just to be polite, then followed the old

lady out to the garage and poured my money into her Hotpoint.

'Now this is just a drier, isn't it, not a washer-drier?' I asked, checking all the buttons to make sure I wasn't condemning my cash to a 40°C non-colour-fast quick wash.

'No, it's just a drier,' she promised, and stuck it on warm and gentle for ten minutes.

We went back into the kitchen and while the old lady got on with making our breakfasts, I took the old boy upstairs and got him to sort us all out with some dry duds. I told him he didn't have to part with his Sunday best or anything, just a few pairs of trousers and a couple of old pullovers from his old lady's jumble-sale pile. Most of it was okay (leastways, it was a damn sight cleaner and dryer than our clothes) but there was one pullover that was so offensive I couldn't see anyone short of a Mozambique gigolo thinking it was wearable.

'It was a present. Please take it, you'd be doing me an enormous favour,' the old boy pleaded, and Goody suddenly became one jumper richer.

We arrived back in the kitchen just as hot plates and greasy food were hitting the table and I got stuck straight in. The food, along with more bread and top-ups of tea, stood no chance against us and we polished the lot off in a little under five minutes (Patsy was so single-minded that he forgot to ask if they had any brown sauce).

'Hungry, were you?' the old boy observed.

'I'm going to take a quick shower then we're getting out of here,' I told our hosts, and disappeared up to the bathroom while the last mouthfuls of food were still sliding down my gullet. This perhaps wasn't the smartest move considering the time factor, but I had to wash myself down. I stank. I stank of sweat, I stank of dirt, I stank of blood, and sap, and shit, and river water, and blackberries, and now I stank of bacon fat and butter, all around my chops. Two minutes under warm water would sharpen me up as much as any meal and dry clothes would and I had to have a shower. It was as simple as that.

I turned it onto hot and let my clothes lie where they fell. I grabbed a bar of soap and stepped under the water. Fantastic. Face, arms, pits and balls all got the benefit of a few suds and a bit of a scrub while the rest of my body had to make do with a thirty-second de-grit. Two minutes later I was stepping into my new dry clothes via a warm fluffy towel and feeling on top of the world.

I tell you; clean, dry, fed and watered – it's so easy to take simple comforts for granted. I always have in the past and no doubt will again in the future, but there's few moments in life better than post-showering after a particularly smelly time of things.

I've always wondered this about tramps. I don't mean the dog-on-a-string brigade with their Gazelle trainers and cashpoint dwellings, I'm talking about genuine, long-bearded, bare-footed, flea-infested, incoherent bin-diners who wander around city centres making Stig of the dump look like Giorgio Armani on a good hair day. Imagine how bad things must be for those poor fuckers. It doesn't even bear thinking about. I couldn't imagine anything worse, not even life imprisonment. And this is probably my point. If I was one of these blokes, the bottom of the pile, on the cusp between man and beast and stinking like a corpse before it's time to, I'd be stealing, robbing and mugging everyone else blind to get myself out of it. Anything, just so that I didn't have to be a smelly old, sore-ridden tramp any more. I mean, what would be the worst that could happen? Bed and board for a few years and a fresh start when I got out. I'd take that over sleeping in my own shit any day of the week. Wouldn't you? Maybe this is just me. Maybe it's my criminal nature, but how could you allow yourself to be that much of a victim? I couldn't understand it. No one had ever given me anything (a hundred grand and a new jumper aside). I'd always had to fend for myself. Yeah, okay, perhaps I wasn't doing a particularly brilliant job of it at the moment but at least I was doing something about it. I wasn't sitting around stinking out the place, waiting for sympathy and an unfinished Burger King to be dropped on the floor near me. I was in charge of my life. That much at least was clear to me. It was all about pride, I guess, at the end of the day. Perhaps that was what was missing with these poor blokes.

Which leads us nicely onto an idea I once had inside.

I thought, if I was an eccentric millionaire with loads of cash and everything it would be interesting to tranquilliser-dart one of those blokes and wash, shave and manicure him up from head to foot, then, while he was still out for the count, stick him in an expensive pin-striped whistle and leave him at Victoria station with a briefcase under his arm. Just to see what he does.

Just imagine how confused he'd be when he woke up.

'What's going on here, then?' he'd probably think to himself. 'What . . . oh, thank fuck for that, I'm not a smelly old tramp after all, I'm a rich businessman, it must've all been a bad dream. Hmm, any Diamond White in the case?'

I don't know what he'd do then – probably go straight back to his old ways, but he'd be the smartest-looking Harold under the arches for a few weeks at least.

I headed back downstairs and got my money out of the drier while Goody took a shower. I made sure I tied it all up in plastic bin liners this time in case Goody took us down any more watery short cuts and told Patsy to jump in the shower the moment it was free. Patsy passed up on the chance to shower and settled for a quick wash in the kitchen sink while I filled a carrier bag with fruit, bread,

tins, cooked meats and bottles, in case – please God, no –
we somehow ended up in the woods again that night.

The old couple eyed us nervously as we got ready to
leave and I had an inkling what was on their minds. There
was no way we could just walk out and leave them to their
own devices when the Old Bill were just a phone call away,
and they knew it as well as I did. We had to take care of
them somehow.

'Car keys?' I demanded.

'The table, by the front door,' the wife replied.

'Okay then. Right, thanks for all your hospitality. This is
for your trouble,' I told them, setting two warm £20 notes
down on the kitchen table in front of them.

'We'd rather not, if that's okay with you,' the old lady said
a little warily.

I looked up at her and couldn't believe she'd just said this.

I don't know what the intention was on her part,
whether she meant it as a deliberate snub to show me how
much better they were than me or whether she thought
they stood a better chance of dodging harm if they allowed
me to hang onto my money. Either way it annoyed and
offended me and made me feel particularly unwelcome in
their house, which I guess we were. But come on, half an
hour, a cooked breakfast, a shower and a few old threads,
we'd hardly ransacked the place. Hadn't we made the effort?
Hadn't we been polite? Hadn't we said please and thank
you and 'here, have some money for your trouble'?

Some people!

Fine, I thought to myself, if that's the way they want it,
that's the way they can have it. Treat me like a criminal and
I'll oblige every time. No problem.

I stuffed the money back into my pocket and put away
my smile. Then I pulled out my gun again.

'Okay, this way, outside,' I ordered them in no uncertain
terms.

Goody appeared at that moment and asked me where I was taking them so I told him. 'The garden shed.' I'd spotted it when we'd cased the place a little earlier and it had stayed in the back of my mind because of the big old shiny padlock on the door. It wasn't unusual for sheds to have padlocks but theirs was wide open, suggesting a rather lax attitude towards protecting their property.

And this at a time when 'criminals' were running loose in the woods.

I marched them down the garden path and told them to get inside, then I thanked them for their hospitality once again (a little more sternly this time) and snapped the lock shut behind them.

Of course, I was always going to have to do this anyway. I mean, even if the old lady had taken my money, we would still have had to deny them the run of the house after we'd left, but at least I would've felt a tad bad about it.

Not that this was too much of an inconvenience. I hadn't tied them up or smacked them about or left them in a place that didn't have buckets or anything. No, things could've been a lot worse for them if someone not as nice as me had come along. Besides, the shed was hardly Alcatraz, they could probably get out of there if they really put their minds to it. And this reflected itself in the last thing I heard the old lady say as I walked back up the garden path. Rather than worry about spending a long hot summer's day in there or starving to death or never seeing her loved ones again, she seemed more put out by the fact that we were taking her old man's favourite jumper with us.

That was until I started chucking petrol up the side of the shed.

Nah, I'm only kidding. What sort of a bloke do you take me for?

I got back in the house and went around locking all the doors and windows behind me. If they did make it out of the shed I wanted to make it as difficult for them to raise the alarm as I could so as to buy us as much time as possible. I told Patsy to have a quick shufti around, gather up all the phones and stick them in the tumble drier, and I was just about to get on when I felt his confused eyes burning into the back of my head.

'You what?'

'Get all the phones, unplug them and stick them in the tumble drier,' I repeated.

Patsy wobbled his legs about in confusion but remained more or less rooted to the spot.

'What? What is it you don't understand about this, Patsy?'

It looked like just about everything, like he'd never even realised those words could be taken and arranged in that particular order up until now, but in the end he decided simply to ask if I wanted the tumble drier turned on too.

'No, don't turn it on, leave the fucking thing off, just hide them in there so that they can't find them when they get out of the shed,' I said, exasperated.

Personally, I thought this explained it all but there was still something Patsy didn't get about the whole idea.

'But they'll find them eventually, you know, next time they come to do their washing,' he told me, then headed off, shaking his head.

You know, I'm the first to admit that I'm no genius but if brains were made of dynamite some of my mates wouldn't have enough to blow off their hats. I put the whole brief but bizarre conversation out of my mind and went to check out the front to make sure the coast was clear.

The odd car, that was about it. This was a secluded country cottage down a quiet country lane. I couldn't make up my mind whether that was a good thing or a bad thing.

'We ready, Eddie?' Goody asked, bringing the money and food up to the front door with him.

'Just about. Let me go first and get the car turned around then you and Patsy jump in when I give you the signal, okay?'

'Cool,' he replied.

'Oh, and by the way – looking sharp there, Goody.'

'Yeah, where the fuck did you find this thing?' he asked, pulling at his new jumper.

'I'll tell you later. Just remember to close the door after yourselves when you come out, okay?'

I grabbed the keys off the little side table and popped open the doors as I strode down the driveway towards the car.

A Rover. Nice car, reliable, roomy, fast. Nothing too flash. Probably the sort of motor I would've got if I'd retired to this place too. It was perfect for our needs.

The only drawback were the number plates – they were personalised.

CL1VE 17.

I took a moment out to wonder how much he'd actually paid for that little baby and decided probably not a lot. I also wondered if this meant there were at least another sixteen Clives out there who were chuffed about their names, though again I had my doubts. Still, no matter how much he, and all the other Clives, had paid for their flashy tags, it would, in my opinion, be every penny too much and then some.

See, I didn't get it, I never had. Why would anyone want to personalise their number plate? Seriously, I understood them about as much as Patsy understood why he had to spin-dry a load of phones. They were such idiotic, inane, pointless things.

Ah, but they're status symbols, you might argue.

How are number plates status symbols? It's not con-sidered particularly flash to walk around wearing a hat with your name on it once you get older than about eight, so how is it otherwise on cars? *Look at me, everyone, look, my name's William Anker, but I've abbreviated it.* Seriously, what's the attraction? Even if I had all the money in the world and my own number plate printing machine I still wouldn't have one. They were that much of a mystery to me.

I was speaking about this to a mate of mine inside once and he gave me the most ludicrous explanation. He reckoned that personalised plates were a good thing because they helped you spot your motor if you forgot where you left it.

I'm sorry, but I didn't buy that then and wasn't buying it now. If I drove my twenty-five-grand motor down the shops and parked it up somewhere I'm pretty confident I could find it again without having 01 1M 0V3R HE4E front and back.

No, personalised plates were simply for people who felt they weren't getting enough attention in life. This was something me, Patsy and Goody had no shortage of at the moment, so CL1VE, with his stupid, easily rememberable, eye-catching plates, had fucked us up a little bit.

We weren't going to get very far in this motor, but then even a couple of miles with our feet off the ground was a real bonus, so that would have to do.

I climbed in and started her up. I took a quick look over my left shoulder and then my right, then I rolled her backwards and forwards a few times until I was pointing in the right direction, and gave Goody the signal.

Goody gave Patsy a nudge and the pair of them came out carrying the cash, the grub and the bottles. Goody even remembered to pull the door shut after him, and they both jumped in.

'We ready, then?'

'We're ready.'

'Right. Smart. Let's see those fucking dogs follow this, then.' I laughed, and pulled out into the lane.

8

The open road – all 500 fucking yards of it

'Here, lads, I found this in the house. Look, you're famous.' I glanced over my shoulder to see what Patsy was talking about and saw him holding up a copy of the *Daily Mirror*. Sure enough, down in the corner of the front page was the headline BANDITS BACK-DOOR BREAK. Someone at the *Mirror* obviously had a sense of humour. There was only room for the headline and a couple of inches of text as we'd had the good fortune to make our bid for freedom on the same day that one of Charlotte Church's knockers had tried to do the same thing at some award ceremony and most of the front page was given over to that.

Unfortunately there were further details inside on pages 8 and 9 (Charlotte's tits did considerably better than us, with pages 4, 5, 6 and 7 and the centre spread dedicated to them) along with pictures of me, Parky and a couple of e-fit mock-ups that would've looked a bit like Goody and Patsy if they'd been made of Plasticine and had come from the moon.

'What's it say? How are we doing?'

'"Members of the Second Battalion of the Parachute

Regiment were last night called in to assist police in the search for the supermarket bandits,"' Goody read out.

'They're not going to keep calling us that, are they?' I moaned, liking my new nickname about as much as I liked our chances.

"'Up to 100 soldiers and armed police are this morning combing woodlands around the New Forest for four members of the gang that made off with half a million pounds yesterday lunchtime. Police say the men are armed and should not be considered . . .'"

'Four men?' I asked in confusion.

'Yeah, er, hang on. Blahdy-blahdy-blah, here we go. "Two of the men have been named as Darren Stephen Miles, 27, and Leonard Royston Parker, 30. They escaped together with two, as yet unidentified men, one described by police as tall, thin, late twenties, with fair hair and blue eyes" – that would be you, Patsy – "and the other stocky, 5ft 10in, mousy brown hair, brown eyes and bad complexion." Eh?'

'They haven't got Parky yet either, then,' I said, trying to look over at the page as I was driving along.

'I haven't got a bad complexion,' Goody moaned, clearly upset at this libel.

'We'll worry about that another time, shall we,' I said.

'But I haven't,' he insisted, and to be honest he didn't. I didn't know where the papers had got their information from but Goody was no scalier than me or Patsy. He'd had a bit of a rash across his boat from where he'd been sweating in his mask all night long but then so had the rest of us. That said, his allegedly mousy brown hair had also changed from sweaty dark to fair following a shower, so Goody's description matched him about as much as his e-fit did. Not a bad thing when you're in our shoes.

'They don't know who we are, then,' Patsy said hopefully.

'Yeah, well, I wouldn't count on it staying that way, Pats, not once your newspaper boys start wondering why you aren't around to stop them stealing fags and why there's a picture of you looking like Bod in the papers all of a sudden,' I told him, pissing all over his freshly lit bonfire.

'Bad complexion?'

'I wonder where Parky is, then,' Patsy said.

'I don't know. Wherever it is I hope he's doing better than us.'

'What are you talking about, Milo? We're doing alright now that we've got a motor,' Goody said.

'You must be joking, this place is going to be ringed with checkpoints. We ain't driving out of these woods, you can bet your Sunday dinner on that.'

If he'd noticed the fact that I was only plodding along at barely 15 mph and slowing down to take a peek around every twist and turn before I made it, Goody might've worked this one out for himself. There were only a couple of roads through these woods and the chances were that the Old Bill would've set up shop somewhere along the line. I didn't know much but I knew one thing, we weren't anywhere near out of this little mess just yet.

A couple of cars passed in the opposite direction and Goody and Patsy squeezed down in their seats, presumably in order to attract as much attention to themselves as they could. Practically on the floor now, Goody continued to read bits from the paper to us, including little snippets like '"BT engineer Mike Mills was last night recovering in hospital with head wounds after he was attacked and abducted by the gang . . ."'and '". . . assaulted at gunpoint. It is believed Mrs Lloyd is now receiving counselling following her hour-long kidnap ordeal.'They were like animals,' she told police officers."'

'Jesus, some people, eh!'

'Yeah, that's a bit rich coming from old Bitey. "Animals"? She was the one who wanted to have a go, not us,' Goody moaned.

'Yeah, well, I don't think we're going to get much sympathy when we come to tell our side of the story. Here, turn over the page quickly. Let's just have a look at Charlotte's ... SHIT! FUCKING HELL!' I slammed on the brakes and quickly reversed back around the corner, out of sight.

'What? What? What is it, Milo?'

'Checkpoint, I saw it. Up there. Old Bill.'

I waited a moment to catch my breath then racked my brains as to what to do.

'What are we going to do?' asked Patsy, not giving me a second to think about it.

'I don't know. I don't know. Hang on,' I said, and weighed up my options.

We couldn't double back because we'd just end up driving backwards and forwards past Clive's cottage all day. If they had a checkpoint in this direction they were bound to have one in the other. By the same token we had no chance getting past those bastards up ahead because they had our pictures and our names. We were boxed in and we knew it. I really didn't want to take to the woods again because I figured our chances of slipping the net were getting slimmer and slimmer by the minute, and if they were now drafting in the A-Team to hunt us down we really needed to be getting out of here some time today, otherwise we weren't going anywhere for a long, long time.

'What are we going to do?' Patsy persisted, hammering home the fact that we didn't have the luxury of time. Two cars had already gone past in the couple of minutes we'd been sitting there and it only needed one of those cunts to tell the boys in blue up at the checkpoint that there were three blokes in a car back here dilly-dallying about like smokers outside a bike shed to tip them the wink. We had to go now.

I half thought about just going for it and putting my foot down, but you can't outrun an entire police force once they know where you are. You might as well just give yourself up and save everyone the hassle. One or two motors you can get away from before they've got a chance to get organised and as long as you bin the motor the first chance you get. But a whole police force? It wasn't even an option.

'Alright, let's hide this thing in the woods and try and make it out on foot again.' I sighed, disappointed that it had come to this once more. How long would it be before I felt nice and clean and dry again?

'Wait, I've got a better idea,' Goody said, though I could see from the expression on his face that it was a work in progress. 'Why don't I take the car through and pick you boys up on the other side of the checkpoint, say half a mile down the road?'

'What? But you'll never get through, this is a nicked motor.'

'Yeah? But it ain't nicked yet, not until it's reported. I could tell them that it's my girlfriend's old man's motor and he lives in the cottage back there. He just lent it to me to go to the shops. "It's alright, Officer, the car's insured for any driver." Give us a seven-day wonder and I'll bring the dockets down the cop shop next week.'

'This is never going to work,' Patsy said.

'It will work. All they're going to want to do is search the motor for guns and money and check my ID. Well, take that lot out with you and I'll show them my old army ID,' he said, fishing it out of his bag. 'I'll even tell them my bird wanted me to come down and stop with the old cunts because they were worried about these super-cool criminals being on the loose in the woods all around them.'

'He's right,' I said, 'this is never going to work.'

'Oh, for fuck's sake, look, you saw it in the paper, the Old Bill are looking for you, blondie Skinny-arse in the back and spotty McDark Hair, and I'm neither of them, so come on, it's got to be worth a try, hasn't it?' he insisted, then clinched the deal with, 'unless you've got a better idea.'

I didn't. And on paper Goody's plan seemed workable enough, but then when was that a guarantee of success? Unfortunately, 'guarantee' and 'success' weren't words we had a right to use any more, so what was there to think about?

'Alright, let's do it,' I said, sliding out of the motor and handing the wheel over to Goody. 'Gun?'

'It's all in the bag,' he said, passing it out.

'Okay, it'll probably take us about twenty, maybe twenty-five, minutes to circle around them and find the road again, so be patient. Drive around in circles and we'll jump out when we see you pass by.'

'Will do,' he said, slamming the door closed and slipping into gear.

'Goody! Goody!'

'What?' he said, looking up at me.

'You might want to put your seat belt on.'

'Oh, yeah, thanks,' he said, then gave me a smile and pulled away.

'This is never going to work,' was all I could mutter as he tore off in the direction of the roadblock.

It took ten minutes of shuffling through the undergrowth for me and Patsy to get level with the roadblock. We'd circled about thirty yards away from the road and we could just about see their motors through the trees. There was a big white police van, some sort of souped-up panda and a black Rover.

Hang on a minute, I thought to myself, that was Goody's motor. He was still there. Surely he hadn't just sat there the whole time we'd been crawling through the bushes? What the fuck was going on?

Of course, I knew what was going on before I'd even

asked myself the question. He'd been detained. Goody's brilliant plan had fallen somewhat short of cop-proof and he was probably in the back of one of those motors with his hands in bracelets. Well, to be fair, his idea had asked a lot of everyone involved for it to work, and the Old Bill weren't likely to be in the mood to give anyone the benefit of the doubt while we were still running around taking the piss out of them.

Therefore, it came as no surprise.

What did come as a surprise was my reaction to Goody's sudden apprehension. Rather than scampering off into the undergrowth and not resurfacing until I got to Rio de Janeiro, I actually found myself edging towards the check-point. This was stupid of me, and I knew it. It went against my every principle as a coward and a Number One merchant, but I just couldn't help myself, I was fucked off. How dare the Old Bill just nick us like that without even having to lift a finger after all we'd been through? The fucking bastards! I could almost see them standing around in a huddle, giving themselves a big collective slap on the back and gloating over my crestfallen comrade in the cuffs, who had nothing to look forward to gloating over himself for the next couple of decades. It made my blood boil and armed me with a steel I never knew I had.

'Where are you going?' whispered Patsy, grabbing hold of one of my ankles.

'We're going to get Goody,' I told him, though by the look on his face I could've told him anything from 'there's a tarantula in your pocket' to 'you've just knelt on a land-mine'.

'What? You can't be serious!' he squeaked, but I pulled out my gun to show him I was.

'I can't do this by myself, you have to help me and you have to do it right otherwise it won't work.'

'But, but, but, but, but . . . but,' he butted for a bit, but my mind was made up. No buts. 'But, but, but . . .'

'Just follow me and do what I do, and for fuck's sake, don't go shooting anyone, particularly coppers, otherwise that'll be our lot for ever. You got it?'

'But, but, but . . .'

'Come on, then.'

We crawled through the bush slowly and carefully, dropping lower and lower the nearer we got until we were barely ten yards away. We watched them for a bit, strutting around like only coppers can, stopping cars and talking down to motorists until we had a fair idea of their strengths and weaknesses.

Their strengths seemed to be that there were four of them and two of them carried sidearms on their belts.

Their weaknesses were that they seemed so intent on the road that they weren't paying any attention to the woods whatsoever.

There was no sign of Goody, but the Rover was parked up by the side of the road with its boot open. One of the armed coppers was nosing around in it while the other was watching him work. The two unarmed uniforms were wearing luminous jackets and standing in the road waiting for the next unsuspecting criminal to come motoring by, while we were in the bushes watching them.

I whispered to Patsy that we had to take the armed officers down first. Patsy asked how.

'Point your gun at them and shout at them to get their hands up, that usually does the trick in the movies.'

'And if it doesn't work in real life?'

I stuck out my bottom lip and shrugged.

'I don't know, use your judgement. Just don't let them draw their guns otherwise they will shoot us if we're still holding ours. I mean it, they will.'

'Milo?'

'What?'

'I don't want to do this,' Patsy said, almost choking on the words.

'Well, me neither, but sometimes a man's just got to do what a man's got to do,' I told him, hardly believing what I'd just said.

Patsy suppressed a couple of panic bubbles and steeled himself for the suicide in prospect.

'Okay,' he finally said.

'Okay,' I agreed. 'I'll take matey going through the boot, you take that lazy cunt watching him. Alright, get into position and make sure you jump out when I do.'

'Got ya,' he said, and I fucking prayed he had. We'd done some dumb stuff over the last couple of days but this was about to take the whole biscuit factory. Even as I crawled into position I was still questioning the sanity of my plan. A voice in my head was screaming at me not to do it, to turn back and leave Goody to his fate, and why not? After all, it had been his idea to get nicked. It had been his plan, not mine. He'd wanted to take his chances, so why did I now have to risk everything to bail him out when it had all gone tits up?

The answer?

The answer was simply this: because I knew for a fact that that big dumb fucker in the back of the van would do the same for me if our roles were reversed. And I fucking hated him for it at that moment because it was guilting me into doing something I wanted to do about as much as Patsy.

God, how I would've loved to have just run off and lived the rest of my life on a beach somewhere and not thought about any of this shit ever again. But I knew I wouldn't be able to. Not if I left Goody behind like this to rot in a ten-by-eight for the next twenty years. Not when I had the chance to do something about it.

And I did have the chance. But that's about the best I could say about it. A chance.

Just a stupid, silly, idiotically ill-thought-through chance that might, or might not . . . oh, what was the use? Come on, let's just get this fucking thing over with.

'GET YOUR FUCKING HANDS UP IN THE AIR NOW!' I bellowed at my target, shitting the life out of him so much that he straightened up and smacked his head on the boot, stretching himself out stone cold across the tarmac.

At last, some fucking luck, I thought to myself, then turned my attention to the other armed copper behind me.

Unfortunately armed cop number two had half a second on me and his hand was already on his gun. I hadn't even turned around yet and the bastard was drawing on me with alarming speed, and it was at this moment that I suddenly realised I didn't have time to shout, warn or threaten him before he had me dead in his sights. My gun was 180 degrees out of the action and there was a fire burning in this guy's eyes that told me that I was in big trouble.

I suddenly started to panic and as I panicked there was one question that kept on popping into my head again and again.

Where the fuck was Patsy?

This was my only thought as I watched in cold horror my plan working out marginally worse than Goody's.

'Noooooo . . .' I heard myself shouting as the guy's lips drew back to reveal gritted teeth and his gleeful intentions as his polished black automatic levelled itself at my chest. I didn't even have time to sling my shooter aside and throw my hands up in the air in surrender – I was going to be shot.

They say that your life flashes through your mind at the very moment of death. I'm sorry to disappoint you but this wasn't the case with me. The only memories that flashed through my mind all featured Patsy and the thousands of opportunities I'd had in the past to punch his fucking lights out. Make hay while the sun shines, that's what I say, but it was all too late for that, and when I heard the crack of gunfire I braced myself to feel white-hot pain the likes of which I'd never felt before.

But it never came.

Just another gunshot, and then a third, but I wasn't the one falling over with a look of horror on his face – PC Armed Cop was. A great cloud of blue smoke hung in the air behind him and when he fell out of the picture I saw Patsy standing there with a look of utter horror on his face.

He'd shot him.

The silly stupid cunt had just shot a copper in the back.

Now we really were for it.

Mad as it seems, this is what went through my head the moment Patsy pulled the trigger. Not that I should be dead now or that my mate had just saved my life, or even that we'd just killed someone, but that it was all up for us now – we were done for.

The two cops in luminous jackets stood like statues in the road, staring down at their floored colleague, and when I looked down at him myself I saw he was still moving. In fact, he was looking pretty lively for someone who'd just been shot in the back three times, and it was then that I noticed the big, black, shiny and slightly used bullet-proof jacket around his midriff.

Patsy had shot him in the jacket. All he'd done was knock the wind out of his sails and the gun out of his hand. The bastard was still alive. Alive and kicking, in fact. And kicking, more specifically, towards the automatic that lay just a few short feet across the ground, attached to his belt by a piece of cord.

It was at this moment that I shook the stunned inactivity from my limbs and was finally able to bring my gun to bear.

'DON'T FUCKING MOVE! DON'T FUCKING MOVE!' I screamed at the top of my voice, pressing the pause button on the whole lot of them. I must've sounded like I meant it too because Patsy froze like a photo and it was only when I got my breath back enough to tell him to grab the automatic that he finally shook his legs into gear.

A couple of cars drove by while he was doing this so I shielded my gun and told the boys in green to wave them through as I ordered Dirty Harry up off the road. The looks on the faces of the passing motorists were confused but hopefully none of them had time to form any sort of impressions as to what was going on. Just a load of coppers fucking about, that's what it looked like.

Patsy pulled the groaning, head-rubbing copper to his feet and we quickly bundled all four out of sight of the road and into the woods.

'Move. All of you, move it,' I told them.

'You won't get away with this, you know,' the guy Patsy had shot in the back said, wincing as we marched them through the trees. 'You can't kill four coppers like this and expect to get away with it. You'll have every copper in the world looking for you and you won't be taken alive.'

'Relax, we ain't going to kill you,' I said, then qualified it with, 'if we don't have to. We're just going to cuff you to a tree.'

'Well, you won't get away with that either,' he amended, making me realise there was no arguing with this twat.

'We're willing to take that chance,' I said, and prodded him in the cluster of bullet tears with the barrel of my gun, poleaxeing him to his knees in pain and making me stumble over his head.

We found a suitably solid-looking tree about fifty yards from the road and told them to stop.

'Radios,' I demanded, and the four of them disconnected their radios and handed them over. 'Mobiles,' I said next, and Patsy patted them down to make sure they hadn't hidden any down their socks, then he slung these over too. 'Keys.'

I removed their luminous jackets and hats last of all, then got them ring-a-ring-a-roses style around the tree and told them to lock themselves together.

'I have to go to the toilet first,' one of the traffic coppers moaned.

'I ain't fucking about any more, lock yourselves together now,' I demanded, then searched all through their pockets for any hidden keys once they had the cuffs on. 'Okay, cool, there's a tree in front of you, go ahead, knock yourself out,' I told piss-wanting copper, flicking my gun in his direction and chuckling at the thought of them all having to stand in his piss for the next hour or so on this gloriously hot sunny day.

The copper stared at me open mouthed in disbelief then looked at the tree and braced himself. He looked back at me once again, then some more at the tree, and I was going to ask him what the problem was when all of a sudden he head-butted it with a sickening thud.

'Argh!!!' he screeched in pain, and fell to the ground dragging the others with him.

'What the fuck did you do that for?' I shouted, and had to pull him back to stop him doing it again.

'You told me to knock myself out.' He blinked, a great dirty scuff across the top of his head. Blood started bucketing out of his nose and I had to find a handkerchief in one of the coppers' top pockets to stuff in his face.

'For fuck's sake!' I gasped, shaking my head in disbelief. I told the others to explain the expression to him and took Patsy back off to the road.

'You can't leave us like this, he needs a hospital,' they called after me, but I wasn't sure what they wanted me to do about it; forget I had twenty years coming to me just because some fucking idiot copper was stupid enough to try punching a tree with his face?

'Anyone that daft deserves to be plucked from the gene pool,' I shouted back, prompting a barrage of complaints.

I stopped in my tracks and turned back to them.

'I haven't gagged you. Be aware of that. Don't make me change my mind,' I warned them. This shut them all up, albeit only until we were out of earshot.

'Did you see that?' Patsy asked, rather needlessly as we started back to the road again. 'What a fucking spastic.'

'I can't believe you shot matey in the back, after everything we'd agreed,' I snapped in reply.

'I saw he had a flak jacket on, I wouldn't have done it otherwise.'

'Wouldn't have done it otherwise? Why did you need to do it in the first place? Where the fuck were you?' I demanded.

'I thought you were going to count to three or something,' he told me.

'Now that doesn't even make any sense.'

'Oh, sorry. Still, no real harm done, though. Right?'

No real harm done? Patsy must've been kidding. The moment it got out that we were shooting coppers in the back open season was going to be declared on us. We'd pulled the trigger. We'd shown the intent. Our chances might have been slight before, but they'd just got even slighter (if that's a word). This wouldn't be stood for. This had just got personal. At least, that's what the Old Bill would be saying. What copper anywhere wasn't going to pull out all the stops to get their hands on a bunch of blokes who'd shot one of their mates in the back?

What newspaper wasn't going to sensationalise this development?

Doubled, that's what Patsy had done, he'd doubled everything. He'd doubled the charges, doubled the seriousness,

the publicity, the number of coppers on the case, the
rewards on our heads and probably our sentences too.

He'd doubled everything. He'd probably even knocked
Charlotte Church's tits off page 1, that's how serious this
was.

We were playing in the big league now.

Still, what else could he have done?

Would it have been better if he'd let that cunt shoot me?
Possibly. Definitely for him, Goody, Parky and the rest, but
probably not for me. Not that there was a single thing any
of us could do about it now. The object of the exercise was
still the same as it had been for the last twenty-four hours.

To keep on running.

We arrived back on the road and found the key that
unlocked the back of the van. Goody looked out at us in
confusion when we cracked open the door and blinked as
if he couldn't believe his eyes.

'Hey, look, it's that fat spotty crook we've all been reading about,' I said as I searched through the keys for the one
that freed him from his jewellery.

'Milo? What the fuck! Where's the cops? What's . . .
what . . . what . . . ?'

'Nice fucking plan, Goody,' Patsy said, rolling his eyes.
'*Pick you up on the other side.*'

'Let's not worry about that now, let's just get out of here,'
I told them.

I finally found the key to his cuffs and loosed his hands
upon the world again and when I looked up at his face I
saw that it was all red, blotchy and tear-streaked to fuck.
He'd clearly been having a tough time of it in the back of
the van but that wasn't anything to be ashamed of. The
façade often slipped when the cuffs went on. I'd known
some real hard nuts curl up and cry like little girls in my
time. That said, I'd also known a few skinny little four-eyed
runts take all the punishment the wing could throw at them

and not even blink an eye. If I had to choose between them, though, I'd probably hang around with the blubbers every day of the week, as you know where you are with them. The other guys are more likely to stab you to death in your bed as soon as look at you.

'Have we got time to go back and smack them all in the mouth a couple of times?' Goody asked bitterly, wiping his eyes with his sleeve.

'Not really but . . .' I pondered, then told him to forget about it. 'Don't worry, they're doing a pretty good job of it themselves anyway,' I reassured him.

Patsy went to climb in the back of the Rover but I told him to forget all about it.

'I've got a better idea,' I said, and handed Goody one of the hats and one of the luminous jackets I'd brought with me. I put the other on myself and gave Patsy a little twirl. 'Let's take the Old Bill's motor. No one's going to stop us in that. We can just motor past all our mates from now on, no problem.'

I thought for a moment that Patsy was going to tell us we couldn't do that but surprisingly he didn't, so for once there was no argument.

The three of us piled in the Armed Response motor and twisted the keys in her ignition. Goody wanted to drive but I told him he could whistle for it, this all was mine and no one else was getting a go. Well, it's not every day you get to drive an Old Bill wagon, is it? Not unless you're actually in the Old Bill, but who could be bothered with that? If I'd wanted to spend my days working with blokes who liked smacking their head against trees I'd go and get myself a job on an apple farm for the short-sighted.

As it was, I had tracks to make.

I pulled out of the lay-by and headed for the motorway. Patsy stayed low in the back and Goody fidgeted nervously up front. I was calmness personified, however. We'd been through so much in the last twenty-four hours, more than I realised you could fit into twenty-four hours in fact, but finally it was over. Finally we had the wheels, the open road and the cash to make it out of the country.

Finally we'd made it.

Part Two
HIDING

Facing facts

'Simon's been gone a long time,' I said, peering through his net curtains and into the street below. 'We should clear out of here.'

'And go where, Milo? Where? We've been through this already. If you can think of something better then shout it out because I'm all ears,' Goody told me, finally explaining his complete lack of brains.

Comical insults aside, he was right, though, we had been through this all before and then some. We were stuck.

It had been two days since we'd had it away with the Old Bill's motor and made it out of the woods, though once we had, we'd found ourselves really no better off.

See, we'd made it through the checkpoints with relative ease. No one gave us a second look and we reached the motorway in under ten minutes. I'd figured at the time that it wouldn't be long before our tree-hugging mates were found and told everyone what to look for so I turned on the rooftop garage music and put my foot down. We made three junctions and about twenty-odd miles before deciding that that was about as far as we dared go. We ditched the car around the back of a small parade of shops just outside Southampton and hoped it wouldn't be found for a couple of hours, then we went off looking for the nearest railway station.

We figured we'd catch the first train out of town, change a couple of times, go up north or to Scotland or somewhere and keep a low profile for a few months before trying to leave the country. But then, it's amazing the things you don't consider in situations like these until you're actually faced with them.

We hadn't made it ten yards from the police motor when we walked past a newsagent's and suddenly realised just how famous we'd become. Every paper – the *Sun*, the *Mirror*, the *Star* and the *Sport* – all of them had the story of the robbery on their front pages and inside they had our names, descriptions and, in mine and Parky's case, our pictures. Goody and Patsy had e-fits and every paper listed the same number, in big print, to call if anyone had any information as to our whereabouts.

This was going to be harder than we thought.

Suddenly, all the little things in life we'd always taken for granted, like buying a ticket, catching a bus, sitting on a train or even walking down the street, were going to be virtually impossible for us to do with any sort of guarantee of safety.

The guy sitting behind the train ticket window only had to have read the *Sun* to recognise us and tip the Old Bill off to the fact that we were travelling by train and to which destination. We could try shaking them by jumping trains every half a dozen stations but there are cameras at every stop these days. They'd follow our trail easier than if we were dropping breadcrumbs for them. And supposing we did lose them, what then? We only had to walk into a pub or a burger bar without thinking and that would be it again, another phone call and another five-minute head start. How were we ever meant to get away?

'I'll get us some hats,' Goody suggested, and bought three

baseball caps and three pairs of sunglasses off the newsagent inside.

'Bit suspicious, don't you think, buying that lot off him?'

'Doesn't matter, Patsy, the Old Bill will know we've been here just as soon as they find their motor, so it don't make any odds.'

'Yeah, but what if old Abdul in there puts two and two together and phones them up before we've had a chance to get out of here?'

'Oh, do me a favour, Patsy, you used to be a newsagent, you know the score. That crooked cunt's probably up to more than us, he ain't going to go phoning no one.'

Goody returned with three baseball caps, three pairs of sunglasses, an armful of newspapers and – God bless him – sixty fags. I put on both hat and shades, as mine was the picture in the paper, and I told Goody to stick with just the glasses for now and Patsy to go with the hat, as we didn't want to make it too easy for the Old Bill.

We found a minicab office just up the street and Patsy got us a cab to Eastleigh station. We piled in and, halfway to Eastleigh, changed our minds. We offered the driver an extra twenty quid if he took us onto Hedge End and, relying on the corruptibility of minicab drivers, hoped he wouldn't tell his control about it so that if the Old Bill came knocking they'd be off in the wrong direction from the off.

Luckily, the corruptibility of minicab drivers is something you can wager your house on.

At Hedge End, we got a train to Fareham, and at Fareham we grabbed a bus to Portsmouth. I was nervous about chopping and changing so much but Patsy and Goody took turns buying the tickets and we did the best we could not to hang about like Fun Boy Three on the platforms or on the trains or buses.

On the way down to Fareham, one bloke kept glancing up at me from his paper a few yards away and I squirmed in my seat when I thought I'd been rumbled. Goody was way over the other side of the carriage and doing his utmost to blend into the walls, and Patsy was next door with his face in a Jackie Collins. I tried to ignore the geezer as best as I could so as not to arouse his suspicions any further (well, who's going to make a cunt of themselves by phoning the Old Bill when they're not sure? Right!) but this didn't work so I gave my shooter a reassuring squeeze to boost my confidence and glared back at him to put the jeepers up him. I wasn't sure what good this was going to do and started to wonder if this was the start of a whole new hostage situation, but then the bloke just smiled at me and I suddenly realised his game.

He was a fucking poof.

I turned away instantly but the bastard came wandering over and sat down opposite me.

'Where are you off to?' he asked.

'I'm sorry, mate, but I'm not actually gay,' I told him, from behind my sunglasses.

'Oh, no, neither am I,' he said, flustered. 'I was just making conversation. I mean, Jesus, can't two guys talk on a train these days without having to be gay?'

They can, of course, but they usually don't. Not unless they're gay.

I apologised for the mistake (as it doesn't do to create a scene when you're trying to keep a low profile) then went back to trying to ignore him.

Patrick, as it turned out his name was, made two minutes' worth of token conversation to prove to me that he wasn't after a kiss before getting off at the next station. Goody stared at us open mouthed in horror the whole time before racing over the moment Patrick took his bow.

'What was you talking to that bloke for?' he demanded, all agitated and panic stricken.

'Relax, don't worry, he was just some bender.'

Goody thought about this for a moment then asked me the same question with a slightly different spin on it.

We arrived in Portsmouth just after lunchtime and lost ourselves in the town centre. We were tired, hungry and worn out with paranoia. Patsy bought us three cod and chips and we found somewhere down by the water to sit down and eat them.

We couldn't keep doing what we were doing indefinitely, jumping on a train or a bus or in a cab here or there, because we weren't clocking up any miles and we were leaving a trail of tickets and CCTV recordings any police force worth their salt could follow the moment they picked up the end of it. We had to put a clear break between us and them so that we could drop out of sight and lie low, and we had to do it quick, because sooner or later some eagle-eyed cunt was going to recognise us no matter how many hats we piled on our heads. But how could we do that?

There was really only one thing I could think of.

We had to nick another car.

Well, we certainly couldn't buy one. We couldn't keep getting public transport and we couldn't hitch-hike, so that really only left us with one option and that was to nick one.

'You sure about this, Milo?' asked Patsy, the consummate worrier.

'No,' I replied. 'But we don't need a souped-up Testorossa or an armoured Rolls-Royce or nothing, just a set of wheels that can get us a hundred miles away.'

And that was about the size of it. Any old Fiesta, Viva or Mini would just about do; something old that didn't have an alarm or an on-board computer to argue with us as we tried to start her up with a coat hanger. We didn't even have to be that sophisticated about getting into it. It was another warm day so we could just drive with the windows knocked in and not look too suspicious. We just needed to get away from here. And once we did that, we could all relax and spend a little time actually planning our next move instead of simply taking evasive action all the time.

'Okay, then, let's do it.'

We threw our chip wrappers in the bin like good law-abiding citizens (although I should point out that I always do this anyway. I might be a thief, but I ain't no litter bug) and circled the town keeping our eyes peeled for possible motors to have away.

I wondered how close the Old Bill were to us at this moment. They were all around, for sure, but the ones specifically looking for us? I wondered where they were.

It had been almost three hours since we'd had it away in their motor so they had to be mobilised by now. Perhaps they'd throw all their efforts into stopping us on the motorways. Perhaps they wouldn't realise we'd ditch the motor so soon after nicking it and try to make it out on public transport. I mean, if they didn't actually find the car for a few hours they might even cast their nets so wide that we'd be able to slip through with relative ease. Just keep our heads down and take the back roads, perhaps . . . perchance . . . possibly . . . feasibly . . . conceivably . . . maybe . . . probably (not).

I didn't know. It was guesswork at best with a few hopeful prayers thrown in for good measure.

They could've been just around the corner or in Timbuktu for all I knew. We had no real way of knowing without the use of a spy satellite. In fact, if we ever did find out where they were, the chances were that information would probably come a little too late to do us any good. We just had to keep our fingers crossed, our heads down and our legs moving.

After twenty minutes of wandering around looking about as suspicious as we could we found a row of cars parked down a little side street. This was presumably the town centre's unofficial car park for people unable, or too tight, to use the Pay & Display across the road. Well, at least one of them would rue their mistake. See, Pay & Displays usually have CCTV and sometimes even the odd attendant (odd in every sense). Side streets usually had neither. This one certainly didn't. All it had was a long, graffiti-daubed stretch of wall on one side and a mish-mash of shop backs and garages on the other. They would've probably parked here in the first place because it was quiet and out of the way, so as not to get a ticket, though when they came back to find their car was gone you could be sure that it would be everyone else's fault except theirs.

People like this deserve to have their cars stolen on a regular basis.

We selected an old Nova that looked like it could be started up with a key made out of leaves and got to work opening the door. Goody and Patsy kept a lookout in either direction while I fished about under the rubber seal with a length of discarded wire we'd picked up along the way.

I must've been out of practice because I took an absolute age finding the locking mechanism and Goody and Patsy kept glancing back at me with mounting concern as I huffed and puffed against the driver's door.

'In your own time, Milo, for fuck's sake!' Goody growled, while Patsy just hopped about from one leg to the other like he needed the toilet really badly.

'Almost got it,' I lied, as I felt the bastard slip again.

I pulled the wire out and reshaped the hook and this time, when I dipped it back in the door, it took only a couple of tentative tugs before I caught the mechanism and pulled it up.

'There you go, still got that magic touch,' I announced proudly to Goody, Patsy and the bloke that had just opened the garage door not five feet away.

He must've been in his garage already or had entered via

a back door because he wasn't there a second ago, but he sure as fuck was now.

We all stopped what we were doing and stood staring at each other like statues for a moment or two as the delicacy of the situation sank in. See, old matey had just witnessed three blokes breaking into a car and three blokes had just seen old matey witness them breaking into a car. And you could tell by the look on everyone's face that none of us were particularly chuffed about it.

We quickly sized up our options, me, Goody, Patsy and old matey — what should we do?

Should we pull out our guns and bundle him into his garage?

Or should we all jump on him and tie him up?

Perhaps it would be best if we ran, cutting our losses and hoping that he hadn't seen us clearly?

And what of the man himself?

What should he do?

Panic? Scream? Phone the Old Bill? Take us on himself?

Up until this point his life had taken him nowhere near us, now fate had thrown us all in the mix together and it was down to us how we reacted to it. Moments like this can often change a person's life, sometimes for ever, and this one could so easily have turned out that way, but we had one thing on our side.

We were all British.

'Afternoon,' matey coughed formally.

'Afternoon,' me, Goody and Patsy replied as one.

Matey averted his eyes from any wrongdoing and reversed his car out onto the road. Me, Goody and Patsy rocked backwards and forwards on our heels with our hands in our pockets, and whistled innocently, while the guy locked up his garage and left us to it. He gave us a respectful nod before he went on his way and got one in return for his troubles, then we got back on with the business of stealing our Nova while matey saw where the adventure we all called life led him next.

'Should we have just let him go like that?' Patsy worried out loud, while I stripped the wires under the dash.

'Don't worry, he won't do nothing.'

'How do you know?'

'I just do. I know the type. I doubt he's a big *Crimewatch* fan.'

'What's that got to do with anything?' Patsy wanted to know.

'Some people are just like that. As long as nobody touches their stuff, their neighbours can get robbed up the ying-yang and they couldn't give a shit. You could see it in his face.'

'I didn't see nothing in his face,' Goody joined in, as I touched copper to copper.

'Well, I did. Besides, you see what a squeeze it was for him to get out of his garage? I doubt he harbours any Christian feelings for the people who park up and down his street all year long,' I said as the Nova's engine rattled to life. I twisted the wires together and tucked them back up into the dash, then I opened the passenger door and told the boys to jump in.

'Don't worry,' I said, as Patsy piled in the back with the bags and Goody jumped in the front. 'Old matey, he's alright.'

I slipped the Nova into first and pulled out into the road.

Finally we had a clean set of wheels (for a few hours at least). So now all we had to do was figure out some place to drive to.

10

Simon who?

It was Goody who finally came up with the idea of calling on Simon.

See, the thing with this being-on-the-run lark was that there was so much to consider that had never even occurred to us. Simple things like: how did we get food? Where did we sleep? Where did we wash? And not just ourselves, our clothes. We were okay for the moment but four or five days down the line without showering and wearing the same smelly old duds and we wouldn't need our pictures in the paper to start drawing people's attention. Besides, other than students and pensioners, who wanted to spend weeks on end in the same old clobber without showering? Things weren't even that bad inside.

With this in mind, the first thing we had to do was find somewhere safe to hole up for a few days while we figured a way out of England.

Unfortunately, we couldn't just book into a guest house or a hotel or rent a room for a couple of nights. We had to assume that everyone in the country had seen our faces and that everyone would blow the whistle on us if they got the chance. So what did we do?

We were stumped for ideas that first night after making our escape in the Nova so we broke into a terrapin and slept there in a walk-in store cupboard (for those of you baffled by the idea of breaking into a terrapin, I should point out that this was what our old school used to call those pre-fabricated 'temporary' classrooms that were actually older than most of the science staff, and just as dilapidated. The names of these buildings change from school to school but you know the fellas I'm talking about). It wasn't especially comfortable – all we had to cover the cold, hard wooden floorboards was a few boxes of exercise books and a couple of curtains – but we made the best of the situation and nested down like gerbils until we were all fast asleep. The day, like the previous one, had been so exhausting that I think we could probably have slept on a bed of nails in the middle of a disco if we'd had nowhere else to lay our heads.

We woke up early the next morning feeling groggy, stiff and irritable. Two nights we'd now slept rough, and the night before that we hadn't slept at all. Oh, for a proper bed and a cup of Horlicks.

'I can't feel my legs,' whined Patsy, rubbing his knees frantically.

'Get up and walk around, then, though watch the win-dows, we don't want to be nabbed by the caretaker,' I told him. Patsy took my advice and gingerly stretched his legs. I looked over at Goody to make sure he'd heard that about the caretaker too but he hadn't even been listening.

'This kid's got no idea,' he said, leafing through part of his pillow and shaking his head. He looked up when he felt me staring and stuck out his lip in confusion. 'What?'

We tidied up the cupboard so that nobody would know we'd been there and set off into the morning. It was half past seven.

The thing I was rapidly coming to realise was that we were stuck without somebody else's help. We needed an outside, uninvolved party to shield us and fetch and carry for us, until we were ready to make our break, and we needed somebody we could trust. I finally understood why all those boys I'd met in prison had been caught under their mum's and gran's stairs. They had nowhere else to go.

And seeing as their mums and their grans were about the only ones on earth who wouldn't turn them in (mind you, mine would, the miserable old cow), it was a logical step. See, of all the people we knew, how many would've been willing to risk being sent down for aiding and abetting a known fugitive? That's some serious prison time, that is. Manny? My brother Terry? Patsy's ex? My Alice? Don't make me laugh, those last two would've turned us in to the Old Bill out of pure malice alone.

Goody's sister Barbara? Possibly, but like all possiblies, she'd have had the Old Bill trailing her about wherever she went. Besides, turning to her, or Terry or Manny or any of those other lot, would've involved going back home. And that was the last fucking place on earth we wanted to be.

No, we needed someone we could trust and someone who was bent enough to want to help.

I knew no end of boys from nick I could probably have called on but I was in no rush to give substantial chunks of my hard-nicked cash to any of those thieving cunts. The same could be said of Goody's old army buddies, who, he assured me, would turn us over for the reward money as likely as blink at us.

'I'd rather trust a pikey than an ex-soldier with empty pockets,' he said, in no uncertain terms.

'Well, who are we going to get, then? We have to get someone.'

The thought had occurred to me to crash in on some happy family and keep the women and children hostage while the old fella ran around and did as we said, but that was a non-starter from the off. See, we could never be sure that he wouldn't say nothing to the Old Bill, and more importantly, the things we needed doing – renting us rooms, buying us tickets, bringing us food and clothes and getting our documents for us – these weren't really things we could wield hostages over. The moment we let them go to use the things we acquired they'd have us. I mean, getting out of the country was going to be hard enough without taking a family at gunpoint along for the ride.

Besides, I'd lost the stomach to be fucking around with hostages any more. My meanness was almost all burnt out. I wanted a friend, someone who'd help us. I was sick of feeling the weight of the world on my shoulders and trying to stay strong.

So, no hostages, but who, then?

'I've got an idea. Simon.'

Simon was Goody's stepdad. Actually, he was just one in a long line of stepdads, number three out of six (so far) and a minor player at that. Put it this way, if Goody's stepdads had been James Bonds, Simon would've been George Lazenby (possibly even David Niven, he was that forgotten). Goody himself preferred to compare them to Dr Whos, as he thought James Bonds were a bit too flash for 'any of those cunts'. With this in mind, Simon would probably have been around the Colin Baker mark; a completely insignificant and unmemorable time lord who wouldn't be remembered at all if it wasn't for the fact that he had the same surname as one of the big players. Actually, he could even have been that McGann brother in that abysmal TV movie, simply because if he ever turned up at a Goodman family reunion or Dr Who convention, he'd be the one there who'd have to constantly remind everyone who he was and why he was there. Hang on a minute, I'm confusing myself now. Anyway, you get the picture.

Simon only lasted four months, back when Goody was about twelve. He hadn't been a bad bloke. He'd never beaten Goody or nicked money out of his piggy bank when he was out at school (unlike Peter Davidson), he'd just liked the sauce a bit too much.

At first Goody's old lady hadn't minded that at all; after all, it had been the boozer where she'd met him. Life and soul of the saloon he'd been, a real good laugh. Darts, dominoes and a drink with the boys; he'd even had hair back then. Yep, everyone liked Simon, he was one of your own. Goody's mum had taken a real shine to him (popularity can be a huge aphrodisiac for women), so in no time at all he'd moved out of his lodgings and hung his hat up at Goody's.

Unfortunately, things didn't work out for Simon and Mrs Goody. I guess she thought she'd have him all to herself once she'd given him a bed to piss regularly at nights, but there's no changing a bloke like Simon. He turned up for the occasional meal and even made it to the first half of Barbara's school production ('What? I didn't know it was an intermission. I thought that was it, Fame School was going well and things were peachy now that Leroy Matey was helping Babs with her homework!') but the writing was on the wall for him in letters six foot tall. See, the thing that Mrs Goody didn't understand was that for a bloke like Simon, being one of the lads down the pub was everything. That was who he was. Take him out of the pub and away from his mates and suddenly he was no one, just another anonymous cardigan mowing the back garden and discussing the weather down the Rotary Club. And who the fuck wanted to be that bloke? Not me, and not Simon, that was for sure. Oh no.

So that was that. After only four months, him, his arse and his hat all got shown the front door before he even knew what the problem was, and he spent the next few years being the bloke down the pub everyone laughed about for letting a good thing slip.

Oddly enough, out of all of Goody's stepdads, Simon was the one that Goody got on with best, probably because he was the one who used to get him a beer when he was fifteen and talk to him like a man, rather than a little boy. Simon wasn't one for authority. He just liked to have a beer and a laugh. What was wrong with that? Not a lot that I can see. That was just Simon.

Consequently, he got to spend the rest of his life alone.

About twelve years ago he left town for good and moved across to Brighton. He was soon forgotten by almost everyone who'd ever known him, even the blokes down the pub, and never ever returned. Only Goody kept in touch, sending off the odd BFPO letter from wherever he was stationed and getting the same short letter back. *Sounds great. You young fellas have got the life. Get stuck into those Belize/Nigerian/Bosnian/Aldershot birds for me and give us a bell next time you're down Brighton way. We'll catch up over a beer or two. Stay lucky, Simon.*

They say that you should never extend an invitation unless you're prepared to have your bluff called. Well, I hoped Simon had heard this too because we were all out of options

Dr Who was about to get some visitors.

The Brighton boozer

11

'D'you think he's gone to get the Old Bill?' Patsy asked nervously.

'No. No, he wouldn't do that to me,' Goody replied, less than convincingly.

'You sure about that? He's hardly living in the lap of luxury here. He'd probably get a few quid turning us in,' I pointed out.

I wasn't kidding about the lap of luxury thing. His flat was a 1960s council job and the furniture looked like it had been around even longer. His carpet was threadbare, the curtains tatty and the stove looked like it was fucking sick of having beans spilt all over it.

'I guess he had to let the cleaner go,' Goody joked when we first saw the state of the place, though none of us were laughing now. A nice fat ten-grand reward for information received was just what this place needed. According to the morning's papers the supermarket's parent company was already stumping up the cash, though there was more than one way to skin these three particular cats. There was money from the papers for the story, a civic reward from the courts, compensation from the criminal injuries board (all he had to do was lump himself in the face with the frying pan – who was going to argue with that?) plus the countless drinks he'd be bought down the local by the law-loving string-'em-up brigade for single-handedly apprehending that dangerous supermarket bandits gang. And of course, on top of that little lot he could always dip his hand into our bags when we weren't looking or just plain try and blackmail us, though he was likely to get a lot more than a frying pan in the face if he ever tried that.

All these thoughts and more swirled through my mind while we waited for Simon to get back from the shops with the stuff we'd sent him out for.

'Come on, let's get out of here,' Patsy implored us.

'He's only been gone half an hour, give him a chance,' Goody said, defending his one-time stepdad.

It had just gone midday and we'd yet to eat. Yesterday I'd been able to send Patsy or Goody into the shops to pick us up some grub but today their sketchy e-fits had been replaced by actual photographs. Goody's was off of his army pass and Patsy's was off of the top of his mum's telly.

'That fucking no-good back-stabbing bitch,' he said when he'd first seen it.

So that was our lot, we were fucked. We could no longer buy food for ourselves or take public transport for fear of being recognised and we had to stay off the streets.

We'd stuck with the Nova for this reason, though we'd swiped some new plates off another blue Nova we'd fortuitously passed in Worthing. After a short scout about, we'd finally parked her up in a quiet street around the back of Hove railway station and walked the rest of the way to Brighton along the beach. If the Nova was ever found (as it would be sooner or later) the nicked plates would hopefully muddy the waters and make it harder for them to trace it back to Portsmouth. They would eventually, of course, but that would take some time, and they might not even recognise it for the lead it was when they did. And this gave me, Goody and Patsy time to drop off the face of the earth.

With Simon's help.

'I wish that bastard had a mobile, we could give him a ring and find out where he is,' I said, the sweat running down my back.

The three of us kept our vigil through the nets for a further fifteen minutes before Simon eventually returned.

'Fucking hell, man, you were gone ages, where d'you go?' Goody confronted him when he stepped through the door. Simon looked confused at this concern and explained he'd been to the shop up the road because he was barred from the one on the corner.

'I owe them a couple of quid, don't I?' He shrugged apologetically.

'For fuck's sake, you should've just said, we would've give you the money to pay yourself off. How much do you owe?'

'Er, about twenty-nine quid. Two months of papers, you see. They won't sell me nothing till I settle up so I have to go to the one up by the pier.'

'But there's shops nearer than that, surely to fuck,' Goody said.

'Yeah, but they're all mates, aren't they? They keep telling each other not to serve me so I'm having to go further and further up the road if I want to get anything, don't I? It's fucking annoying really.' He frowned.

'What a loser!' Patsy muttered to himself, summing up all our thoughts in one perfect phrase.

'Anyway, here's the papers and some sarnies and stuff, and I thought we could have a beer too so I took the liberty to get a few in,' Simon explained, setting down two local property papers, three cheese and ham sandwiches, a family pack of Cheesos and sixteen cans of Tennent's Super.

'Didn't you get anything other than cheese and ham?' Goody asked, emptying out the bags. Simon looked at the packet of Cheesos and then at the Tennent's Super and then thought better of it.

'What's up, don't you like cheese and ham? I could go out again if you like,' he offered, but me and Patsy weren't up for that so we broke open our sandwiches and swapped our ham and cheese about until we had the problem sorted.

'Everyone happy now?' I asked.

'My ham tastes a bit cheesy, I hate cheese,' Goody moaned, but he ate it anyway.

'Well, no point standing on ceremony,' Simon announced, and cracked open the first can of Super. 'Cheers, then, boys, good luck to you.'

When we were done with the sandwiches we gave Simon £50 and told him to go and pay matey-boy over the road and bring us back some more grub. Ten minutes after that he returned with six Cornish pasties and a bottle of vodka.

This was the bloke we were trusting our lives to.

First things first, we had to get a place to stay. We couldn't stop at Simon's even if he'd had the room because the Old Bill would eventually get around to checking out our extended families and friends, and Simon would be in there somewhere, so we had to get a place of our own. I'd told him to pick up a load of local papers for us while he was at the shops and we set about scouring them for flats as we ate our Cornish pasties. We got on the blower to each in turn and asked about the possibility of a short-term lease, cash up front, but unbelievably every landlord we pitched this to turned us down. They all wanted references and bank statements and employment records and suchlike and everything else so we were at a bit of a loss. Patsy suggested Simon rented the places in his name but he had no job, no money and council accommodation to begin with, so who the fuck was going to give him a second flat?

We lowered our sights a bit and started phoning around

a few real 'DSS welcome' rat-holes that we thought would
ask fewer questions, but even these cunts were reluctant to
take us. Somewhere along the line cash had come to be
worth less than government cheques.

'Go to the Social Security or Home Office and they will
give you forms. If your friends cannot speak English, this is
not a problem, I will fill in the forms for them. Good day,'
one helpful old thief told us.

We went through every paper and rang just about every
suitable flat/house but all to no avail. Then Goody noticed
we'd missed a paper.

'Why did you buy the *Gay Times* too, Simon?'

Simon didn't know. 'I just grabbed every paper and
magazine that said Brighton on it. I don't know.'

'Do we look like three benders?' Goody demanded.

Simon shrugged. 'I didn't know you robbed supermarkets
until yesterday so how should I know what you get up to?'

'There's a big difference between robbing supermarkets
and being a fucking bandit,' Goody pointed out without
any trace of irony.

'Hang on a minute, chuck it over here,' I told him.
Goody looked at me funny and asked what I wanted to
look at a bender mag for. 'To see if it's got any accommodation in it.'

'What? Fuck off, I ain't staying in a bender house,' he
objected, but Patsy snatched it out of his hand and tossed it
over.

I flicked through the issue, averting my eyes whenever
some bloke in tight pants smiled back at me, and found the
ads at the back. There was indeed accommodation in the
mag and, unlike Goody, I could see a few benefits to hiding
out in a bender house. See, we wanted to stop somewhere
where people minded their own business and weren't going
to ask a lot of questions. Wasn't this what half the gays in
Britain wanted?

The other thing about them was that they were a right old secretive bunch who mistrusted the Old Bill and the media almost as much as crooks and darkies did, so that even if they tumbled who we were, it wasn't a stuck-on cast-iron certainty that they'd go dialling three numbers on us; especially if they'd been given a bit of a hard time themselves off the Old Bill in the past. Just look at when that serial killer was going around London murdering gays. I can't remember his name, Colin something, but he got about five of them over the course of a month or two, so it was big news back then. Even with all this going on, though, the lads in the loafers still wouldn't cooperate with the Old Bill and that was the major stumbling block with their investigation. Mad, isn't it? Still, if they weren't prepared to go running to the Old Bill over someone who was deliberately murdering them, what was the likelihood of them shopping three blokes who'd done nobody any real harm except take a load of supermarket money and slightly shoot a girl?

Anyway, that was the theory and I explained it to the lads, but Goody was still less than convinced.

'I don't know, what if people find out?'

'Find out what? That we once rented a flat off some bloke who was gay? Yeah, imagine the scandal. Fuck me, Goody, we ain't going to have to wear dresses and dance with each other every time Abba comes on the radio. Sort it out.'

We spoke to a couple of landlords and explained the situation to them. Not that we were fugitives on the run from the law or nothing, but that we were new to this sort of thing and wanted to exercise a little discretion.

'I quite understand, young man, my tenants' privacy is sacrosanct. I don't give out names to anyone,' one particularly camp landlord reassured me.

'All the same, we'd rather, for the first couple of months

at least, just deal in cash, if that's okay. I really don't want anyone finding us and I'd really rather not use my name or details, if that's alright. This is very important to me.'

I heard matey thinking this over on the other end of the line, then he asked if someone was looking for me. I had a sudden brainwave.

'My father,' I told him. 'He's a policeman. A chief inspector, actually. And I understand, according to my sister, that he's got a couple of private detectives looking for me too. I can't go back. I'd die,' I minced.

'There, there, okay, let's see what we can do. Oh, you poor thing. Is it just yourself?'

'No, it's me and . . .' I looked over at Goody, who screwed up his brow at me. '. . . my friend.' I left Patsy out of negotiations for the moment as I couldn't very well tell him there'd be three of us staying there or this cunt would likely as fuck invite himself round for a bit of a party, so I reassured him there was just the two of us. Inseparable. Loving. Faithful. That was me and Goody, the big dopey fuck. We'd sneak Patsy in through the back later.

'Oh, how romantic,' he said, and I almost slammed the phone down on him. 'Listen, you'll still have your council tax to pay but if you let me have a hundred pounds a month on top of the rent, I'll pay it for you in my name. Just for the first couple of months, mind, just until you're safe.'

'Oh, thank you,' I wept. 'Thank you so much. You've saved my life. Listen, I can't get down to you for a couple of days myself but I'll send my uncle down to pay you and collect the keys. That way we can just move straight in, if that's okay?'

'Very good. When will your uncle call by?'

'Later this evening,' I said, then looked over at Simon, who was now stumbling around his flat as drunk as fuck. 'Er, actually, we'd better make that first thing tomorrow.'

All the latest

We sent Simon over the road (after he'd had a bit of a lie-down) to pick us up some dinner from the kebab shop and settled in for the night. Simon had a telly so we stuck it on to see what we could see. This was the first time we'd had a moment to watch the telly since we'd pulled the job and we were interested to catch the news to see if they had anything to say about us. They did.

According to Katie Derham (who is a fantastic bit of alright – and she'd heard of me! Smart) we were still at large. Goody made a good joke about us being 'at king-size, darling' as we tucked into our kebabs, and even Patsy laughed at that one. Detective Sergeant Haynes made it onto the telly and we all shouted 'wanker' at him and threw bits of lettuce at the screen until Simon started clearing them up and we remembered we were in someone else's flat. Anyway, Weasel (I would've loved *News at Ten* to have captioned him like that) told the on-the-spot reporter that every port, airport and train station was being watched and that we were going nowhere.

'That's all we can say for the moment, except to reiterate that these men are armed and should be considered highly dangerous. If anyone has any information at all they should contact the police immediately,' he said rather unoriginally.

Katie reminded viewers of several numbers they could phone and Simon asked if any of us had a pen. He got a laugh for that but it was a rather half-hearted, guarded laugh. Some things just shouldn't be joked about.

That was all that made it onto the national news. Simon told us that news reports had been a lot longer the last couple of days and that was quite reassuring. Yesterday's news, that was us. Give it a few more weeks and we'd slip out of the nation's conscience altogether until the next exciting development.

There was a bit more in the local news and a lot more in the next morning's papers, and piece by piece it all added up to a fascinating jigsaw puzzle.

We were getting spotted all over the place: London, Bristol, Glasgow, rather unsettlingly Brighton, and even as far away as Spain and the Med. According to some reports we were living rough in the countryside and according to others we were being sheltered by underworld connections. Simon smiled at the thought of being regarded as an underworld connection, then he went and made us all a cup of tea. There were also more offers of money for information in the papers so I tore these all out while Simon was in the kitchen. He hadn't informed on us yet, that much was obvious (if he had the Old Bill would've been here in droves by now) but there was no sense in leaving this sort of temptation out for him to see. Even so, I knew we were going to have a problem with him at some point. After all, even when we'd left Simon's place and moved into our own gaff, Simon would still know where we were, so what did we do?

Money, that was the obvious solution. We'd have to give him a few quid and, more importantly, the promise of a lot more to come and hope that this would be enough in itself to buy his trust. We'd hope, but we wouldn't know.

Getting back to the news, though, the stuff that really

interested me wasn't the ongoing manhunt or the question of our whereabouts, it was all the rest of it the papers reported on.

The supermarket had been closed on police orders for two days following the robbery. I guess they wanted to check it out for fingerprints and forensics and stuff. The bomb squad'd had to clear the place first and had actually carried out a controlled explosion on our 'bomb', which apparently, and rather amusingly, caused a further £25,000 worth of damage to the store (they must've really hated us). The papers all went on about how our 'bomb' could've killed hundreds had it gone off but not a word was given over to the fact that it was just a fake, a bluff to stampede the cattle. Yet another charge we'd have to answer to if we were caught, no doubt.

Some twenty-odd people had been hurt in our escape, most with cuts and bruises but a couple with stitches and broken bones, and I did feel bad about that. I remembered getting squashed in the loading bay just before we all ran and only realising then that this was a somewhat dangerous idea. I took some comfort from the fact that none of the injuries were really serious. The worst case seemed to be two blokes who'd knocked heads in mid-sprint and who were concussed, but were expected to make full recoveries.

Then there was the girl we'd shot. She was in all the papers in full colour and declared a national heroine when she returned to work the first day the supermarket reopened. Jesus, the fuss they made of her. Anyone would've thought she'd bayonet-charged a machine-gun nest with dynamite strapped to her back the way they carried on; all she did was stack a few beans while six dozen photographers took her picture and she got a medal off the *Sun*. Jesus, it's not like we even shot her that badly. Still, there you go, that was her fifteen minutes of fame and something she could bore the tits off her grandchildren about in years to come. I just hoped we weren't all still inside when she was doing it.

What made her all the more heroic, of course, was that about a third of the shop's staff refused to do the same, citing emotional trauma as the reason for their absence. Now obviously, most of them would've just been swinging the lead, hoping to get a few weeks off work on full pay and land themselves a nice little compensation lump at the end of it, but presumably one or two of them would be genuine. Goody refused to believe this and reckoned they were all at it but I wasn't so sure – everyone loved a confidence-shattering experience. Just look at daytime TV. There seems to be no shortage of people willing to bare their souls and cry their eyes out in front of the cameras. Victims of alcohol, victims of drugs, victims of crime, victims of broken homes. People loved being victims. It's comforting and it brings them attention, sympathy and support; things they might not otherwise have in their lives. We live in an age when people are inventing newer and more obscure things to feel fucked up about just to get a taste of this support. My favourite new trauma is the trauma of birth (that's the babies being traumatised, by the way, not their mothers, they have their own separate trauma for that). Yes, the trauma of being born. Fine, yeah, very clever, give yourselves a big research grant, but I'm not buying this one because what do you want us to do about it? I mean, there is no way around it as far as I can see, so what do you do?

Goody had an excellent solution.

'Cum on her tits.'

Which you have to take your hat off to.

So yeah, a few of our 'victims' would milk it for all they were worth and make a big deal out of how we'd ruined their lives and so forth, so that consequently, anything that went wrong for them in the future would now be all down to us.

Lose their jobs? That would be our fault.

Marriage falls apart? That's us again.

Start hitting the Scotch? It wouldn't have happened if we hadn't held them prisoner.

Put on eighteen stone? They're not to blame.

Get done for theft? It was only a matter of time.

They could do anything, anything at all, and blame us for it. They had their perfect Get out of Responsibility Free card, and refusing to go back to work was just the start of it for these moaning cunts. I don't want to seem harsh, but seriously, we're top of the food chain here, don't you know? Nothing's going to hunt us or eat us or lay its eggs in us while we're paralysed, so can't we all just count our blessings and give it a rest? This is Britain, after all, not the United States of boo-hoo-hooo America. Whatever happened to our world-famous stiff upper lips? The Dunkirk spirit? Dancing around with a big smile on our faces while all our houses and mates are blown to smithereens? Honestly, it makes me fucking mad, as you can probably tell, so that's enough of that.

There was also a little interview with our old mate Clive in the paper; you know, the old guy we'd locked in the shed. It turned out his surname was Kinsey and that his wife's name was Rose (funny how it's only old ladies who are called Rose and Doris and Ethel and Peggy and so on, isn't it? I suppose every generation has its clutch of names and in fifty years' time the only people to be called things like Jo and Jackie and Mel and Nicki will be the smelly old birds in the post office). Anyway, they told their side of the story about how we fell out of the woods and how we made them cook us breakfast and give us some old clothes and so on and to their immense credit they were actually pretty fair about us. Clive reckoned we treated them well and that he never really felt in any sort of danger from us, and Rose added that we were even quite polite, considering, which was all good, and yet in another way, it wasn't. See, if they'd never really felt in danger from us then we obviously weren't very convincing as hostage takers and this didn't bode well for the next time we had to impose ourselves on some poor bastard.

Supposing that, like us, our next lot of hostages had read Clive's words: 'At no point did I fear for my life'? They might then think, 'Well, I know they're not actually going to kill me because old matey in the paper said so, so they're just full of shit. I'm gonna try it on,' and do precisely that. And if they did, then all of a sudden the game gets upped and we really would have to do something about it. And that could prove dangerous, know what I mean? Because one thing was for certain, I wasn't going back to prison for twenty-five years just so some little cunt could pull the birds with a George Cross. Oh no. Anyone wanted to get some medals off the back of us they were going to have to get them posthumously.

Fucking polite . . . ?

Anyway, that was Clive and Rose. I took a moment to wonder if they'd been paid for their interview and if they had been, had they any sort of problem taking the paper's money? I was pretty sure they probably would've been because the old bastards would've viewed that money as clean, whereas ours was nicked, so that just goes to show how even the most respectable of people can live their lives by double standards.

Still, at least they hadn't booed their eyes out and called us 'animals' like others had, so you had to give them some due.

The following day one of the papers carried an interview with the wife of the copper Patsy had shot in the back. Obviously she went and got a baby from somewhere so that she could have her picture taken with it and then proceeded to bawl her eyes out about what monsters we were and what a hero her old man was. This really narked Patsy, especially the part where it said that PC Colgan's life had only been saved by the fact that he'd been wearing a bullet-proof jacket.

'Fucking wankers,' spat Patsy. 'I knew he was wearing a bullet-proof jacket, that's why I shot him in the back. I wouldn't have shot him if he hadn't been wearing one.'

Patsy wore his face all day and even wanted to phone up the news desk and put his side of the story across, but me and Goody wrestled the phone out of his hand and told him to stop trying to get us all nicked. It wouldn't have done him any good anyhow. Shooting at cops is shooting at cops, no matter how reasonably you phrase it. I told him to save it for his memoirs, but Patsy had trouble letting it go. The papers hated him. The cops hated him. The country hated him. Patsy wasn't a person who enjoyed being hated.

'Fucking wankers,' he continued to grumble as he sat in the corner and sulked.

There was more stuff over the next couple of days about me, Goody, Cop-killer and Parky. I was fascinated to know where the fuck Parky had got to and scoured all the rags hoping to find out but nothing ever came up. I guess that was probably a good thing as far as Parky was concerned. All his family were in the papers going on about what a scandal it was that their poor innocent son/brother/ boyfriend/etc. should be linked to such a heinous crime and that the police were only picking on him because he was a black man with a record. It was an outrage. Me and Goody pissed ourselves laughing when we read this, and when we saw his mum on the telly standing next to some bloke from the Nation of Islam we almost wet ourselves. Fucking Parky was the biggest fucking villain I've ever met, and I was proud to call him my mate, but he couldn't leave the old race card alone. Fair do's, I probably would've as well if I'd been in his skin, but it did make me laugh.

I liked it when the reporter asked Mrs Parkinson why, if her son was so innocent, he'd fallen off the face of the planet? Obviously he'd done that because he was scared, scared of getting arrested and wrongly convicted of armed robbery. 'My son does not trust British justice,' Mrs Parkinson defiantly declared, then was subsequently arrested herself on suspicion of harbouring a known fugitive. That was when matey from Islam had his say and just annoyed us so we turned over and watched *EastEnders*.

Funny, though, I really did wonder where Parky had got to. The last time I saw him he was stretching his legs across that waste ground like he had a lion at his back. Old Parky can run when he wants to. I wondered where he was and I hoped he was safe, though I qualified this by hoping we were safer.

Things were probably easier for Parky than for us. One person can disappear a lot easier than three, but then three can hold hostages a lot better than one, so that meant his family had to be helping him. I wondered if he'd told them the truth. Knowing Parky I truly doubted it. His poor mum, all banged up in a cell with nobody for company except Malcolm X next door, probably genuinely believed the Old Bill were victimising her poor, helpless, overgrown idiot of a son and trying to pin something on him just because there had been a black man involved in the robbery. Yes there had, and that black man had been Parky. Where else would he have gotten fifty grand in cash and his pricing gun from, Mum? I'm sure even if we all gave her a good shaking and convinced her that he had been there she would probably still have argued that it had been against his will, that we'd somehow forced him to participate. 'My Leonard wouldn't do something like that. My Leonard's a good boy.'

That's right, blind wishful thinking can overcome all obstacles — like reality.

I wondered if the Yorkshire Ripper's mum still sent Peter a tangerine at Christmas.

There was nothing from my old lady in there, or my old man or brother, come to that. I guess they all knew I'd done it so what was there to talk about? They weren't going to win any friends and they certainly weren't going to get paid for it like Clive and Rose had so why bother adding to it? I guess that's what they thought because that's exactly what they did. Terry probably thought this too because there was nothing from him except a picture of him coming out of the newsagent's with a copy of the *Mirror* under his arm and a caption saying, 'Terry Miles, keen to read all the latest about fugitive brother Darren in yesterday's *Mirror*', which I guess was just their way of bigging up their own coverage, but that was about it. He didn't smile, or wave, or try and punch out any photographers or anything, he just looked out of the page in confusion as if trying to work out why someone was taking his picture.

Old Terry, poor bastard, I'd really dropped him in it. He let me stay at his place when I got out of the nick and I was still living around there when we came to do the shop. He'd lost his job about a month earlier and as far as I knew still didn't have one. I wondered how his new-found fame would help or hinder him there. Poor Terry. Sorry, brother.

I had thought that Alice might try and get in on the act but even she opted to stay out of the papers, which I found even harder to deal with. I actually wanted her to get involved, to tell the papers how we'd been together for seven years and how she knew me better than anyone. Even if she ended it by saying that I was a complete cunt for behaving the way I'd behaved, that would at least have been something. But she didn't. She just stayed silent.

She'd come down to the supermarket while we'd all been barricaded in there, and tried to talk us out, but I guess that had been Weasel's idea. Plus there had been people's lives at stake then, now there was only me, so who cared?

I was tempted to phone her and let her know I was safe and sound but I figured she'd just hang up on me or call Weasel, so I didn't bother. She was gone and I had to let her go, but some things in life are even harder to shake than the Old Bill.

There were a dozen more sightings of us up and down the country over the next week or two but these gradually disappeared deeper and deeper into the paper, then all of a sudden a story broke that had us right back on page one.

MEGASAVER MANAGER ARRESTED.

Duncan, our friendly night manager, had been arrested and charged after the Old Bill had found two grand stashed in a toolbox in his garage. Me and Goody had given it to him to look the other way after we started helping ourselves to a rather more than equal share of the pot. The two of us had made our way down to his office behind a human shield of shop girls and had them all stand against the windows while we emptied the safe. As a tiny bribe to get them on our side (for whatever reason, I don't know, probably fancied a couple of them, I suppose) we gave each of the girls £250 to stick down their knickers and Duncan £2,000. I remembered at the time that one of the girls wasn't particularly cockahoop about taking the cash but that all the other girls had browbeaten her into it so that they could safely take theirs, but now this had backfired on the lot of them.

The girl – or Julie Green, as the papers named her – had felt so overcome with guilt about taking her multimillion-pound annual-turning-over employer's money that she'd decided to give it back. Not to Duncan, though, not a quick 'here you go, I don't want this. Slip it back in the safe when no one's looking'. Oh no. No, she'd gone to the day manager. The guy we'd terrorised and tied up along with his wife and kids. This bloke was never going to have a sense of humour about anything to do with the robbery and the moment she opened her gob she was sacked and arrested.

I personally can't believe that anyone could've been this stupid, and you know the funny thing, she was in tears in the paper when she was led away. What did she think was going to happen?

'Thank you, Julie, that's very honest of you. You're an example to us all. Here, have a big fucking pat on the back.'

And that was what it was, she wasn't just looking to give the money back because she wasn't comfortable with it, she was looking for that strange inexplicable kudos that honest people think comes with not taking advantage of an illicit windfall. I've never understood it (that old lady's tenner. Fuck!). This was some sort of act of attrition on her part but in order to be absolved of her crimes she had to drop everyone else in it. What a selfish cunt! She'd spilled the beans on the lot of them, which, of course, she was always going to do anyway; I mean, how could she look good if nobody else looked bad? Every girl and Duncan got a pull, but only Duncan was found to have a large sum of unexplained cash hidden in his house (I guess all the others had done theirs up the wall in no time) so that he was the only other one to get charged besides Julie Green.

And that was beautifully ironic: Julie Green, the only honest girl in the room and now also the only one to have a criminal record. The rest of the girls had all stuck to their denials and got away with it in the end (great), but not without a probe. They'd all been suspended from work while they'd been investigated, but at the end of the day it all boiled down to their word against Julie's, a self-confessed thief, so they had to be given the benefit of the doubt.

Even Duncan, to his great credit, refused to grass them up, though this was probably because he was still frantically trying to wriggle off his own particular hook, but nevertheless he showed more loyalty to those girls than the law-abiding Julie Green, so what does that tell you about law-abiding people?

I have to admit, I did take an enormous amount of perverse pleasure seeing Julie Green crying her eyes out on the telly and pleading with the great British public for forgiveness, but that's probably because I always love seeing honest people get their comeuppance.

'But I gave it back,' she sobbed on the steps of the police station. 'I was the only one to give it back.'

'Yeah, well, darling, it ain't the giving it back that everyone was bothered about, it was the taking it in the first place,' I told the telly. 'Don't you think we'd give it all back like a shot if we could put everything right again?'

Huh? Huh?

Wouldn't we?

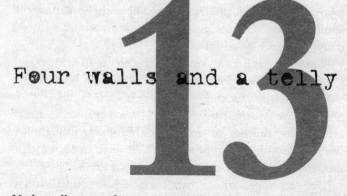

Four walls and a telly

Yeah, well, most of it anyway. I'd probably try and hold onto a few grand because I was fucking skint before I pulled this job. Probably the reason I did it in the first place now that I come to think of it.

And talking of money, things got a little bit tricky when Patsy finally asked for his share. He'd been expecting around fifteen grand (as we all had) but the safe had contained a lot more than that and the average equal share now ran to something in the order of thirty-eight grand. Plus, like I said, while me and Goody had been emptying the safe, we had awarded ourselves a few performance-related bonuses so that I alone had around a hundred grand in spun dry notes all to myself (my share of thirty-eight plus Patsy's thirty-eight plus my twenty (or so) grand I had off the top). The question was, how much did I give Patsy?

Now, equalitarians among yourselves might think that this is actually quite an easy sum to figure out and that the answer's a nice round fifty grand.

Well, I laugh in your faces. Fifty grand? I didn't go to all this arse-ache just to give away half of my hard-earned beer tokens to the first sweet-shop monkey who asked me for a share. No, fuck that. Patsy had originally signed up for fifteen grand. That was what he was entitled to and that was what he was going to get. Now obviously I'm not such a total cunt that I'd rip him off completely so I dropped another fiftee . . . er, ten grand on top of his pile and pushed it across the table to him.

'There you are, now don't go spending it all on stickers,' I warned him, wagging a finger in his face.

'Thanks, Milo, fucking hell, you're a star.'

Now the reason Patsy said this was because he never actually saw the size of my pile and probably thought we were on around the same amount. At least, that's what he thought until Goody opened his big fat mouth.

'But you took a whole share for him, Milo, and all you're giving him is twenty-five grand? That's out of order.'

Patsy was somewhat confused by Goody's remarks as he'd just been given ten grand more than he'd been expecting and was as happy as a bunny at springtime. Suddenly, thanks to Goody, reality had snared his short-lived happiness and Patsy was now faced with the lip-wobbling prospect of having to chew his own leg off in order to avoid taking a hot bath with some carrots. Hang on, that doesn't make any sense. Well, you know what I mean.

'Equal share? What are you talking about, Good? Milo, what's he talking about?'

'He's just winding you up, don't listen to it,' I tried to wriggle, but Goody was up on the moral high ground and he had me in his cross-hairs.

'No, fuck that, Milo, thirty-seven grand, that was what you took for Patsy, that was an equal share. Pats, we actually got three hundred grand in all and Milo brought out your thirty-seven with him when he came, didn't you, Milo, so don't go trying it on. Go on, give it to him.'

This was unbelievable; the fucking hypocrite. He'd happily lined his own pants while we were in the office with an extra bonus share, now he was dropping me in it with Patsy over twelve grand. Admittedly, he wasn't giving me up about the bundles we pocketed in the office, just Patsy's legitimate share, but that was only because he knew that particular admission would hit him in the pocket as much as me. No, he was just pissed off that I was scamming Patsy and that he wasn't in on it. Probably.

But was I scamming Patsy?

Like I said, he'd done a runner. He wasn't in the super-market when we were all in there. No, Patsy had said, 'See you later, lads,' and left us all to it. In fact, the only way I'd managed to get the little bastard to come back for us in the end was through sheer, unapologetic blackmail.

And he thought that was worth an equal share?

'Patsy, for fuck's sake, you're only in it for aiding and abetting after the fact. It's me and this cunt over here who are looking at serious time for armed robbery. We need the extra spondulicks because we're looking at twenty years,' I explained.

'After the fact? I shot a copper in the back for you, if you remember. You really think they're going to let me off with a bit of a bollocking and no telly for three months? If you're getting twenty years for scratching a shop girl's arm, you can bet your tinned pudding I'm looking at double that.'

'He's got a point there, Milo,' said old Big Mouth help-fully.

'Alright, alright, you couple of cunts,' I said, and went and fetched him an extra thirteen grand from my bag. I would've fetched it from Goody's but he anticipated this move and followed me into the bedroom to make sure his bag went unmolested.

'There, go on, then, have it, now that's you square, alright?' I told Patsy with as much ill-grace as I could muster, and dropped myself sulkily into the chair. 'And don't go looking at me like that, I am a thief, you know, as everyone loves reminding me all the time. What did you all fucking expect?' I asked, and we all sat in silence.

Fantastic. Brilliant. Lovely atmosphere. Just what three blokes in a poky little flat needed to make their eleventh straight night under the same roof together a real humdinger.

By this time, of course, we'd moved into our 'gay flat' and hadn't seen the outside world except through some extraordinarily clean net curtains. That first wonderful sigh of relief at finally having a safe place to ourselves soon turned to sighs of utter despair as we started bouncing off the walls and each other after only a few days.

To be honest, I was okay. Compared to the nick, a two-bed flat in Brighton with a view of the railway tracks was something of a luxury for me. No, it was Goody and, in particular, Patsy who felt it the most. See, Goody had always been an outdoors sort of bloke, whereas Patsy had never had his freedom taken away to this extent, not even when he said 'I do', so it was pretty hard on him. He'd sit by the windows for hours on end watching the world go by and pining to feel the sky above his head again, and every now and then he'd ask me what we were going to do and how long we were going to be doing it for.

'We've just got to lie low, Pats, we don't want to do anything stupid. We could be here months before it's safe to make a move again. Just . . . I don't know . . . grow a moustache or something, that should keep you busy.'

We were totally reliant on Simon bringing us food and supplies and by and large he'd done okay by us (though we were still only too aware that he was the weak chink in our ointment). He'd brought us clothes, grub, books, magazines and videos, anything we'd asked for. He'd even got us a swanky flash games console and a few silly games, but no matter how hard we tried to distract ourselves, the simple fact was that we were in a prison of our own making and there was no getting around that.

I'll tell you a little secret here; hiding out is actually a lot more claustrophobic than prison. In prison, it's all about walls and bars and screws and fences and stuff, whereas hiding out is purely about discipline. Walls, fences and bars can be a lot easier to deal with in your mind than your own self-imposed restrictions because it's someone else who's doing it to you so there's something there to fight against. When it's just you, how can you fight against yourself?

If you don't understand what I'm saying, think of it like this: smoking is bad for you. We all know this, we all accept this and we all shit ourselves at the thought of waking up one morning with lumpy lungs, yet how many of us smoke? Oh, sure, we could give it up if someone was to lock us in a room for a couple of years and not give us any fags, but how many smokers are able to quit, completely and overnight, without any sort of outside help? Not many, I bet, and even the ones that do would probably admit it was a slog. Most things involving discipline generally are.

Of course, the other thing about prison is that, for most prisoners, there's a light at the end of however long a tunnel the judge awarded you. This is something to look forward to.

Sitting in our flat in Brighton, watching the trains go past and eating takeaways three times a day, the only lights waiting for us at the end of our tunnel were light pockets when our money finally ran out. And then, my friends, we would be fucked.

I'd told Simon after the first week that what we really needed were three fake passports to get us out of the country and Simon said he'd ask around. I told him to be subtle, with a capital 'S', and gave him another ton for his troubles on top of the shopping money.

'Will do,' he winked and skipped off down the stairs.

Simon wore his best jacket and a healthy glow for the next few days so I figured he'd been doing most of his asking in the pubs around town. I didn't begrudge him this (where else were you going to find dodgy blokes with false passports?) but I did feel jealous. Tins of lager were all well and good but I would've given anything for an afternoon in the boozer. Anything.

That evening, when I walked in the bathroom and found a fully clothed Patsy reading a book in the bath 'just for a change of scenery', I decided we couldn't go on like this for much longer, we had to stretch our legs.

'We can't just go to the pub, Milo, use your loaf. Someone'll see us and blow the whistle,' Goody objected.

'I'm not suggesting we go to the pub, just that we take a stroll around town, after dark, like, around midnight. Go and sit on the beach or something. Anything just to get a breath of fresh air. What do you say? We'll all wear our hats and keep our collars up. Avoid the main drag and just take a walk. Well?'

'Yeah, I'm with you, Milo, let's go for it,' Patsy agreed enthusiastically, and started looking for his coat.

'Twelve o'clock. That's when we'll go. When the good people of Brighton are tucked up in their beds. Okay?'

Patsy stared at the clock for the next five hours and put his clobber on at half eleven because he couldn't sit still any longer. It was like watching a schoolboy getting all excited about going off on a school picnic. The only thing that really surprised me was that he didn't make a load of sandwiches and then eat them on the stairs on the way down to the front door. Goody stuck a bottle of Scotch in his inside pocket and we tiptoed past the other flats and out onto the street.

It felt weird being outside again and I half expected the neighbourhood to suddenly light up like Colditz – but it didn't. A car drove by, a gust of wind blew down my neck and Goody asked me which way was the sea. Those were the highlights.

'Downhill, I would imagine.'

'I love the seaside,' Patsy told us. 'It always makes me think of *Hart to Hart*.'

This made no sense whatsoever so I decided to ask him why.

'I don't know, just does. I remember going on holiday with me mum and dad and Denise, when I was little, and staying in this caravan in Bognor. We used to watch *Hart to Hart* on a little black-and-white telly and sleep on these orange sofas that folded out.'

'Jesus!' muttered Goody to himself. Patsy didn't seem to notice, though, and carried on with the anecdote, so that we got to hear all about the clubhouse sing-alongs and the time he got his hair caught in the fold-out ironing board. Fascinating stuff, it was.

On the way down to the sea, we passed a big old pub that still seemed to be open and it tugged at my heartstrings as we stood outside. I went on tiptoes and peered through the window, and sure enough the place was still serving.

'Looks a bit trendy, doesn't it?' Goody remarked, joining me at the window. I had a good butcher's and had to agree, it did. It was mostly full of people our own age drinking bottles of lager at around three pound a pop and standing around a few old sofas that seemed to take up more floor space than they were worth.

'Loads of birds in there, though, isn't there. Look. Fancy that thing in the cardy, she's alright.'

'It's four pound, lads,' a voice from out of nowhere told us, and we all jumped out of our hats and stumbled back a few yards when this whacking great bouncer stepped out of the doorway and onto the street.

'No, no, we're fine thanks, just looking,' we said, and scurried off as quickly as we could. We legged it the moment we were around the corner and criss-crossed the road a couple of times to avoid groups of people coming this way and that before finally making it to the beach.

The streets were surprisingly busy for twelve o'clock at night and it was up to Goody to remind me that it was the weekend.

'Is it? Fuck! I'd lost all track.'

'Friday, innit.'

'Oh well, we'd better steer clear of it down there by the pier because it'll be chocker with people milling about,' I said as we looked down the beach. The lights from that part of town looked bright and inviting and I could hear music and voices from even this far away above the crash of the sea. It sounded like it was all going off down there and we weren't invited.

'We'll get ours in Bangkok,' I reassured the lads, though we kept on staring down towards the lights.

'Shall we go and have a look at the water, then?' Patsy finally suggested.

This was about the most exciting offer open to us so we crunched across the pebbles to within a dozen yards of the wash and sat ourselves down.

We passed the bottle of Scotch around between us and smoked a few fags but none of us really had anything to say. The idea of getting out of the flat had been to relieve the claustrophobia, though seeing and hearing everyone whooping it up just a few hundred yards away and enjoying themselves in places we couldn't just made us feel all the more miserable. We sat around for about thirty minutes, as long as it took our arses to numb off completely, then stood up and dusted ourselves off.

'What do you want to do, then?' I asked the lads.

They thought about it for a few seconds then decided they wanted to go home.

'See if there's something on the telly, yeah?'

A pint

Another week slipped by and there was still no news of our passports. Simon reassured us he was dealing with some dodgy bloke and that everything was getting sorted, though even Goody was starting to catch a whiff that something wasn't as it seemed.

'If it's all getting sorted, why hasn't he asked us for any photos, then, the lying bastard?' I asked Goody and Patsy after Simon's latest visit.

Goody made excuses for him and suggested that perhaps he was only at the negotiations stage of proceedings, though I had a rather more plausible explanation.

'Yeah, or perhaps he doesn't want to see his golden goose fuck off before he's had all the eggs. Think about that,' I said, and I could tell by the lads' stony silent reaction that they already had.

'What are we going to do, then, Milo?' Patsy asked, not unreasonably.

Goody snapped.

'Let's have it out with him. Tell him we want those passports by next week or fucking else.'

'Or else what, Brains?'

'Or else . . . er . . . we don't give him no more money no more.'

'We can't do that, Good. We do that and he might just turn us in for the reward money after all.'

'He wouldn't do that,' Goody objected, but I stared him in the eyes and asked him if he was sure.

'Wanna bet your life, mate?'

Goody ran his fingers through his hair by way of a reply and Patsy said nothing.

'All we've got with Simon is a carrot, no stick. We can't take a chance on pissing him off because we're in too precarious a position.'

The lads agreed to stay shtum on this one for a couple more weeks, though the seeds of ill-feeling were well and truly sown.

The one positive that came out of our midnight wanderings the other Friday night was that we discovered it was reasonably safe to leave the house under cover of darkness. This was great because for the first time in Christ knows how fucking long we could all get away from each other. I could go down and wander along the beach while Goody could go off and stalk some side streets and Patsy could have a quiet night in and knock several out in front of Channel Five. It was great; such a relief to be able to get away by myself again. I sometimes spent the whole night away and would only return once the sun started coming up.

It was a bit like being a vampire.

I never saw anyone on my travels, or if I did I kept my head down and crossed the road. I just wandered around and mulled things over in my mind.

It had been more than three weeks since the robbery and we were out of the papers for the time being. The other lads, Norris, Jacko, Jimbo and Bob, had all been charged with armed robbery, false imprisonment, possession of firearms, resisting arrest, wounding with intent and every other offence the Old Bill could make stick, and were on remand in custody awaiting trial. They were all at different nicks too; the Old Bill had split them up as they often did in situations like these so that now the four of them were scattered around a bunch of southern prisons. I wasn't entirely sure why the authorities did this but I guess it made it easier to grind people down if they didn't have their mates around to lean on. The bastards. Anyway, that was their lot and this was mine.

I wandered around the darkened streets thinking about things like this and what I would do if I had my chances all over again and all the rest of that stuff a person tortures himself with when his life's turned to crap, when all of a sudden I came to a halt and found myself standing across the road from that selfsame trendy pub again.

It was a Saturday night and the place was rammed. People were spilling in and out of the pub and paying no more attention to me than they were to the lamp-posts that lined the street. I smacked my lips longingly and weighed up the risk.

Surely, if I kept my head down and myself to myself, I could get away with one pint, couldn't I? I mean, who was going to recognise me? The picture the papers had kept using was over four years old. It was my last mug shot and I'd aged (considerably) and done things with my hair since then. As if to prove this to myself, I stroked my newly cultivated goatee and ran my fingers over the prickly stubble that sat where my barnet used to.

A pint.

That was all I wanted.

Just one pint.

A pint.

A pint.

'A pint,' I shouted, pointing at the Stella tap and rattling my twenty under the barman's hooter. He searched about underneath the bar for several seconds then told me he was very sorry but he didn't have any more Stella glasses.

'Will a normal pint glass do or would you prefer another lager?' he asked.

'Oh, for fuck's . . . yes, yes, anything, put it in anything, I don't care. Just a pint of Stella, okay?'

The barman pulled the tap and stuck a sponsorless glass underneath. He held it at just the right angle to maximise the bubbly head like a big fucking amateur and had to scoop it off several times with a straw and refill it again and again to overflowing before moving off to play in someone else's beer. I wiped the side of the glass dry with my sleeve and picked it up. When I came to set it back down again the glass was half empty.

Or half full, depending on how you look at these things.

It tasted good. Very, very good.

It wasn't exactly an *Ice Cold in Alex* moment because I'd had four cans of lager before I'd come out, it was just being in a pub again, surrounded by people and enjoying a pint. It was very, very good.

Of course, I would've hit the roof if I'd found out that Goody or Patsy had gone and done the same thing, but then that was just because I didn't trust them as much as I trusted myself. I was only going to have the one (or maybe two) and keep myself to myself, whereas Goody would probably have been putting his money down on the pool table or smacking the fruit machine about. No, I wasn't here to interact with anyone, I just wanted to stand at the end of the bar, nice and anonymous, like, and have a couple of quiet pints.

Now if that was wrong, how could anything else in this big old world be right?

The pub wasn't as ram-jam packed as it had looked from the outside. People weren't fighting for floor space or standing six deep at the bar, it was just comfortably busy. All the stools were occupied, of course, and every sofa had an arse in it (literally), but I wasn't bothered about that. I just wanted to keep out of everyone's way and have a pint.

And a bag of nuts.

'Sorry, sir, we don't sell bags of peanuts, we only do bowls.'

'Er, well, a bowl then, please, and another pint of Stella.'

'That'll be five pounds forty-five,' he said in all serious-ness, then set an elephant's dinner down in front of me.

I almost coughed beer in his face when he told me how much, but I managed to hold it together enough not to kick up a scene and paid the silly cunt. Jesus, two-fifty for a bowl of nuts! What was going on in the world?

I polished off the last of my first pint and started on my second, and wondered if a man standing alone at a bar eat-ing a whole bowl of nuts to himself looked a bit odd to anyone.

Apparently not.

Most eyes were too focused on the legs and the tits that stuck out in every direction from the sofas in the middle of the room to pay me any attention, so that was something at least.

I ate as many nuts as I could, turning my lips horribly greasy in the process, then pushed the bowl away and decorated the remainder with my fag ash to stop them from being resold, before having a sneaky peek around.

Young and hip, that was these people. If a place like this had opened up back home I would've probably gone to it on the weekends too, but only because places like this attracted all the skirt. It wasn't actually a pub, more like an overpriced student union for people too frightened to mix with the hoi polloi. I wasn't sure I liked it, to be honest, and the unpub-like feel to the place soon kicked my euphoria into touch. In fact, my good mood vanished so quickly that all I was left with was this overwhelming feeling of paranoia.

What the fuck was I doing in here surrounded by all these people? Any one of them could've recognised me at any time and called the Old Bill. There was a big reward on my head, didn't I know? Wouldn't I want to cash in if ten grand walked into my local and started eating nuts at the bar?

What was I thinking about?

Okay, so I'd fancied a pint. So I'd fancied a night out of the flat. So I'd been bored and lonely.

Jesus, didn't I think I'd be even more bored and lonely spending the next twenty-five years in a fucking cell? God almighty, where was my head? After all I'd said about Jack Sheppard and the stupidity he'd exercised when he was on the run, I'd gone and done exactly the same thing myself. The realisation came crashing over me like a winter's wave hitting the rocks.

I had to get out of here.

I had to get out of here now, though I couldn't do it too fast in case people stopped and stared.

Though they were stopping and staring right now.

I could feel them. I could feel every eye in the pub surreptitiously glancing over towards me and recognising me for who I was. I could even hear what the bastards were thinking.

'Okay, he's looking this way, pretend we haven't spotted him. Just carry on as before.'

'And you're sure the Old Bill are on their way?'

'Yeah, I just rang them, when I was in the bog. Quick, laugh like I just said something funny, he's looking.'

'Ha ha ha ha ha. Is he still looking?'

'Yes. No, don't turn around, offer me a fag. Pretend we're just sitting in a pub having a quiet chat. We're not grassing up a dangerous criminal or nothing, no, sir. We're just having a chat.'

'Where are your fags?'

'They're in my pocket.'

'Well, why don't we smoke them, then?'

'That would look too suspicious, just what he'd be expecting us to do. No, don't, he's looking edgy as it is. Go on, quick, give me a fag.'

'Oh, for fuck's sake.'

'Good, now go to the bar and get us both another drink. Don't look over at the criminal, though, as I think he may be onto us. No, no, I said don't! Fuck's sake, that was a close one. Well, go on, then. Two more Scotch and cokes. And get us a bowl of crisps while you're at it.'

'Do you want to stop telling me what to do?'

'No. Give me a light.'

'What?'

'A light, give me a light.'

'Get you own fucking light.'

'I need a light, can I borrow a light?'

'Er . . . what?'

The redhead pointed down at my lighter and smiled optimistically. I looked down at where she was pointing and finally snapped out of my own little world.

'Er . . . oh, yeah, sure. Sorry. Help yourself.'

'Thanks,' she said, then looked at my peanuts. 'You've got ash all over them. Been a long day, has it?'

My jaw seized up completely and I didn't know what to say or whether to try and cover my face. In the few seconds I'd been scanning the rest of the pub before making my escape, I hadn't seen her sidle up until she'd stopped right in front of me.

'Yes, a long day, yes,' I finally confirmed, and stared into her eyes for a flicker of recognition. Redhead smiled back and sympathetically told me that she understood. This I severely doubted. When I didn't add anything further she looked back towards her friends and I thought that was it, but there was more to come.

'Do you want to join us?' she said, pointing to a table in the corner of the boozer with two birds and a bloke around it. They all looked over my way and I tried to put Redhead's red head between my face and them in case they paid more attention to the papers than this one did.

'Erm, no, I'd better not, I've got to get going anyway,' I told her.

'Do you live around here?'

What the fuck was this?

'Er, no. I'm just down for the weekend to see a mate.'

'Oh yeah, where's he?' she asked, looking from side to side like I was talking about the Invisible Man.

'Er, he's had enough and gone home,' I said, then added, 'I'd probably better be doing the same.' I jabbed my thumb over my shoulder to underline this fact and picked up my fags and lighter.

'Have you got a girlfriend?' she asked, almost kicking me sideways. This sort of thing had never happened to me before, not even when I wasn't on the run, not never. It was very unsettling.

The redhead's eyes glistened as she waited for an answer and she pulled on her cigarette provocatively. She was an attractive girl, of that there was no getting away from. Her hair was short and her waist was slender. She had long shapely legs protruding from an A-line skirt and rich ruby lips that I would've loved to have felt against mine. Her smile was genuine, if a little apologetic, and when she caught me with it again I felt my resolve start to weaken.

I had to get back to the flat, I tried to tell myself. I had to get back to safety. That was the sensible thing to do.

Unfortunately my little redhead friend was one hell of a persuasive distraction. Sometimes, some things are worth the risk, I started to hear myself think. Sometimes, life just has to be lived.

I wondered if I dared.

It had been so long since I'd been with a woman (and years since I'd been with one this pretty) that I didn't know if I had it in me to say no. Not that I was even bothered about sex, just a little female company would've done nicely. A chat, a drink, a few laughs and a little kiss. God, how I would love that – even more than an afternoon in the pub. But what the fuck was I doing?

My head was dancing all over the place, this way and that, and I felt like a rabbit caught between two onrushing headlights.

Did I stay and risk all, or did I run and kiss off the chance to connect with a beautiful woman, which, let's be honest, is what life's all about?

'I . . . I . . .' I started, now standing so close to her I could almost feel the heat from her body against my chest. 'I don't at the moment, no,' I told her, hardly daring to blink.

I hadn't felt this sort of pull on my heart since those first few awkward dates with Alice, and I so wanted to topple over and plunge right through her, kissing her on the mouth as I fell, and landing on top of her in soft warm sheets.

I didn't know why I felt this way. Maybe it was all the loneliness and all the despair I'd felt in the last few weeks, or maybe it was the fact that she was holding herself in a way that reminded me of Alice, but suddenly I was hooked, and no matter how much I fought, I was rapidly being reeled in.

'Good.' She smiled excitedly. 'Because my friend over there really fancies you,' she said, and discreetly flicked her thumb back towards her table.

I looked over her shoulder and saw Olive from *On the*

Buses smiling back at me, also apologetically, though she had a lot more to apologise for.

'Fuck! I mean, sorry, no,' I almost screamed. 'No no no no no, I really do have to go, I'm not kidding. Can't be helped, I'm afraid. Yes, lovely to meet you I've got to go 'bye,' I told her, and headed for the door before she had a chance to get another word out. I looked back at her just as I reached the door and saw her shrug towards her friends, but I don't know what else she'd been expecting.

I mean, Jesus!

Perhaps she had recognised me after all. Perhaps she knew all about me and had read the same newspaper reports as I had done. After all, every time he'd been interviewed Weasel had described me as a desperate fugitive.

This may have been the case, but one thing was for certain, I wasn't that fucking desperate.

A day in the sun

A day or two later our landlord called around unexpectedly. He knocked on the door and we all stayed quiet so that he'd go away, but the cheeky bastard started letting himself in.

'Wait! Don't come in,' I yelled, dragging Goody onto the sofa with me as matey stepped through the door. Patsy had already launched himself into the bedroom and me and Goody did our best to try and hide our eyes and look like we'd just been caught making the beast with two backs (and two of everything, in fact).

'Oh, please excuse me, my dears, I'm so so sorry,' he said, falling back through the doors with mock shock and shielding his eyes. 'I'm Bernard [which he pronounced Bern-*ard*, though he probably wasn't], your landlord. I'm afraid I must intrude upon you today as I have a young man from the gas with me here this morning. He needs to check your gas,' he explained a little unnecessarily.

'Just a minute. Hold on.'

'Of course, I quite understand, we'll call on number five first while you make yourselves decent,' he said, then exited stage left.

'The fucker's going to see us,' Goody pointed out, pushing himself up off of me. Patsy looked out of the bedroom and pointed out exactly the same thing, then they both asked in perfect harmony, 'What are we going to do?'

'I don't know. I don't know,' I said, scratching my head and running around the flat like a rumbled chicken.

'Maybe he won't recognise us. After all, it's been a few weeks and we've all changed a bit from our pictures in the meantime,' Patsy said optimistically, tugging at his newly acquired beard.

'From a distance perhaps, but we still all look like our-selves up close,' I replied, staring at Darren Miles as he stared back at me from the mirror.

'Yeah, but he probably ain't going to know what we look like up close, is he? He might not even read the papers,' Goody argued.

'Yeah, and then again he might be our biggest fan with pictures of us stuck all over his headboard. Are you willing to take that risk?'

Goody and Patsy ummed and ahhed as I pulled on my trainers. One thing was for certain, once we'd let him see our faces our nice safe flat was utterly compromised. Better to get recognised outside and have somewhere to bolt to than be recognised inside and have nowhere to run.

'We can't go out now,' Patsy objected, but I told them we just had no choice. Bern-*ard* was coming back in a matter of minutes and we couldn't all simply hide in the bedroom. For one thing that would've looked even more suspicious and Bern-*ard* didn't strike me as the sort of bloke who'd let two young dears (because he still didn't know about Patsy) evade his curiosity for very long once he had them cornered.

The three of us rushed into our hats and coats and legged it down the stairs and out towards the front door before Bern-*ard* and his young gas man had a chance to poke their heads out of number five. We got out onto the street and kept on going as fast as we could in case he tried to make it after us, but there was no sign of him. I knew this was going to look a bit off, but I hoped that the nosey cunt would see it as a flight by two bashful homos rather than three wanted villains.

We made half a dozen turns down this street and that before finally figuring it was safe to slow up.

'Where are we going?' Patsy asked, looking up and down the residential street.

'Let's head for the beach, get away from the road and all the houses,' I said, and pointed down the hill.

'Here, why did you bring your money?' Goody asked, grabbing the satchel I'd slung over my shoulder on the way out.

'Well, I just figured I'd rather keep it with me than leave it back home with them two going through the flat,' I explained.

'Oh, thank you very much for that. Thanks a fucking lot. You could have told us to pick up ours as well,' Goody moaned, while Patsy turned white.

'I didn't think, I only grabbed mine at the last moment. Sorry, mate,' I said, though to be honest they should've thought about this themselves. I couldn't be there for them their whole lives.

'I'm going back,' Goody suddenly announced, but me and Patsy grabbed an arm each and told him to think about it.

'Chances are they're not going to be looking in bags in wardrobes when they're checking the place for gas. I only grabbed mine because it was a reflex action and so that we'd have some cash today in case we wanted to get an ice cream or something. Come on, think about it.'

Goody did just that and reasoned it would be riskier going back than staying away. Besides, if they were only taking five minutes in number five, how long were they likely to take in ours? Even if they checked out all eight flats

today and took their sweet time about it trying on everyone's pants, they were still only going to be a couple of
hours. We could sweat it out until then.

We strolled down to the beach and walked across the
pebbles to the water's edge. The days were certainly cooling
off and the beach was fairly quiet. It would be busier farther
down by the pier but we avoided that end and stayed out of
harm's way.

It felt nice to be out in daylight again. Nice, but weird.
I'd been out of the public eye for so long that I kept on
instinctively looking for places to shelter (or rocks to crawl
under, as I'm sure a few of my less charitable acquaintances
would've said). On the beach there was nothing of the sort.
Just a seawall near the road and a few assorted huts.

We had no newspapers or books or food to eat, just a
load of stones and a big load of water, so we spent a loose
half-hour doing what came naturally and returned as many
of the stones as we could to the sea before this got too
boring.

'I'm fucking starving,' Goody moaned, clutching his guts
before going on to explain at tedious length how and why
he'd missed breakfast this morning. We could smell the
aroma of fish and chips wafting towards us from the direction of the pier and we all went quiet for five minutes. I
knew what the lads were thinking because I was thinking
exactly the same thing; could we risk getting a bite to eat
off one of those takeaway bars down by the pier without
blowing our identities?

Like I'd said, there was hardly anyone about, it was a
work and school day rolled into one and the sky was
covered with a blanket of grey clouds, so most people had
decided to give the beach a miss today. We had our hats
with us and our sunglasses, and we weren't exactly going to
engage anyone in a conversation save for 'cod and chips
three times and three cans of Fanta, please, mate', and I

could do that from under the brim of my cap while the
others stayed down by the water. We'd done much the same
thing when we'd landed in Portsmouth, starving hungry
and knackered out, and the bloke in that chippy had hardly
battered a sausage in our direction. Surely it was worth a
go?

Obviously not. I mean, fish and chips are nice and everything but they're not worth doing twenty years for, even if
they are seaside fish and chips.

Perhaps a better way of phrasing the question was, how
realistic was the risk?

Not very, I concluded, but only after my guts kicked in
with a bad case of the rumbles, so I explained the plan to
the chaps and they seemed well up for it. We hauled ourselves up off the pebbles, dusted the grit off of our trousers
and started on down the beach.

Now, I know what you're thinking here, and I would've
been thinking exactly the same in your shoes; that we
must've been barmy. Here we were, on the run, the whole
country looking for us, and we were happily wandering
along in broad daylight going for fish and chips. I'm sure
if I read about people in the paper who did something
similar in similar circumstances I would've shaken my head
and called them wankers, especially if, at the end of it, they'd
all got themselves nicked. But try and see things from our
point of view.

We were bored.

We were so, so, so, so brain-numbingly, moon-
screamingly bored.

You have no idea what it's like to have to cut yourself off
from the rest of society and live life in the shadows. It does
your head in. It certainly did mine. To not be able to do any
of the things you'd spent your whole life doing? It was like
trying to fight against our instincts. Fine, it's doable and
we'd all been managing it for weeks on end up until this

point, but occasionally you can't but let your better judgement wander off for a copy of the *Racing Post* just when you
need him most. Take my pint the other night, for example;
how sensible had that been? Not very, you'd all probably say,
but I'd done such a fantastic job arguing myself in circles
convincing myself that a pint was such a little thing and that
being on the run was such a big thing that how could the
two have any bearing on each other?

I know, I know, I know. At least, I know now, but back
then I didn't. I mean, who would? It wasn't like I was trying to reserve my usual table at the Saveloy or something ...

... it was only a bag of chips on the beach.

'Didn't they have any red sauce?' Patsy moaned when I
dumped his grub down in his lap.

'Oh, sorry, Pats, I forgot.'

Patsy exhibited his bottom lip, then told me to go up and
get some for him.

'Let's just leave it, shall we, I'm not going back there
again, risking being recognised twice just 'cos you want
ketchup, alright?'

'But it ain't the same without it.'

'I'll have yours if you don't want it, then, Pats,' Goody
volunteered, making a grab for his grub, but Patsy held it
out of range and began forcing it down under protest. Jesus,
it wasn't like I'd forgotten the salt and vinegar or nothing.

There had been tables and chairs outside the takeaway
but we'd come and sat well away from them, on the beach
in the shadow of the pier. Even this close to the centre of
the action, there still weren't that many people about. There
were loads of legs fifty feet above us on the actual pier, but
down here on the pebbles and by the stone-cold murky
chop, there weren't above a handful.

'Where shall we go when Simon comes across with the
passports?' Goody somehow managed to ask with half a cod
sticking out of his face.

'If he comes across with the passports,' I corrected him, wagging my chip fork under his nose to underline the point.

'Alright, if he comes across with the passports?'

'I thought we were going to Thailand?' Patsy said in confusion.

'Yeah, well, we are eventually, but we can't fly straight there from here, can we? We'd be picked up at the airport the minute we showed our noses through the door. No, we'll have to fly out from somewhere safer, Italy or Spain or France or somewhere.'

'But they'll be looking for us there as well, you know,' Goody reminded me. 'Interpol,' he said, finally finding the name for them.

'I know that, but not with such . . . wasser name . . . determination. We ain't going to have been in every frog paper for the last four weeks, are we? Over there we'll just be Tom, Dick and Harry Bloggs, three more moaning Brits trying to find egg and chips on the menus and sending their grub back when it tastes funny. They ain't going to know us or give us a second look if our passports check out, are they, they've got their own villains to worry about.'

'I can speak a bit of French,' Patsy then told us. Me and Goody looked suitably impressed so we told him to give us a twirl.

'*Je suis désolé, mais je suis sorté sans mon portefeuille,*' he said, then added as a finale, '*une plus de fois.*'

'Go on, then, I'll bite. What's it mean?' I asked.

'I'm very sorry, but I've come out without my wallet . . . again.' He laughed.

'Very handy. Anything else?'

Patsy thought for moment but told us no, that was his lot. 'Went on holiday with Jackie and her tight-arse French cousin, didn't I,' he muttered, by way of explanation.

'Well, we'll leave you to get the tickets over there, then,

Pats, eh?' Goody said, making us all laugh chips through our noses.

We ate and talked for the next ten minutes or so, discussing things like where we were going, how we'd be getting there, what we'd do when we got there and so on, and it was very pleasant indeed. We kept a good eye out over our shoulders but nobody came within earwigging distance of us or even looked in our direction, so slowly we began to unwind.

Like Patsy, I'd always liked the seaside, though for reasons other than *Hart to Hart*. The sound of the sea is a very soothing sound, and just staring out across a big expanse of wobbly water is enough to make a person forget all their recent troubles – if for only a few minutes. I guess this is why mental people come to convalesce by the seaside and why yuppies listen to tapes of it in their penthouses. It's very therapeutic, I believe cleverer people than me have said.

So, while we were sat there on the pebbles, enjoying our fish and chips and talking the way old friends talk to each other (i.e. bollocks), we were completely unaware of the events that were unfolding not fifty feet above our heads which would have a dramatic effect on any of us ever seeing Thailand in this lifetime.

Milo the hero 16

'. . . so I said to Tony, "Oh, I've seen this one, Tone, they all did it," and he flings a paddy, chucks the remote across the room, breaking it, and storms out of the living room. Can you believe that? But then that's Tone for you. Personally I thought everyone had seen *Murder on the Orient Express*, so how was I supposed to know he hadn't?'

Only Christ and the seagulls knew what Goody had been banging on about for the last couple of minutes because I was far too busy trying to figure out what the palaver up on the pier was all about. When Goody finally stopped talking and saw me squinting upwards he joined in too, and the pair of us stared up at all the feet running about in circles and listened to all the screaming that was going on.

When it had first broken out I'd just thought it was high spirits, I mean, there were bumper cars and hoop-la-hoops up there and so on, but then it carried on for a bit too long and I recognised the voices as those of adults. There was just one voice at first, but then this was soon joined by another, and then another, and then another still. There was a definite level of panic in the words they were calling and suddenly everyone was clunking backwards and forwards across the boards and shouting at the tops of their heads.

A cold, clammy fear suddenly descended on me and instinctively I made to bolt. I didn't think it was us they were screaming about – I mean, even when we were on form, we weren't that scary – but there was definitely trouble up there. And where there was trouble, the Old Bill were never that far behind.

'What are they all shouting about up there?' Goody asked, himself more than me. 'It sounds like "Jenny".'

'I don't know, mate, but I really think we should get the fuck out of here now. Come on, let's get going,' I said, hauling myself and then him up to his feet.

It did indeed sound like 'Jenny'. In fact, it sounded more like 'JENNY! JENNY! JENNNNNY!!!'

At that moment Patsy returned from taking our wrappers to the bin. The bin was up by the takeaway so it was a risky mission in itself, but we hadn't wanted to attract unnecessary attention to ourselves by littering. Patsy told us that the geezer in the chippy had grabbed him as he wandered past and told him that they'd rung down from the pier to say that a little girl had gone missing and to keep his eyes peeled for any oddballs. Patsy was still in a state of nervous shock at being spoken to by someone other than me and Goody but had calmed down enough to pass on the appeal.

'I think we should definitely get out of here, right now,' I said. 'If some fucking weirdo's picked her up the whole place is going to be swarming with Old Bill any second and everyone within a mile of this place is going to get a pull. Come on, let's get out of here.'

I tried pushing them along in the direction of Hove, but Patsy was holding back and shaking his arm free from my grasp.

'Come on, Pats, for fuck's sake, let's go!'

'Wait. No, wait a minute,' he was saying, staring out at the water just underneath the pier. 'Milo, wait.'

'Patsy, let's go,' Goody joined in, but Patsy suddenly shrieked.

'Shit, Milo, look, there she is.' He pointed out at something about thirty yards away, bobbing up and down in the swell and drifting under the pier. I looked at where he was pointing and saw it immediately. The girl was on her front and her face was in the water. She didn't appear to be moving and she was clearly out of sight of the folks above.

Nobody could see her but us.

Isn't fate a wanker?

'DOWN HERE! DOWN HERE!' Patsy started calling up, but nobody seemed to hear him. The girl drifted under the pier and started towards one of the encrusted supports.

'DOWN HERE, SHE'S DOWN HERE!' Goody then joined in, but it didn't matter anyway. Even if they'd heard us and looked down to see the girl, it would've been a good three or four minutes before they were able to get to where we were, and by that time it would've been too late. We were the only people in a position to do anything about it and if we didn't we'd not only have our consciences to live with, we'd also have an angry lynch mob out to string us up for our cowardly dereliction.

And personally, I didn't fancy that. There were enough people in this country who fucking hated us already, the last thing we needed was a few more.

'Ohhh, BOLLOCKSSSS!' I growled as I pulled myself out of my hat, coat, shoes and trousers.

'What are you doing, Milo?' Goody had the intelligence to ask, but I didn't have the time to answer. From the moment I'd spotted the girl in the water to the moment my toes touched the fucking freezing cold stuff, barely ten seconds had passed. Well, I like to think of myself as one of life's quick thinkers and I'd worked out all the angles in a millisecond and knew it was all down to me.

Me, that was, not us.

See, my one other talent in life (other than getting locked up for long periods of time) has always been swimming. I was like *The Man from Atlantis* when I was a kid, you could hardly get me out of the water, so I knew I had the tools to do the job. Besides, I don't know if I've ever mentioned this before but I'm not a complete disbeliever in the Big Fella upstairs, and if I had to answer to him as well after all this, I really would be pissed off.

He put us here on the beach, he made a conniving self-preservationist like myself a good swimmer, then he tumbled a kid into the drink to see what I'd do. This was his little game and one way or another we always had to play.

'Back in a mo', I shouted to Goody and Patsy, and launched myself head first into the water.

The shock of the cold washed over me in an instant and I almost pulled up, screeched like a little girl and turned back for the beach, but unfortunately I couldn't do that as there was a real little girl out there and she was unnervingly quiet. The only thing I could do was kick my legs, flap my arms and live with it, so that's what I did. All other considerations were put on the back burner for the moment as I focused all my strength on one task. In actual fact, I soon got used to the temperature. The waters around Britain are never that cold, even in the winter, and it had been an exceptionally long and hot summer. It was really just the initial shock that sent my spuds fleeing for their lives.

'Kick your legs, darling. Kick your legs. I'm coming,' I called out to the girl, and I could hear Goody and Patsy way off behind me shouting similar encouragement. I didn't realise it at the time but my rescue attempt was drawing quite a crowd up on the pier too. I wouldn't normally have minded this, because everyone fantasises about this sort of stuff from time to time. You know what I mean, risking your life, saving the day, being a hero, getting your picture in the paper and shaking hands with the mayor. Perhaps even getting a big hamper of meat from the Co-op as a reward. Well, who wouldn't?

Unfortunately, my picture had already been in the paper rather a lot just recently, so the last thing I needed was more publicity. I just hoped I could snag the girl, get her back to the beach, get Goody to do his army medical bit on her, then leg it before anyone else got within back-slapping range of us.

I pushed on and kicked up a storm behind me, thrashing my arms through the water and dragging myself to within grabbing distance of the lifeless bundle of flesh now only ten feet in front of me.

The salt stung my eyes and a wave gushed into my face just as I was taking another breath, so that I got to swallow a great lungful of acrid brine, but other than that I was making good progress.

Five feet left to go, then four, then three, then two, then I measured my strokes so as not to whack her in the face when I caught hold of her legs.

The poor little thing was freezing cold and horribly stiff. I turned her over in the water and looked into her eyes for signs of life, but they just rolled back into her head, completely dead.

It was a doll.

It was a little kiddy's fucking doll.

It took a full moment for this to filter through, but when it did a shock ran over me far colder than the water I was treading.

I looked up and saw around four dozen faces gawping down at me and cheering while back on the beach Goody and Patsy were urging me back towards them, still oblivious to the fact that . . .

. . . it was a fucking doll.

That big bastard upstairs, he'd certainly got us this time, and now we were in real schtuck because a trickle of people had started wandering down to the waterline by Goody and Patsy to see what this particular retard was doing swimming about in the sea half dressed on a windy day.

We were in trouble.

I launched myself back to the lads, clutching hold of the doll, and chucked it at Goody when I was within range of the beach. Goody stumbled blindly into the drink up to his knees in order to catch it, then looked at me accusingly when he saw what I already knew.

'It's a dolly,' he said, open mouthed in confusion. 'It's just a little dolly. A toy!'

A few of the onlookers laughed with enormous smugness and I wanted to blow every one of their fucking brains out. My fingers touched shingle and I hauled my heavy body upright and out of the water. Goody waded in a little further to steady me up and helped me out when he saw how shaky I was, and together we splashed out of the water and up towards my clothes.

I used my jacket as a makeshift towel in order to get my trousers and socks back on, though even when I had I was still soaking wet for the most of it.

The people around us were still chuckling to themselves and nattering to each other about what a trio of losers we were, but so far no one had tried to approach me. That was probably just as well considering the mood I was in and the handgun I had in my bag.

'I thought it was real,' Patsy was murmuring to himself, checking the dolly over again just to make sure we hadn't missed something. 'I saw it out there and I thought it was real.'

'Well, never mind that, let's just get out of here before anyone recognises us,' I said, wiping the water from my eyes and tying up my trainers. Patsy dropped the dolly where he stood and him and Goody helped me to my feet.

More people were now wandering in from all areas of

the beach to see what all the hullabaloo was about and more and more fingers were now pointing in our direction. I pulled my hat down over my eyes and turned to walk away when a voice called after us and told us to hold on a second.

I turned to look up the beach and dropped several bricks when I saw this young woodentop striding purposefully across the beach towards us with a big grin on his face.

'Hold on, lads, you alright?' he was asking with amused concern. 'Just a sec.'

And there was me thinking I couldn't have got any colder. Icicles suddenly ran through my veins and my heart started smashing against the inside of my chest as I stood stunned and horrified in complete inaction.

'Milo . . .' Goody started, but I grabbed him by the arm and told him to stick a sock in it.

'Son, are you okay?' the copper asked rather patronisingly (son? He couldn't have been more than three years older than me) when he got up to where we were standing.

'Yes, I'm fine. Just want to get home now and put some dry clothes on before I catch my death,' I replied, averting my eyes and shifting about like a cat on hot bricks to try and stop him snapping a close-up of my mush. Goody and Patsy were somewhere behind me, doing their best to study the distant horizon, while casually making tracks towards it.

'We saw you from the pier, I thought you must've been mad. Very good of you all the same but you shouldn't have done a silly thing like that over just a dolly. That sea's a lot rougher than it looks, you know, you could've drowned,' the wanker lectured me, a big condescending smile plastered all the way across his hat-warmer.

'Yes, well, thank you, I'll bear that in mind . . . er, Officer. I thought it was the little girl who was lost, that's why I went in there. I didn't know it was a doll at the time, did I?'

'You what? You thought it was the girl? Ah, ha ha ha ha

ha,' the bastard laughed, and Patsy and Goody took the opportunity to put a few more yards between them and us while he wiped the mirth from his eyes. 'Oh, that's classic, that really is. Oh, I can't wait to tell the lads. Oh dear, no, no, I'm sorry, son, you're a hero, really you are. I never realised. No, the little girl's quite safe. She went looking for her dolly but I guess you found it first. Here, come with me, she's up on the pier with her mother. Why don't you reunite her with her toy? I'm sure she'd appreciate it coming from you,' he said, and actually tried leading me off up the beach with him.

I tell you, what a wanker! Even if I hadn't been in trouble with the Old Bill, I still wouldn't have gone with him. I hated that sanctimonious, superior, smug way every copper I've ever dealt with has looked and talked down at me. It's like they see us, the public, or 'civilians', as simple-minded children who need to be patted on the head and herded down the straight and narrow by them, the bastions of society, the brave boys in blue, our moral guardians and heroic protectors. I don't know where they get this attitude from – it must be something that's drummed into them at police academy because most of them are fucking flids at school, who spent most of their deservedly painful teenage years fishing their bags out of trees or inspecting the insides of bogs while they're flushed repeatedly by everyone from Remedial B. I hated them. And not just because they kept on nicking me and putting me away for years on end, it was more because of the sheer pleasure they exhibited when they did so. There was no sympathy, no 'well, that's the game and this time you lost', no professional neutrality, no nothing. They fucking loved it. Every time. Loved it. Smiling at me through the hatch in the cell door, rubbing their hands with glee that I was about to be deprived of a good chunk of my life, coming down to gloat over me after sentencing. I hated them.

Fucking wankers to a man, every one of them.

Now this bastard was chuckling at me because I was all wet and dripping and ordering me to come along with him so that he could show me to his mates and have a good laugh at my expense. What right did he have to talk to me this way? What right did any of them have?

'No,' I told him. 'I'm all wet, I'm going home, I'm going to get changed.' I put a little more steel into my voice to show that I wasn't fucking about and started off after Goody and Patsy, but the cunt wouldn't let me go.

'Alright, alright, you win, come on, I'll give you a lift back home,' he said, picking up the doll and flagging me back.

'No!' I insisted. 'I don't want a lift, I'm fine on my own.'

Now this really must've pissed him off because suddenly he flexed his authority and told me to hold it just there. Like old ladies with children, if there's one thing coppers hate it's unappreciative 'civilians' wandering off while they're trying to talk down at them.

'Right, do you just want to stop right there for a moment, please, sir? I haven't quite finished with you yet. You two as well, please, gentlemen,' he said, talking to all three of us. I turned around and saw him pointing to a spot about three feet in front of him. This was his way of telling me where he wanted me to stand, and the look on his face told me just how long he was willing to give me to get there.

I crunched back towards him and stood where he wanted me, shivering for a number of reasons and trying to hide my face with my cap.

'Gentlemen, you too, please,' he said, and allocated Goody and Patsy a bit of beach of their own. 'Right, we'll start with your names, then, shall we, and while I'm taking those you'll all empty your pockets, please,' he instructed the three of us.

It was clear he still didn't know who we were, but from our reluctance to play kiss-chase with him he'd assumed we were probably up to something, smoking dope or sniffing glue in all likelihood, so now he was going to give us the quick once-over.

The three of us looked at each other while he got out his pad and I gave them a little nod. I was still hoping we could talk our way out of this one but if we couldn't we had to be ready.

'Colin Beale,' I told him, and turned the pockets of my jacket and jeans inside out. Fags, keys and a few coins, that's all I had.

'Dennis Jessop,' Goody said, and did the same.

'Anthony . . . er . . . Hopkins,' Patsy stuttered, sending all our bullshit names up the Swanee without a paddle between them.

PC Smug smelt a rat and asked Mr Hopkins for some ID.

'And from you two as well,' he added.

'Fuck me, this is police harassment. All I did was jump in the water because I thought a little girl was drowning, now you're looking for some excuse to chuck the book at me. This is going to make interesting reading in the *Brighton Herald*, I can tell you that, Police Constable . . .'

'Miller,' he said, folding his arms in impatience.

'Yeah, sure, I made a fool out of myself, but just because I want to go home and dry myself off instead of having my nose rubbed in it in front of that load of wankers,' I said, indicating the interested spectators, 'I've got to go through the third degree. Well, no, you cannot see any ID because I didn't bring any with me. I left my wallet at home because I deliberately didn't want to spend any money today. I am a student, after all.'

'Oh yeah, and what are you studying?'

'Politics and law,' I told him defiantly, hoping that this combination would make me sound like a sufficiently big enough pain in the arse for him to send us on our way before a three-hour soap-box debate broke out.

'And what about you two, I suppose you've left your wallets at home too?' PC Miller surmised, and for the briefest of seconds I thought we were actually going to get away with it, but then Goody said:

'Yeah, well, I thought Milo was bringing his, didn't I?'

The three of us froze the moment my name was spoken and PC Miller furrowed his brow in confusion, not quite sure what he'd just heard. Then suddenly the curtain lifted from in front of his eyes and recognition dawned across his face.

'Eight-one urgent assis . . .' was all he managed to shout before I shoulder-charged him and his radio into the surf. Miller went under head first to cheers from half the beach, and me, Goody and Patsy turned tail and ran. We worked our legs like blue bloody murder, but running on pebbles is an awful lot of effort for very little gain and I just hoped and prayed we could reach solid tarmac before Miller managed to cough enough of the English Channel from his lungs to call for help.

And so that was our lot for Brighton. Thanks to a few pounds of pink plastic from Taiwan, Patsy's eagle eyes and Goody's big dopey gob, our time lying low was prematurely at an end. Our cover had been blown and rest time was well and truly over.

Suddenly, we were back to where we'd started.

Suddenly, we were running again.

17

Brighton handicap

'STOP THOSE MEN! STOP THOSE MEN!' Miller started shouting behind us while we were still crashing our feet through the pebbles. 'SARGE, SARGE! IT'S THEM. IT'S THE SUPERMARKET LOT. SARGE!'

I couldn't tell you if Miller's sarge heard or not, all I can tell you is that I suddenly wished I hadn't had fish and chips for breakfast. My guts were as heavy as my feet, and my legs were raw from where my pants were soaked inside my trousers. I'm not sure how I'd managed to do it but I'd somehow plumbed the depths of discomfort before the race had even begun. At least when we'd all run through the woods I'd started out feeling okay and had gradually got worse as that particular nightmare unfolded; here I was in the middle of a town not ten seconds into the chase and my thighs were already feeling like someone had had a good go at them with a block of sandpaper. It's unbelievable, isn't it; where's the justice?

'Come on, come on, let's go!' Goody was urging us. Naturally him and Patsy were way out in front again and it was left to old Sloppy McTight Pants to bring up the rear as usual. Goody shouted the whole way across the beach but it didn't make things any easier for any of us. See, on pebbles, every three feet you step forward, you sink back

two. It's like running in jelly in lead boots, or more applic-
ably like in one of those horrible dreams you have where
the big scary monster's charging up behind you at a hundred miles an hour, but no matter how hard you try you can
hardly lift your feet. That's what it was like, though I'll tell
you something for nothing, it's a lot fucking scarier in real
life.

I didn't dare look over my shoulder to see where the
monster was or even off to my right to see if the sarge had
got the message, all I concentrated on doing was reaching
those steep stone steps that led up to the promenade and
disappearing off into town.

If we could just make it back home . . . if we could just
get changed . . . if we could just pick up our money . . . and
if we could just nick the first car out of town . . .

'HEAD THEM OFF! HEAD THEM OFF!' the cunt was
shouting, making me wish I'd smacked him in the gob
when I'd had the chance.

Startled faces watched us go by but no one tried to stick
a foot out to collect a reward, for which I was truly grate-
ful. This was also just as well for them as I'd dug my pistol
out of my bag and wasn't in much of a mood for fucking
about. I figured it was probably safe to do this for the
moment because all the coppers around (at least until word
got out about the Supermarket Bandits) were likely to be
unarmed so, if the worst came to the worst, the only people
at risk of getting shot were everybody else in the world
except me.

'Make way! Make way!' I shouted, sliding both arms
through my rucksack and motoring on towards the steps.

The footing got firmer the closer we got to the steps and
we were able to measure our strides a little better. This was
just as well because all of a sudden I felt a gnawing clawing
at the back of my throat and before I knew it my fish and
chips were landing all over the beach. I pulled up sharply

and ejected the rest in three great bucket-loads, ruining my shoes and poleaxing myself in the process as my lunch made its own bid for freedom.

I could see Miller running up the beach towards me through a vale of tears but there was nothing I could do. The fear, the sudden exertion, the sea water and my swollen belly had combined to stop me in mid-flee and there was fuck all I could do about it until my gut stopped going over like a tumble drier.

I pointed the gun in Miller's direction while another great load of semi-digested batter hit the deck and shouted a warning to him in between heaves.

'Stay back. Don't come any, uhhhgggghhhh . . . any, uhh-hgggghhhh-h-h-h . . . any, uhhhgggghhhh . . . ooh, fuck me!'

'Milo, for fuck's sake, knock it on the head,' Goody was shouting at me from the steps, but all he got back for his troubles was another: 'Uhhhgggghhhhhhhhhhhhhhh!'

I spat the residue from my mouth, took a couple of deep breaths and soldiered on as best I could. My guts tried jumping out of my throat one last time but there was nothing left to juggle, so I was able to swallow it back down and keep my legs moving. Incredibly, within a couple of strides I actually felt a hundred per cent better. My stomach no longer felt bloated, my legs no longer felt heavy and I had a spring in my step that helped carry me to the lads waiting at the bottom of the steps.

'You alright?' Patsy asked pointlessly.

'I am now. Come on, let's get going, shall we.'

We charged up the steps as Miller passed my sick and headed for the road. All of a sudden, though, there, three steps from the top and blocking our progress, was one of Miller's mates. He stretched out his arms and danced from side to side like he was getting ready to grab the first of us who tried to make it past him, and I saw that there really was no alternative. I aimed the gun at the concrete two feet from where he stood and blasted a great chunk of it into his face.

The noise of the shot and dust it kicked out must've made him reorder his priorities because he stumbled back in surprise and left a sufficiently wide gap for us to pass through. Goody planted one right on his nose as he went past, just for good measure, and the bloke collapsed down the steps.

We reached the promenade and spun our heads from side to side. Charging up from the beach was Miller, while a hundred yards off to the right a couple of coppers were holding onto their hats and sprinting off the pier and in our direction.

People all around were turning in confusion, probably wondering who'd thrown the firework they'd just heard, while the traffic in the road was motoring along obliviously and going about the usual business of using up the world's oil.

'This way,' I shouted, smacking Goody on the arm and running straight out in front of several oncoming cars. The cars braked sharply and were able to swerve to avoid me, but they had only been going at about 20 mph. I wouldn't have tried the same thing on the M27, but by the same token I wouldn't recommend running out in front of slow-moving traffic as a long-term survival strategy. It was just something I had to do and I was desperate enough to do it.

Goody and Patsy were right behind me and the three of us sprinted across four lanes until we reached the other side.

Miller and the other Old Bill saw this move and were straight on after us. Only our friend with the broken nose stayed where he was, holding his face in place and screaming furiously into his radio. Neither me, Goody or Patsy hung about long enough to hear what he had to say, but it was fairly obvious from what I'd just done that it would be something along the lines of 'bring guns'.

We ducked around the first corner and headed into town. People stopped and jumped out of the way as we sprinted past and most looked suitably wary. I don't know how many, if any, passers-by recognised us for who we were, but three blokes running full pelt in broad daylight is always a bit of a giveaway that something naughty's just happened.

'Which way? Which way?' Patsy was panicking, but me and Goody weren't worrying about that just yet; the coppers a hundred yards back needed shaking first before we could even think about plotting a course.

With this in mind Goody took matters into his own legs (as the cunt had overtaken me again) and threw himself around the next right he came to, then ran straight across the road and took the next left, fifty yards farther on.

We all had to jump around half a dozen parked motors to make this run, and by the time we reached the next corner the Old Bill were already coming around the first and they saw which way we were disappearing.

'Again,' Goody shouted, and sprinted out into the road, straight in front of some Captain Lycra on a bike, who got to find out if his crash hat was worth the money or not. I jumped over his spinning front wheel while Patsy leapt the bloke himself and we all ducked between a Mondeo and a Mercedes on the other side of the road.

Patsy somehow managed to run wide and went careening into some bloke and his bird, pushing the pair of them through a curry-house window before finding his feet again and carrying on after us. That little blunder probably cost him a dozen yards, though it was up to him to make it back up, not up to me and Goody to slow down to let him catch up.

I myself was having all sorts of nightmares trying to keep up the pace in dripping wet clothes with a big heavy revolver in one hand and a half-empty rucksack jumping about on my back, and all too soon I felt my legs start to weaken.

I turned around again and saw that one of our cops (it looked like Miller) had stopped to assist the assorted casualties, though this was of little consolation as I knew motorised reinforcements would be pouring in from all directions in a matter of minutes.

Goody hung another right, and then fooled everyone (including me) by taking another right, instead of crossing the road and taking the next left, as he had done previously. Here, the crowds were starting to thicken as the shops increased, and it was getting more and more of a job to avoid running straight into the bastards, particularly as Goody, five yards in front of me, was scattering them in all directions. More than a few ended up on their arses and a couple of the braver ones shouted after us to watch where we were going (one little old lady shouted 'arseholes' at us, which was really weird) but all these calls ended the moment the Old Bill went steaming past in hot pursuit.

Much of this was lost on me, though, as I was deafened for the most part of it with the slap slap slap of my feet and the wheeze wheeze wheeze of my lungs.

'Oi, watch where you're going, you fucking clumsy cunt,' someone was shouting after Goody when I leapt around him like a gazelle, sending him flying face first into three other people who'd also been caught by the pace man. 'What the fuck . . .!' was all I caught of his next observation, and I hoped he kept his head down until Patsy had passed him by otherwise he was on for a hat trick of whacks.

Goody turned yet another sharp right and sent some bloke, his shopping and his glasses flying across the pavement in the process. I trampled through his shopping when I rounded the corner two seconds later and, three seconds after that, Patsy took care of his glasses. As much as I felt sorry for the poor fucker we had our own problems to worry about, so there was nothing we could do for him except hope that the rest of his day turned out a little brighter than his lunchtime had.

This new road Goody had led us into seemed to be some sort of high street and it seemed to be leading us down to the sea again. This helped us slap our feet a little faster, but we were clearly putting distance between ourselves and the possible safety of our flat, so I shouted after Goody to double back and make for home. I figured we could run around in circles once we were into our neighbourhood, but I wanted the opportunity to duck out of sight the moment we had a two-second blind lead on the cops.

'The flat. The flat,' I told him, and Goody seemed to understand this because he veered out right between two parked cars and dashed straight across the road. Several more cars braked suddenly to avoid Goody and one of them swerved into an old Nissan, which was a real shame because there was a brand-new Porsche with personalised number plates parked not three feet off.

I leapt through and around the angry beeping confusion and into the alleyway I'd just seen Goody duck into. It was good to get away from the assault course that was the high street and get a little open air in front of us, but I suddenly didn't have a clue where we were going. I didn't know this town particularly well to begin with, and ten minutes of running around in circles had done for my senses completely. I vaguely knew that down was towards the sea and that we lived somewhere off to the left of the pier, but I'd never been into this busy bit of town before so my legs were starting to lock with disorientation.

'This way,' Goody yelled, as we emerged from the other side of the alleyway and into some sort of paved shopping area. There were just as many people here as there had been on the high street, but at least they were a little more spread out so it was easier to duck and dive between them.

'Oi, watch it!'

'Slow down!'

'Hey, come back here!'

'You bloody morons!'

Normally I would've shouted back something like 'sorry' or 'fuck off' but I figured I'd be needing that breath sooner, rather than later, so I saved it for that moment.

Goody was now peeling off to the left and heading in a direction that felt like it was the right way. This gave me the tiniest sense of hope, but I wasn't allowed to enjoy it for even a second as a distant wailing suddenly rose above the shouts and screams of our shopping-laden obstacles.

The sirens still sounded pretty far away and the traffic around the town centre was slow at the best of times, but that probably only gave us a window of just a couple of minutes before the bastards were here in all their glory.

'Up here, this way,' Goody was still confidently declaring, dashing out between two more parked cars and across the next road. I followed blindly, even though I wasn't sure Goody knew where he was going any better than I did, but it helped to have someone to keep up with, so once again I left the safety of the pavement and ran straight across the road. It was okay, though, the nearest oncoming motor wasn't within twenty yards of me, so that gave me plenty of time to dodge a busted nut. I reached the opposite pavement and was just heading up the hill after Goody, however, when I heard the unmistakable sound of a car braking, then hitting something solid.

'MILO!' a voice behind me cried, and I stopped in my tracks and turned back, expecting to see Patsy, but all I saw was a car pulled up in the middle of the road and a load of gawping faces.

Oh no.

Oh no no no.

No, please, don't do this.

'GOODY!' I yelled, and raced back to the front of the car.

A few Samaritans had dashed to Patsy's aid but I screamed at them to get away and held out my gun to show them I wasn't fucking around.

'He just ran straight out in front of me. It wasn't my fault. I didn't see him,' some near-hysterical woman was saying through shivering hands.

I bent down to Patsy, who was flat on his back and puffing like Ivor the Engine.

'Can you stand?' I asked, grabbing him by the lapels and heaving him up. Patsy screamed and clutched at his right leg and straight away I knew it was serious.

Goody suddenly appeared and grabbed one arm, heaving him up by the shoulders, while I took the other. Together we dragged him through the gap between the cars and onto the pavement, but Patsy howled every painful step of the way.

'Stop right there! Police! Hold it!' two approaching voices were shouting at us, and we spun as three to see our plucky pursuers sprinting across the paved shopping area towards us.

'Shit, Milo . . .' Goody started to say, but this wasn't a time for pointless observations. I aimed the gun in their direction and fired three shots over the bastards' heads, causing panic and pandemonium all around. People screamed and ran in all directions while Cagney and Lacey dropped to their faces and tried to hide behind their arms.

'Arggghhh! Arggghhh! Arggghhh!' was the common consensus, and I couldn't fucking believe it. We'd started the day worrying about wandering around in hats and dark glasses on a deserted stretch of beach, now here I was screaming at the top of my lungs and firing a gun in the middle of a busy shopping centre. How on earth had we got to this point? It was ridiculous.

Also, I'd lost my hat.

'STAY BACK. COME ANY CLOSER AND I'LL FUCKING KILL YOU,' I warned the coppers, and at that precise moment in time I think I actually meant it.

We turned again and tried continuing with Patsy between us but even Patsy knew the game was up for him.

'I can't, Milo. I can't. Put me down,' he was pleading with me, but I refused to listen for at least a dozen steps. 'Please, Milo, it's no good. Just go. Go on, now.'

'No,' I objected, but even as I was saying it Goody was backing Patsy against the wall in readiness to set him down.

'We have to, Milo, his leg's busted. Come on, we can't help him, we have to go.'

I knew Goody was right and I surprised myself by just how stubborn I was being about it. I guess, at the end of the day, I really had believed all three of us would make it out together, and seeing Patsy fall by the wayside like this suddenly brought home the reality of my own chances.

'Set me down. Set me down. Easy. Easy,' Patsy insisted, so I finally agreed and we lowered him to the pavement while I kept my eye and my gun on the cowering Old Bill.

There wasn't the time for a dozen long lingering kisses goodbye as the sirens were getting louder and with them our prospects were getting quieter. We had to get going and we had to do it *now*, that was all there was to it. We'd see Patsy again, I was sure about that. In the next life perhaps . . . or the next five minutes more likely.

'See you, Pats, take care, man,' Goody said, ruffling his hair, and set off up the road.

'Remember, after the fact. Just tell them you were there after the fact,' I added, then turned and ran for my life.

Patsy called after the pair of us, telling us to 'Run, Milo, run, Goody', but his voice quickly faded into the background rhubarb. The last thing I heard him shout was to me and it was about the money he'd left behind back at the flat.

'Don't spend it all on stickers, Milo,' he told me, as I'd once told him.

And then he was gone.

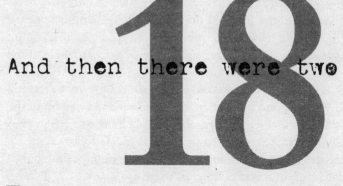

And then there were two

We ran.

We ran and ran and ran. What else was there to do? Luckily, neither of the cops that had been chasing us fancied meeting the Queen so for the first time since we'd chucked Miller into the drink we were alone again.

We put a couple of hundred yards between us and the Old Bill and ducked down this way and that, until we were all over the place.

'Wait. Come on, let's get that cunt,' I told Goody, and he spun around to see me doing a stand-and-deliver job on an approaching motorbike courier. The courier screeched to a halt in the middle of the road and I screamed at him to get off his bike. Goody saw the plan and knocked him off sideways before he had a chance to weigh up his options, and a moment later I was on the back and we were on our way again.

The bike was heaven-sent as the chaos we'd caused back where we'd lost Patsy had backed up the traffic something rotten. Goody used the small corridor between the lines of cars and the pavement as he saw fit to put some serious distance between us and those oncoming sirens, and three minutes later we were on familiar ground again. I recognised my local and the road down to the beach and bashed

Goody on the shoulder and pointed. Goody was already leaning into the turn and twisting back the accelerator to take us up the hill, and the suicidal fucker almost knocked me off the back in the process. I just managed to cling on for a few seconds longer, and suddenly we were there, at the front door of our flat.

Goody revved the engine a last couple of times and steered us into the garden. I jumped off and raced up to the door as Goody ditched the bike behind our hedge and made sure it was hidden from the road. He followed me up to the flat and a moment later we were both peeling out of our wet duds and pulling on some dries.

We changed our tops as well and grabbed the rest of the money so that two minutes after entering we were once again ready to leave.

We were just making to do so when Bern-*ard* appeared at the door.

'Knock knock,' he knock-knocked. 'I heard you come in. I was up in number eight. Just thought I'd pop down and say hello, if that's alright.'

Boy, did we not have time for this. Hmm, but then again . . .

'Bernard, do you have a car?'

'Why, yes, I do. Why do you ask?'

'Let's go, then,' I explained, sticking my gun in his face.

'What? Wait. What's going on?' he asked, not unreasonably, as Goody pulled back the slide on one of the cop automatics we'd taken from our mates at the New Forest roadblock, clicked on the safety and tucked it into his belt.

'We need a car and we're taking yours,' I told him, grabbing him by the collar and sticking my gun in his neck.

'Take it, take it. I don't mind. Just please don't hurt me.'

'We ain't going to hurt you, Bernard, you're a nice bloke, but we can't leave you behind, so just do as we say and come with us.'

We marched him down the stairs and peered out of the front door. Those sirens were still wailing somewhere, but they'd yet to make it to this neighbourhood so we walked him out to his Mercedes (and who says they all drive Citroëns?) and climbed inside.

'I'll do the driving if you don't mind, Bernard,' I said, pushing him over to the passenger seat and starting her up. 'Nice motor.'

'Where are we going?' Goody asked.

'Well, I know this place is going to be crawling any time soon but we have to see if Dr Who's got those fucking passports yet. Because we're going to be fucked if he hasn't,' I said, and pulled out into the road.

I wasted as little time as possible on road etiquette and pounded the pedals, yanked the gears and spun the wheel until we were outside Simon's. It had taken only five minutes to get there but even in this short space of time we'd still seen one police motor flash past us along the main drag. It wouldn't be long before they started setting up roadblocks so we had to be quick. Stopping for the passports was a gamble but it had to be done. If he had them, we stood a great chance of getting out of the country. If he didn't, it would've cost us just five minutes. It was worth it.

We should probably have invested in a couple of pay-as-you-go mobiles but Goody had always vetoed these on the grounds of triangulation and eavesdroppers. These had seemed like reasonable objections at the time but that's probably just because we hadn't needed phones back then. Now we did, it was decidedly inconvenient.

I didn't even know what triangulation meant.

'Stay here and look after him. I'll be out in two,' I told Goody, and rolled out of the Merc and up the stairs to Simon's flat.

He answered after three knocks and breathed Gold Label in my face the moment the door was no longer between us.

I pushed him inside and asked him straight out, 'Have you got those passports because we need them now?' It had been four weeks since he'd promised them and he'd originally estimated an eight-day wait, so I couldn't decide whether he'd just been sitting on them or bullshitting us all along. Now was the time to find out.

'Er . . . what? Oh, no. Chappy says they'll be ready by the end of the week. Latest Monday . . .' he started to explain, and that used up the last of my patience. I slammed him against the wall and jammed my gun underneath his chin.

'No more fucking lies. Where are those passports?'

'They're coming. End of the week, I promise,' he yelped in fear and surprise.

'We haven't got till the end of the week. Patsy's gone. He's been nicked. We're leaving now, so either you can lay your hands on those passports or you can't. I don't want to know about the end of the week or even the end of the day. I want to know yes or no and I don't want to have to hang around to hear it.'

'What? What?' he asked, almost tearful with confusion. Personally I thought it was a pretty good speech, although I will admit that it did go around the houses a bit, but that was just me getting swept up in the moment. These things can happen, you know. I decided to simplify things for the drunken bastard.

'Yes or no? Can you get those passports? Yes or no?' I jammed my gun into his throat even harder, though this was a pretty pointless exercise. I mean, it wasn't going to make getting shot hurt any more, was it? But it seemed to have the desired effect on Simon because finally (and most reluctantly) he 'fessed up.

'No,' he admitted through a veil of dread.

'You wanker!' I spat, backing off and dropping my gun to my side. Simon stayed squashed against the wall as if still pinned in place by an invisible hand. 'There were never any fucking passports, were there? Come on, admit it.'

Simon choked back the tears and started to babble about some bloke down some pub who reckoned and blahdy-blah, until I pointed my gun at him again and he confirmed there were never any passports.

'You fucking shit!' I growled, and Simon started to whimper like a mangy mutt in fear of its life. I had half a mind to twist the knife and make him piss his pants with terror, but that was just because I was angry. Simon, for the most part, had been there for us when the rest of the world hadn't. Nobody could blame him for not wanting to see his gravy train leave town when he had so little else going on in his life, not even me, so I told him to calm down and put my gun away.

'You should've told us the truth, Simon. Lying to us has helped no one. Especially yourself.'

I held his stare for a few hard seconds then reached into my pocket. Simon screwed up his eyes when I pulled it out again and almost fainted on the spot when he felt something dig into his chest.

'Don't . . .' he started, but tentatively opened his eyes again and looked down when he found the thing didn't hurt as much as he'd been expecting.

'That's five hundred quid and that's the last of it. Get yourself a drink.'

Simon blinked a couple of times when he saw that he was stuck with himself for a few more years yet, then took the money and waited to see what happened next.

'Okay, I'm off. If anybody ever asks you anything, just act stupid,' I told him, advising him to play to his strengths. Simon nodded and I turned to leave when he said rather quietly, 'Sorry, Darren. Please tell Trevor I said sorry.'

'Forget it. You take care of yourself. Just tip a glass to us once in a while, okay?'

'I will do,' he promised, so I left him alone to get on with precisely that without further delay.

Goody's anxiety levels had rocketed since I'd been away and he told me before I'd even slipped behind the wheel that a police car had rolled by not a minute earlier.

'I'd ducked under the seat. This cunt tried to do the same until I reminded him that nobody was looking for him.'

'Well, we're moving now.'

'Did you get them?' Goody asked.

'What do you think?'

'Well, I don't know. That's probably why I asked.'

'No. I didn't.'

I filled Goody (and Bern-*ard* by default) in on what had happened and Goody was even more furious than I had been. We put half a mile between us and Simon's gaff but Goody wanted me to turn the car around and go back for his stepdad.

'Forget it. It ain't worth it,' I told him.

'But it's down to that cunt that Patsy's been nicked. We would've been out of here weeks ago if he'd just told us straight up.'

'Would we?'

I doubted that myself. I mean, we had nowhere else to go and no other means of getting there. In fact, if it wasn't for Miller collaring us on the beach we would probably have sat in that flat indefinitely, or at least until we stumbled across some other ingenious way of getting ourselves nicked.

'You didn't even smack him?' Goody complained.

'I didn't need to. Look, Simon did for himself as much as he did for us,' I told him as we passed the first signs for the A27.

'How d'you figure that one out?'

'Simple. The answer's sitting right beside us chewing his fingernails.'

'What? Me?' Bern-*ard* jumped, spitting out bits of his fingers in surprise. 'I haven't done anything.'

'Yes, but you will. Our flat was rented in Simon's name. You'll report us to the police and they'll trace it back to Simon.'

'I won't. I won't,' Bern-*ard* lied pointlessly, but I told him to untwist his knickers.

'Yes you will, why wouldn't you? We've nicked your motor and kidnapped you at gunpoint. I'd go to the Old Bill if I was you.'

'I promise . . .'

'Oh, shut up, you promise. Promise whatever you like, mate, we ain't going to kill you. Why would we? To protect Simon? I don't particularly want you to grass him up but I ain't going to murder someone to stop that from happening.'

Goody leaned forward between the seats and Bern-*ard* balled himself up, as if readying himself for a couple of whacks across the nut, but none were forthcoming.

'Hang on a minute, I still don't understand how Simon's done for himself,' Goody said.

'Well, he kept us around, didn't he? He should've taken what money was on offer, helped us out of our spot and packed us off as quickly as possible. Instead the silly cunt kept us around for as long as possible because he thought he could keep on milking us. He didn't seem to realise that the moment we were rumbled in Brighton, it was always going to lead back to his front door.'

'I'm not going to say anything . . .' Bern-*ard* insisted through a river of tears. Me and Goody just looked at him and replied, 'Whatever.'

'Aiding and abetting. He's looking at some serious time. A couple of years probably. I hope he doesn't hang about spending that monkey.'

We rounded several roundabouts and found the dual

carriageway, and mercifully there were no Old Bill about. I stuck my foot down and set about clocking up the mileage on Bern-*ard*'s motor, but he seemed too preoccupied with confusion to appreciate this.

'I won't tell your father, I promise I won't. I understand about these things, I really do,' he was pleading with us.

Goody furrowed his brow and burst out laughing.

'Don't you even know who we are?' I finally asked. Bern-*ard* stopped crying for a moment and looked at both of us, but he didn't have a clue.

'Fuck me, Barnard, don't you watch the news?' Goody asked, slapping him on the back of the head.

Bern-*ard* yelped, then told us he didn't really get the time. This was such a load of shit. There are newspapers, radios, TVs and the Internet these days, we're surrounded by headlines wherever we go. Anyone who says they don't get the time to watch the news is a liar. What they actually mean is they have no interest in the outside world as they're far too preoccupied with themselves to care about anything else. Bern-*ard* may have disagreed with this but it was fairly obvious to even me that he was a man who planned to spend the rest of his life forgoing reading newspapers for trying on different hats in the mirror.

'We're the supermarket robbers,' Goody told him, with great pride, so I joined in and flashed him a smile.

This was funny – all these weeks of keeping our heads down and trying to blend in like a couple of nobodies, the first chance we got to tell someone who we were and we couldn't be more chuffed about it.

Bern-*ard* had never heard of us.

What the fuck do we do now?

Good question, and one which Goody lent a voice to every five minutes or so for about thirty miles.

Well, first things first, I turned on the radio. I tuned it into a local Sussex station, as I figured these boys would give the greatest weight to our latest exploits, and sure enough we weren't disappointed. Bern-*ard*'s horizons opened up in front of him as he now listened intently to stuff he wouldn't have given a fuck about just an hour ago.

'Darren Miles . . . Trevor Goodman . . . Tom Patterson . . . police chase . . . shots fired . . . one man arrested . . . daring escape . . . motorbike recovered . . . witness accounts . . . area combed.'

All the ingredients were there and then some. They actually made us sound quite edgy, but any sense of pride we felt over this was tempered by the phrase 'one man arrested'. Poor Patsy. I'd done for him just as surely as Simon had done for us. Patsy had actually made it away scot-free during the hold-up and it had been me who'd dragged him back into it all. Admittedly if I hadn't, me and Goody couldn't have got into the mess we were in now, so that went some way to excuse my actions, but I doubted that would've cheered up Patsy any.

I wondered what he'd get charged with. Would they try and pin the attempted murder of a police officer on him? I hoped not. Without it, he'd only be up for aiding and abetting after the fact, and that would only be a couple of years. Then again, there was also the little matter of the car thefts, carrying an illegal weapon, theft of police property, aggravated burglary, assault, kidnap and every driving offence in the book, so perhaps not.

Poor Patsy.

Poor Bob, Jacko, Jimbo, and even poor Norris.

Poor me, Goody and Parky, who were still running.

Poor all of us.

What had we gotten ourselves into?

Well, now was not the time for self-pity. I'd have plenty of that to come if I didn't concentrate on the tasks in hand.

'Milo, what are we going to fucking do?' Goody asked again.

'I don't know, I'm thinking. First thing we've got to do is drop off Bernie somewhere, we can't take him with us and we can't very well discuss options in front of him.'

Bern-*ard* looked suddenly fearful and reiterated the fact that he wasn't going to say anything to anyone.

'Bernie, you are. We know you are, and we don't care.'

'Please don't hurt me. Please,' he wittered on and on.

Jesus, how did some people make it through life?

We found a dirt trail that led into the woods just outside Peacehaven and I headed up it. A hundred yards out of sight of the road I pulled over and killed the engine.

'Get out,' I told Bern-*ard,* pointing my gun at him.

Bern-*ard* started hyperventilating and shaking so bad that he could hardly get a grip on the door handle.

'Just calm down, Bernie, calm down. Deep breaths, okay.'

Bern-*ard* nodded a couple of times, sucked in a lungful of air and tears and opened the door. He looked like a man headed for his own execution and I guess that's what he thought was coming. I couldn't see why, though, we hadn't done anything other than point a couple of guns at him, steal his car and drive him out into the woods. Well, whatever.

Goody held open the door for him and manhandled him into the trees while I popped the boot and searched for stuff to tie him up with. There wasn't much, to be honest, a few bin liners, a tennis racket and one spanner. We were going to have trouble tying him up with that lot.

Or so I thought.

Goody had obviously watched *The A-Team* a few more times than me, though, because he pulled the racket to bits and used the strings and the bin liners to secure Bern-*ard* to the base of a sycamore thirty yards from where we'd parked. Bern-*ard* continued to plead for his life long after we'd tucked our guns away, and banged on to such an extent that I actually considered shooting him a couple of times, just because he was getting on my nerves so much.

'Please, I'll do anything. Anything at all,' he was sobbing.

'I don't doubt it,' Goody remarked.

We took his wallet and mobile as we figured these things might come in handy and thanked Bern-*ard* one last time before turning to leave. I made it about five yards when a thought suddenly occurred to me and I rushed back to ask Bern-*ard* a question.

'Bernie, tell me something, are you a benny tied to a tree?'

Bern-*ard* was somewhat confused by the question but tentatively confirmed that he was. Goody grabbed hold of his head with both hands, stunned to disbelief that I'd trumped his earlier effort with a real, genuine, bona fide bender tied to a tree, then he went on to call me a cunt several times.

'I don't believe it. I can't believe I didn't see it.'

Bern-*ard* had obviously never heard this silly schoolboy

joke because his face was the picture of fog. We left him to figure it out for himself and strolled back to the motor, happy in the knowledge that we, at least, were still on the loose.

(In case you're still in the dark, the joke went something like this: 'Are you a benny tied to a tree?' 'No.' At which point you run off shouting, 'Urgh, benny on the loose! Benny on the loose!' This joke usually stops being funny at about eight years of age and is best kept separate from adult conversation.)

With Bern-*ard* out of the motor we were free to discuss our options. Goody wanted to put as much distance between us and Brighton as possible and head north. He suggested we went to Manchester and call Len, the guy we'd bought the guns off in the first place. I wasn't too keen about this, though, and not just because of the risk a long drive involved. I was more worried about Len. What easy targets me and Goody would've made with our hundred-and-sixty-odd grand in used notes and precarious predicament. Ripping us off would've been the easiest thing in the world to a guy like Len. I personally didn't fancy wandering within a country's length of him.

I also didn't want to turn to anyone else. As soon as Simon's involvement came to light, the Old Bill would double their checks on our extended kith and kin so that we were better off on our own from now on.

'Hostages, then? Barge in on a place and sit on a family for a few days?' Goody suggested.

'Oh no, I'm fed up with hostages. Let's not take anyone else, I can't deal with that any more,' I replied.

'Well, what, then?'

'Actually, I do have an idea, but I'm not so sure about it,' I mulled.

'Well, shout it out, don't keep it to yourself.'

It was like this. I figured we were just about done with this country and had to get out. We couldn't do it with passports and false noses any more so that left only one alternative – we had to smuggle ourselves abroad.

Goody made a face at the suggestion but I'd been thinking about it for some time. How difficult could it be? Asylum seekers were arriving in this country by the lorry-load all the time, and although some of them were getting caught, a hell of a lot more of them were getting through. And that was with every customs man, immigration officer and *Sun* reader in the country keeping an eye out for them.

We were just two blokes. And we would be heading in the other direction.

Who fucking smuggles themselves, or anything else come to that, *out* of Britain? It stood to reason, then, that the vast majority of checks and sniffer dogs would be pointed at the Bosnian buses coming into Folkestone, Ramsgate, Dover, Newhaven and all the rest of the ferry ports, not going out.

'All we've got to do is find ourselves a lorry, climb in the back and hide ourselves under a load of potatoes until we hear Frogs outside.'

'I don't know. I mean, once we're in there, that's it, we're trapped. It's do or die,' Goody objected.

'Yeah, maybe so. But there's a very good chance they'll never check and once we're in France, things will be so much easier. We can take the bus, ride the trains, be down in Spain before you know it. Bribe some dago to run us over to Africa and from there on in we're on Easy Street. That whole fucking continent's bent as a nine-bob banana, so we can just find ourselves a nice quiet little corner by the sea, buy ourselves a bar and spend the next twenty years stiffing the tourists. Do a Lord Lucan or a Shergar.'

'I don't think Shergar went willingly, you know.'

'Well, whatever. That's the plan, anyway. What do you think?'

'Not Thailand, then?' Goody asked.

'Bit difficult to get there without passports. I think Africa's our best bet. Maybe in a few years' time we'll be able to get Ivory Coast citizenship with a few well-bunged bribes, get over there then, but for now I think we should just worry about getting out of Britain.'

Goody was still less than convinced but I told him people wandered across Europe all the time without papers, and who were they? A load of backward cabbage eaters who still thought it was okay to buy stuff with chickens. We were British, for fuck's sake. We were out ruling the world while they were still peering around the backs of mirrors. No, if an Albanian or a Georgian could make it to Britain, we could make it to Africa. It was as simple as that.

'You in?'

Goody mulled it over for a few more miles before he finally agreed.

'Alright, I'm in. How do we do this?'

Dover. I figured we'd try it there. It was the busiest ferry port and the shortest Channel crossing. These things could only work in our favour.

It took another hour and a half to get to Dover, so we arrived a little after four. The first thing we did when we got there was park the motor up in a busy residential side street. We sandwiched it into a small gap between three dozen other cars and didn't look back. This was it. If we were going to try for the ferry, then we couldn't hang around. The moment they found Bern-*ard*'s Merc, they'd know we were in Dover and would probably use their experienced police brains to guess why.

Actually, that wasn't strictly true. Bern-*ard*'s Merc wouldn't be reported as being stolen until Bern-*ard* was himself. And that wasn't likely while he was tied up in the back of beyond.

As we walked I thought this over. The police had found our BT engineer and old Naggy-tits when we'd tied them up in the sticks because they knew roughly where we'd disappeared. This wouldn't be the case with Bern-*ard*. We'd shown Brighton plod a clean pair of heels relatively early during our last chase (we were more practised by this stage) so it seemed fairly unlikely they'd even know to look for our latest tree hugger. Bern-*ard* might end up dying out there if he weren't found, and nobody wanted that – least of all Bern-*ard*.

I pulled Bern-*ard*'s mobile out of my pocket and was just about to dial a number when Goody asked me who I was calling.

'Terry.'

'Terry? Your brother Terry? Why the fuck are you calling Terry?'

'Look, we can't leave Bernie out in the woods like that, we have to tip off the Old Bill and let them know he's out there,' I explained. 'So, better than calling them myself and getting myself triangulated, I'll call Terry and tell him to pass it on.'

Goody agreed it was something we had to do, but questioned my timing.

'I don't know how this triangulation works really, but what if they're able to backdate it? Terry tells the Old Bill, they call up his phone records, check out the last call he got, triangulate us and that's it, they've got us just as much as if you gave them a bell yourself.'

Goody had a point (I think). It certainly sounded reasonable enough. They could do funky things with phones these days, so why not triangulate us after the fact? I mean, who would've believed that one day we would all be able to watch *Match of the Day* on our mobiles? Mind you, who would've believed that any but the silliest of cunts would've wanted to?

'Well, what do you suggest?'

'Give Tel a bell, yeah, no problem, but do it from the boat, and wait until we're just outside France. That way, even if they are able to triangulate us, it'll take 'em fucking ages to get their skates on and by that time we'll be halfway up the autobahn and home free.'

It sounded like a better plan than mine, and one which couldn't do us any harm, so I agreed to wait a while.

And that's how these things have always happened to me; a tiny little harmless, innocent suggestion, which didn't look like it could get a fly busted, ends up dropping me in the toilet even deeper than before.

You'd have thought I would've learnt my lesson by now, wouldn't you? That I'd steer clear of any ideas that weren't my own, but no, not me. Not the genius that is Darren Miles.

Oh no.

Once a doughnut, always a doughnut.

Brian of France

We found signs for the port and made our way towards it as briskly as possible. We kept our heads down, our arms moving and took side streets and alleyways wherever possible. After a few minutes we got to the hill that overlooked the port and surveyed the place. There were gates, fences and lights all around, and a steady hum of traffic going in and out of the gates.

The port looked like a big spread-out affair, large enough (you'd think) to afford us the odd gap in the fence, but half an hour of walking backwards and forwards along the perimeter soon shot that theory out of the air.

Goody suggested scaling the fence, but it was broad daylight and there were people about all over the place. We felt quite unbelievably self-conscious already, so neither of us could find the courage to try going over the top. We left the port to its business and went back up the hill to have a think.

This was a tad frustrating. I'd taken for granted that the British side would be slack, so much so that I hadn't given any thought to how we were actually going to get into the port itself. Just beyond the fence was lorry after lorry, but that fence was tall and spiky and there were lights (in case we fancied coming back after dark), and cameras and plenty of nosey witnesses wandering around the shop. We simply didn't have the tools or, more importantly, the information to risk breaking in. We also only had one crack at it. We had to get it right first time.

It was about this time that my guts reminded me how hungry I was. The only thing I'd had all day had been those fish and chips, but that had only been a temporary deal. My belly was empty to concave and I was having difficulty concentrating on anything else while it was like this.

'Why don't we go into town and get a bite while we plan our next move, then?' Goody suggested.

'Well, there would be several reasons why, Goody,' I replied, and steeled my resolve to resist all temptation of trying to buy food from somewhere. We wandered back into town anyway, in the hope of spotting a possibility or two, and several presented themselves right away. Scattered about the edges of town were a number of car parks. There were a fair few lorries parked up in them, along with cars, vans and coaches to boot.

Most, if not all, of these boys would be heading across the water, so it occurred to me that we could simply jump aboard here and wait for the driver to return from his latest fry-up and take us out of the country. Hey presto, off we go. Again, who was going to check a lorry leaving the UK?

We wandered into the car park and took a stroll among the lorries. Some of the cabs had drivers, some didn't. Some were reading the *Sun*, others were napping. A couple eyed us suspiciously through their windscreens, so we picked up the pace to make it look like we had a purpose, and found ourselves back by the entrance.

'This is bollocks,' Goody pointed out.

'Let's give it another go, down the road, in that car park.'

We wandered off in that direction and set our stall out to be more positive in our approach. We couldn't do this if we were just going to go tiptoeing through the tulips like a couple of pansies, we had to spot a mark, crack it open and get on board. That was the only way.

This time we checked out the lorries from the other side of the fence before going into the car park and spotted a likely-looking horse tucked away in the corner, a decent distance from prying eyes.

We hurried around to the car park entrance and made our way over to it. The cabin was empty and the day's *Daily Sport* was on the passenger seat.

'What does that prove?' Goody asked.

'Well, they don't sell the *Sport* over in France, do they? That means he must've bought it over here. That means he's going in that direction,' I said, pointing out towards the sea.

'How do you know they don't sell the *Sport* over in France? He might've got it on the boat. He might just be resting up after a long sea crossing and getting something to eat before going on his way. Seriously, Milo, we have to be careful here. If we're not we could end up in fucking Grimsby, and who wants that?'

I reassured Goody that I'd thought it all through and explained it all again in words of less than two syllables.

'Most of these GB lorries are going to be heading across the water. If they were coming back, they would've got a bite to eat on the boat, wouldn't they? No one's going to be resting up in a car park in Dover for the fucking fun of it after they've done the crossing, are they? Come on, don't worry, honestly, we'll be alright.'

Goody was finally convinced, so we took a scoot around the back and tried the door.

'It's locked,' Goody informed me, rattling a big golden padlock.

'I can see that.'

'Well, how are we going to get in?'

'Er . . . hang on a minute,' I told him, and gave the lorry a thorough going over. Goody ended up hanging on for

about ten before I finally conceded defeat. He looked at me
accusingly, like a big spoilt child who hadn't got his balloon,
and said:

'I thought you said you'd thought of everything.'

I thought I had, for fuck's sake!

Honestly, they make it look so easy in the films, don't
they? Yank open the back, jump in, jump out, and off they
go. I guess not being able to get in the back of a lorry when
James Bond needs to (and more importantly, not being able
to close it from the inside without signs of a break-in) just
gets in the way of the rest of the plot, so in movieland
everyone leaves their lorries unlocked.

In Dover, they generally don't.

'Well, hang on a minute, how do all the Abduls manage
it coming the other way? They must get in somehow,'
Goody said, but he'd overlooked the rather obvious.

'They pay.'

'Pay?'

Their life savings usually, and half of them are nicked
before they get anywhere near a Brick Lane curry-house
kitchen.

'Well, why don't we pay? Bung the driver a couple of
grand to take us over to France. If it's as low-risk as you
reckon then it's money for old rope as far as that cunt's concerned.'

'Have you seen how much the papers are offering for our
capture?' I asked the idiot, and found it wasn't a cliché –
your hands really do go straight to your hips when you talk
down to someone.

'Yeah.'

'Yeah, and I bet every lorry driver in the country has too.'

Goody thought about this for a few moments then asked
me that question again.

'Well, what are we gonna do, then?'

What are we gonna do? What are we gonna do? What are we gonna do?

'You know, they're going to stick that on your grave-stone. *Help, I'm dead. What are we gonna do?* I don't fucking know. Come on, let's get out of here before someone clocks us.'

We walked back to the entrance of the car park, but before we got halfway I was hit by a smell straight out of heaven — fried onions. I looked around for the source and saw a good old British burger van parked up on the other side of the car park. I stared at the van for a few seconds and weighed up a quarter-pounder with cheese, onions, mustard, ketchup and a cup of tea in a polystyrene cup against twenty years in Parkhurst, and for the briefest of gut-tugging moments it didn't sound like the worst trade-off in the world.

'You hungry?' Goody asked, licking his lips.

'I'm starving, man.'

'D'you think we should . . .'

'No, I don't,' I answered, without letting him finish. I had turned my back on the van and started in the other direction when I almost went tumbling arse over tit over some skinny little Frog boy in a multi-coloured knapsack who'd been standing right behind me.

'*Pardon, monsieur, parlez-vous français?*'

'What the fuck?' I said, almost staving his head into the tarmac as I tried to avoid him.

'Er . . . sir, do you speek *français*?' he asked again hopefully, as I righted myself, only for Goody to demonstrate the full range of his French and tell him to 'fuck off'.

'No, wait, hang about. *Allez* here, mate, come here a second,' I told him, shutting Goody up before he could get into his stride.

'What are you doing, Milo?'

'I've got an idea,' I told him. 'Mate, *français*? No. No *français*. You speaky English?'

The kid nodded cautiously, so I asked him what he wanted.

'Where are ze bathrooms?'

Me and Goody blinked at each other for a few moments and I tried to decide what it was with the Frogs. Would an English kid, standing in a French lorry park, busting for a piss, need directions to a bog? I doubted it. In fact I doubted many would use 'em even if they were standing right next to 'em, not when there were Renaults to be Jimmyed all over.

'Just go over there, mate, round the back of that motor.' I pointed. The kid looked at me suspiciously, so I told him it was fine, everyone did it, and eventually he believed me. Once he'd splashed Perrier all up the fence and all over his shoes, I called him back and gave him a tenner.

'See that burger van over there, get me and him a quarter-pounder *avec fromage* each and two cans of Coke and you can keep the change. Savvy?'

The kid creased his forehead to show that he didn't savvy, so Goody had a go and between us we knocked it into him.

'Okay,' he said, and rushed off towards the van.

A big, greasy burger and a can of Coke later I felt so much better. The kid seemed happy enough to have made a couple of quid and he practised a bit more English on us until Goody told him to shut up.

'Where are you going now?' I asked, and again the kid frowned at me.

'Honestly, I'm gonna wallop him in a minute,' Goody said through a mouthful of onions.

'You go France now?' I asked, pointing out to sea, and the kid replied, 'Okay,' and started walking off. 'No, no, mate. *Allez* here, you fucking doughnut. What I'm asking is, when . . .' I looked at Goody and asked him if he knew the

French for when. He didn't. 'Look, when . . . you know, *when* . . . do you go to France? What time?' Almost inevitably matey looked at his Mickey Mouse watch and told me the time, but I persisted and finally he understood.

'*A cinq heures et demie,*' he replied, and even I recognised that as half five.

'Where's your bus?' I asked, and Goody suddenly saw the angle.

The kid pointed over to the other side of the car park and we all went and had a look together. There, parked in among a row of cars and lorries, was matey's coach. It was a big, flashy type, with lots of comfortable seats, a bog and a TV up front, but I was more interested in the luggage compartment down the side by the wheels.

'Mate, what's your name?'

'Brian,' he told me, which sounded like just about as un-French a name as you could get, but there you go.

'Brian, how would you like to make yourself a hundred pounds?'

Brian held his enthusiasm in check until I'd reassured him it had nothing to do with my cock, his arse or the Internet and that all we wanted to do was to smuggle our-selves across to France. Brian wanted to know why we had to smuggle ourselves over so I grabbed his English/French dictionary and after five minutes of page-flipping managed to get it across that it was part of a dare. Dares are some-thing every kid in the world understands and Brian seemed suitably excited at the prospect of being part of something stupid, risky and pointless.

'*D'accord,*' he readily agreed, then ran off to get things ready while me and Goody sank back amongst the lorries.

The one-way ticket

21

The coach stopped and started half a dozen times over the course of the next hour and I bricked myself every single time. I couldn't tell why we were stopping, as me and Goody were lying on our faces in complete darkness, but every time we did, I expected the panels to be yanked open and growling customs dogs to stick their snouts in.

We were right on the far side of the luggage compartment, buried under forty or so multi-coloured knapsacks and lying head to head so that we could whisper to each other if we had to.

We both had our guns out and were like two coiled springs waiting to take someone's eye out, but we had no call to do so. The panels stayed where they were and no one bothered checking for contraband, but then why would they? Back home in France, these kids could buy flick knives, knuckledusters, hard-core porn, cheap booze, fags and huge slabs of chocolate and finger-obliterating firecrackers. What could they pick up in Britain that they couldn't get over there? Yorkshire puddings, sticks of rock and the *Radio Times*. And that's probably about it. Even our drugs were more expensive than theirs, so who was ever going to smuggle anything over to France from Britain?

Calais's customs officers must've had the easiest jobs in Europe.

The coach started up once more and we drove around in a few circles for a short time, then over a series of bumps, then up a steep slope, then into an echoey cave, then over to the right a few inches, then finally stopped again. This time the engine stopped with the coach, and when it did we felt the unmistakable rock of the sea way down below us.

'We're on the ferry,' Goody whispered to me. 'We fucking made it.'

We hadn't made it yet, of course, but we'd taken a giant step towards our goal and I couldn't help but feel elated and relieved at where we were. Only this morning we'd had Brighton's finest an arm's length from our collars, now here we were, stowed away on board a Calais-bound ferry with the whole of Europe opening up to us.

We lay in the dark and listened as cars and lorries parked around us, then the front door of the coach was popped and the kids stampeded out in search of the arcades. A few moments later the door was closed again and the coach fell into silence.

'Think the driver's still on board?' Goody asked, but we couldn't hear anything so we presumed he wasn't.

'Have a search through some of these bags, see if anyone's got anything to eat or drink,' I said, so we spent the next five minutes feeling about in the darkness and amassed a little pile of sweets and crisps and a couple of bottles of something between us before tucking in. We couldn't see what anything was because of the blackness, but happily no one had decided to bring stool or urine samples back from England with them.

'What flavour are your crisps?' Goody asked.

'Beef flavour Hula-Hoops,' I told him. 'What flavour are yours?'

'I've got fucking prawn cocktail normal crisps,' he moaned, like the hardest-done-by man in the world.

'Well, do you want to swap, then?' I asked, and Goody said he did. He handed me his packet so I emptied three-quarters of my Hula-Hoops in front of me in the darkness and handed him the remainder. Goody moaned that I hardly had any Hula-Hoops left so we swapped back again, though not before I'd tipped half his packet onto my crisp pile.

'Now I can't find my Mars bar. I had a Mars bar here just a minute ago, now it's gone,' he moaned next, though that didn't surprise me in the slightest seeing as I'd just eaten it. And it had actually been a Snickers.

'You've probably accidentally pushed it under those bags,' I told him. 'Have a feel behind you, you'll probably find it back there.' I had his tangerine away while he was doing so.

'Oh, fucking hell, now I've lost my orange.'

'Don't worry about it,' I told him, peeling it two feet from his face. 'You can have a couple of segments of mine if you like.'

'Ta. Cheers, Milo.'

I checked the time on Bern-*ard*'s phone when we were done stuffing our faces and found it was a quarter past six. The boat's rocking had picked up a bit of a momentum so I figured we were finally on the move. This swept another tidal wave of relief over me, though surprisingly this one was tinged with regret.

We were leaving England.

Our home, our country, our island, and we were leaving her, quite possibly for the rest of our lives.

How could that be?

I loved England. The place hadn't been that great to me, to be honest, but I loved her all the same. England was where I was born. England was where I'd grown up. England was where I called home.

I was (and still am, as far as I can make out) an Englishman, and will be until the day I become part of a foreign field. You can forget about Britain as a whole, or the proud Celts, or the lucky Irish, or the sunny Aussies, or the wealthy Yanks, or the thieving dagos or any of them other lot. I was English. I'd won life's first prize and now I was having to hand it back. How had it come to this?

I once heard someone say that you never truly appreciate what you've got until it's been taken away from you. Actually I can't remember who said that, but it was probably someone in nick as those blokes were always coming out with profound clichés like that, but it's true. And it can be anything, anything at all, no matter how tiny. Look at the panic that grips most households when the telly breaks down, everybody's suddenly lost and sticking their heads in the oven to avoid having to talk to each other. Well, think about that on a much larger scale.

Remove any of the following from your life – spouse, job, home, hobby, mates, routine, health or kids – and see if it wouldn't affect you. Now obviously, the cleverer clogs among you have selected kids when you haven't got any but that just proves my point, that you couldn't bring yourselves to drop one that does apply.

Also, I'm sure there's no shortage of people scratching 'job' from the list and laughing at the suggestion that they wouldn't be able to cope without it, but are you sure?

My old granddad on my dad's side worked in a cable-making factory his whole life. They made everything from the little wires you get in your phone to the bigger wires you get in your . . . er, . . . well, I've never really given it a great deal of thought, to be honest. Anyway, the point is that I remember every time we went around to see him he would always moan about his 'crummy' job. He'd say it was really hard work or that the management were a load of wankers or that he'd lost his passion for the work (for wires? Really, Granddad? And that only took you forty years?) and all the rest of it.

'Looking forward to retirement, I can tell you. Get some golf in. Spend more time with your grandmother too – but mainly golf.'

Then when it came to it, he couldn't do it. The silly bastard got special dispensation from the factory and put his retirement back indefinitely. Worked on until he was seventy-three and would've probably still be there today, moaning about his stupid line manager and his crippling arthritis, had the company not given up the ghost before he did and folded. See, old Granddad Harold couldn't do it. For forty years, all he'd done was dream about the day when he could finally jack it in, but when that day had come along, he just couldn't do it. Mad, isn't it? I find this sort of behaviour especially incomprehensible, but then I've never been what you would call one of life's workers.

I'm sure everyone's heard or read of similar stories; old Gertrude, who goes to Buckingham Palace to get a CBE for working in the same village post office for seventy-eight years (only to get home and find she's been sacked for taking the day off) or smelly old Alf, who's still sweeping the same streets he's been sweeping since the Blitz and refuses to stop despite being forcibly retired twenty-five years earlier and all the rest of it.

I mention this because working is just one thing, one aspect of our lives, and one which most people claim to hate, but secretly can't live without, and I use it as an example to try to demonstrate exactly what me and Goody were having to leave behind:

Everything.

Every – single – thing.

Admittedly neither of us had a spouse, job, home, hobby

(outside of going to the pub), routine or kids. Health and mates were the only two that really applied to us, and we weren't losing the former and the latter was lying two feet away from me, feeling about in the darkness for where his Curly Wurly had got to ... so I guess it was a bad example. All I'm saying is that everything we knew and took for granted – the weather, the people, the familiarity, the homeliness, the countryside, the language and everything else about England that we loved – we'd never see again.

It was a sobering thought and one that other men have had to face before me. Burgess and Maclean, Biggs, Edwards and Reynolds. Florida Phil. Even lucky old Lucan. They'd all had to leave this sceptred isle of ours knowing (and fervently praying) they'd never see the fucking place again, and they'd all had differing rates of success. I wondered how I'd fare.

At that moment, light suddenly flooded into the luggage compartment and Goody and me cracked our heads together ducking out of sight.

I reached down to my belt and found my gun, but wasn't sure what I was going to do with it now that I had a hold of it. I certainly wasn't going to shoot anyone, but I wasn't about to allow myself to be taken without a fight either, not after all the crap we'd had to go through to get to where we were. I peeked over the bags to see who had opened the door and saw Brian's inquisitive face peering in.

'*Allo,* mister, are you in here?' he sang quietly.

With him were two of his mates. All of them were crouching down by the side of the coach and all looking like they'd come to see the monkeys eat.

'Brian, is that you?'

'*Oui,* mister. I get key. I open door for you,' he said, completing his side of the bargain. Well, with the panels locked all the way to Brian's school, I didn't fancy our chances if we had to jump out in front of a load of French parents and teachers. We would've just started the whole thing all over again, and this time over in France where the *Vieux* Bill had guns. So Brian had been detailed to get the key, unlock the panels and return the key without anyone noticing, and the little beauty had only gone and done it. I'm not quite sure how he'd done it, to tell the truth. Perhaps he just went up to the driver and asked if he could borrow the key to let some *rosbifs* out of the luggage compartment. I didn't ask. I just gave him his ton and told him to *allez* off.

I did it politely, mind, as it doesn't do to upset teenage boys who are in a position to get you locked up for life.

'Do you want a burger?' he asked, and I saw the little chancer's angle. I reached into my bag and pulled out another tenner and told him to go and stick it in the fruities.

'No burgers for us, thank you. Just leave us and don't tell anyone we're here, okay?'

'*D'accord,* mister,' he said and replaced the panel.

'That little cunt, what's he bring his mates with him for?' Goody growled, but I told him to forget about it.

'Couldn't play the big man later if he didn't have witnesses,' I told him, but Goody worried about the rest of them talking. 'There's nothing we can do about it. Look, Brian knows he'll probably be expelled if he's caught and his mates know it too, so the only people they're going to tell are other naughty kids. By the time it reaches any of the do-gooders we'll be in France and well clear of the coach, and no one'll believe them by then.'

Goody still wasn't convinced but, like I'd said, what else could we do? Wait in Dover indefinitely until we'd found a completely risk-free way of crossing the Channel? It didn't exist. This was as close as we could manage.

'Don't forget to phone about Bern-*ard*,' Goody reminded me, so I said I'd do it at quarter past seven, when we only had about twenty minutes left to go. Goody concurred so I checked Bern-*ard*'s phone for the time and worked out what I was going to say to keep the call as brief as possible.

Other people's suggestions

22

At a quarter past seven I dialled my brother Terry's number, but the phone beeped three times and disconnected. I checked out the little screen and saw that I didn't have a signal.

'What are we gonna do?' Goody asked, presumably because he hadn't asked it for five minutes. 'We've got to call someone, you know that, don't you? We can't leave the poor geezer tied up out in the woods otherwise he'll kick the bucket.'

'I know, don't worry, I'm going to call. I've just got to get a signal,' I told him, trying it several more times with similar success.

'Maybe it's the coach. Perhaps you need to get out and phone from outside?' he then suggested.

This sounded logical enough so I crawled over the kids' bags and carefully popped the side panel open. I poked my head outside and flung my eyes from left to right but no one was about, so I dropped out and straightened up.

My legs, back and arms demanded a much-needed stretch before I did anything else, so that's what they got. Once I was done, I checked the phone and saw I still had no signal. I really didn't fancy going up top to make the call, not least of all because I could've got lost and found myself stuck on the ferry if the coach left without me, so I decided to leave it and make the call when we got to France. Well, they had mobiles over there, didn't they, and presumably networks and signals of their own, so it seemed feasible enough. Actually, with hindsight, I can't think why this didn't occur to me in the first place, but then that's often the way with these things; you visualise doing something so specifically that you don't see the simpler and safer option until your original idea's cost you every penny in the bank or hospitalised several family members.

I was just climbing back into my hiding space when I heard the one thing I really didn't want to hear – a man's voice.

And it was asking me what the hell I thought I was doing.

'Just getting my bag, mate, what's it to you?' I asked him right back.

'Oh no you're not. You didn't come on that coach. You're stealing. SECURITY! Can we get some security over here, please!' the man yelled.

The blood drained from my face at a sickening lick when it dawned on me the horrific position I was in. Here I was, sandwiched between two borders, with armed coppers on either side, and I'd just been tumbled again.

Oh – my – fucking – God!

I pulled out my pistol in a flash and shoved it in his face in the hope of silencing him before he could bring the whole crew down on us but it was too late – half a dozen people popped up out of nowhere between the cars and lorries to clock me waving my weapon about and that was all they needed.

'Quick, get the police,' they all shouted in unison,

scattering to the four corners of the boat to spread news of me to everyone who would listen.

'Goody, we're in trouble,' I shouted into the coach, but Goody was already climbing out with the bags of money.

'I fucking know,' he growled in annoyance, and I was a bit cunted off that this annoyance seemed to be directed at me. 'Here's your bag.'

My original witness still hadn't budged so I whacked him across the head with the barrel of my gun – more out of a desire for payback than anything else – laying him out cold across the deck, then ran for the nearest set of stairs. Anyone in our way got out of it quick and we muscled our way past dozens of families and booze cruisers and into the ship.

I lost track of which floor we came out on. We found ourselves in a long corridor with shops and amusements on either side. People turned and stared at us, then someone started screaming and we had to barge some slow-moving bloke over onto his face to get through the doorway before him.

We ran up a corridor, no longer caring who we had to shove out of the way, and were horrified to hear urgent French voices charging up behind us.

'Milo, they're coming!' Goody screamed, so we veered right and took the next stairwell at a huff and a puff, pushing over two sophisticated Parisian types and scrambling over their faces to make it up to the next deck.

More startled screaming met us on this deck and I threw my head left and then right in a desperate attempt to spot a way out of this tightening noose, but none were apparent, so I headed left, as that seemed as good a direction as any.

'*Arrêtez-vous!*' came the voices behind us, and even though I didn't understand the words, I got the general gist.

'Jesus Christ!'

'Look out!'

'He's got a gun!'

'Arghh!' These words were more familiar to me as I'd been hearing them a lot lately, and they welcomed me and Goody into the aft bar as we crashed through the door, knocking half a dozen tables over and scrambling to our feet.

Immediately, everyone stood up to get a better look at what all the fuss was about so that every escape route was now well and truly blocked.

'GET OUT THE FUCKING WAY!' I screamed, lashing out at the nearest figure and trying to fight my way through the scrum.

'*Il n'y a pas d'issue!*' voices screamed behind us, and me and Goody turned to see two French police crash through the same door we'd just crashed through.

The bar was such pandemonium that they didn't spot us at first, but that all changed when Goody let off two shots in their direction, blasting out the windows behind them. The gunshots were insanely deafening, what with the enclosed space and all, so that it was a good three seconds before I got my hearing back, but when I did all I could hear was screaming. Everyone in the bar, it seemed, had their lungs open and turned up full volume. Luckily they'd all decided to do this from the comfort of the floor so that me and Goody were able to leap, stumble and blunder over a tangle of bodies and reach the door on the other side of the room.

'*Arrêtez ou on va tirer!*' one of the French cops yelled after me, pulling out his shooter, and I saw that we'd just upped the stakes considerably.

We ran down another short corridor and hit the stairs, then ducked down a floor and sprinted across to the other side of the ship. Our best hope was to try and lose them in the maze of corridors and decks and then see what we could do once we got to France.

We came out in a long winding corridor that spanned

the length of the ship and ran along it full pelt, jumping through doorways and over the bodies of yet more scream-ing shoppers, so that it felt like we were making good progress. It reality, though, we weren't at all. The French coppers behind us were keeping pace every step of the way and, worse still, we turned the corner straight into two more. I raised my gun and fired before I even knew what I was doing, and to my utter horror the nearest of the gendarmes went down clutching his shoulder.

Oh bollocks.

Goody did a 180 and fired yet another shot in our pursuers' direction in order to buy us a little more time, but all he got back for his troubles was two French bullets. The lead ricocheted off the ferry's steel and rattled around us like flies at a picnic, almost making me bring up Goody's Curly Wurly out of sheer terror, and I dived at Goody so that the pair of us tumbled down the adjacent stairwell.

When I landed at the bottom I sent another shot up the stairs to keep them at bay and fled in blind panic once again towards the rear of the boat.

'Get out the way! Get out the way!' I screamed at any-one and everyone as we rapidly ran out of space to run into.

'What are we gonna do?' Goody was blithering, but he was blithering at the wrong guy. I was all out of ideas and just running for my life.

At the next intersection we turned right and found our-selves back in the same corridor with all the shops and amusement arcades we'd run through already. This helped me out a tad because at least now I knew roughly where we were in the ship and which way we had to go to avoid the crowded bar area again. The next set of stairs headed up top so we took them at a leap and a bound, hoping to lose the cops in the bowels.

I wasn't sure what we were going to do once we got up

top, I was just hoping the sea air might help us conjure ourselves a way out of this nightmare.

We left the ship by a side door and legged it to the front. I guess the passengers must still have been unaware of the chaos we'd caused below because someone in a uniform shouted 'No running!' at us as we tore past him like our backs were on fire. I think he would probably have come on after us but suddenly there was no need – four coppers and three security bods were doing it for him.

That kind of put a dent in my plan about lowering one of the lifeboats and paddling the fuck out of here, so we were back to running around in circles. People stopped and stared as we raced past, confused, bemused and exhilarated as they saw someone's day unfold into a real fucking pain in the arse.

We clambered up one noisy set of tin steps and then up another, smacking our ankles, knees, toes, fingers and just about everything else that protruded from our bodies that brought a tear when you smacked it on various bits of the boat as we went.

'*Allez, allez, allez!*' the bastards on our arses were yelling at each other as they split up at each staircase and slowly, but surely, they were boxing us in for the final grab.

A mile or so straight ahead was land (probably France) and the boat started to veer to the left. I figured we were getting ready to dock and I figured once we did, a garrison of gendarmes would pour on board and kick the shit out of us (if we were lucky). There was no way we were going to be able to sneak out now because the port authorities would've been notified and nothing and nobody was getting off this boat without having a torch shone up it.

We jumped over a chain that seemed to be protecting a big empty area of the boat from the passengers and ran across to the other side. The cops behind us did the same thing, though rather worryingly there were now only two of them. Where had the rest of the bastards gone?

If they were waiting for us it was an even-way bet they'd have their shooters out and at the ready. Me and **Goody** still had ours in our hands and we made for inviting **targets** so I told Goody to sling his gun, sling it over the side and make sure the coppers behind us saw him do it. Goody was reluctant at first, but these were only the crappy old guns we'd bought off Len, we still had our police automatics in our bags. Probably a good idea not to get caught with them anyway, not unless we fancied being linked to every shooting in Moss Side that had taken place in the last ten years.

I launched my gun out to sea with a huge swing of the arm and Goody did likewise so that, to all intents and purposes, we were now unarmed. I just prayed that counted for something in *la France* and carried on running.

The other side of the boat was much like the side we'd just come from, only it had stairs going down where ours had gone up and the sea was somewhere else. Other than that, we knew what to expect and what to try and avoid smacking into, but did so anyway with unerring accuracy.

And this is where the last of our luck finally ran out. Waiting for us at the bottom of the second set of steps were our missing gendarmes. They were looking pretty smug about their cunning trap and pointed their guns at us shouting:

'*Il n'y a pas d'issue, vous feriez mieux d'abandonner!*' which I imagine means something along the lines of, '*We've got them, we're fantastic. Snails for everyone!*'

But they hadn't got us yet.

They were close, but others had been close too, and where were those cunts now? Where indeed?

See, there's something about looking at an enormously long stretch that can inspire people to incredible feats of desperation and stupidity. It's quite amazing what people are

capable of. Everyone's heard the stories about women picking up lorries when their silly fucking kids have got themselves trapped underneath them, and this is a similar sort of
desperation. It's also not something you want to get in the
way of.

I'm not talking about me, of course, acts of heroism aren't
really my cup of tea, I'm talking about Goody. See, there I
was, just skidding to a halt at the fifth from bottom step
when this great dopey blur whooshed past me on the outside and knocked all four coppers onto their arses. The
defective bastard dived straight into them, swinging, kicking
and biting as he went, so that they all scattered about on the
deck, leaving a little gap for me to leap through.

I landed on the other side and turned to help Goody, but
suddenly he had coppers all over him. The bastards were
systematically pinning him down limb by limb and our two
pursuers were just arriving on the scene as well. If he'd had
one or two coppers holding him down, I might've been
able to help out, but six? There was nothing I could do
short of getting myself pinned down next to him. It was a
hopeless situation. And I'd seen enough hopeless situations
in my life to know it. Goody looked up at me as I wobbled
over my options and his eyes told me to go. Maybe I was
just seeing what I wanted to see, because the fat selfish cunt
sure as fuck didn't say anything along those lines, so I did
the only thing I could do under the circumstances . . .

. . . and ran.

My two pursuers and one of the coppers who'd taken
out Goody broke off and came after me. They were maybe
two dozen yards behind me, but I soon stretched this lead
to three. I looked around, wondering why they were taking
their sweet merry time over my pursuit, and saw why. I'd
legged it so fast that I'd run straight past the last doorway
without taking advantage of it and now I was rapidly
running out of boat.

The coppers fanned out when they hit the open deck and blocked off my last exit, cornering me at the stern. Two of them had their guns out but had them pointed at the deck rather than at me, so I guess they could see I was unarmed.

'Put your hands in ze air,' one of them said, finally figuring out I couldn't speak French. 'Do it now!' he ordered, pointing the gun at my chest to emphasise the point. I did as he said and all the fight drained from my body. This was the moment I'd been dreading all these weeks. This was it. I was caught.

We'd come so close. So very, very close to getting away, but one silly mistake with the phone and that was it. Next stop prison.

For a very, very, *very* long time.

The other three coppers appeared behind my lot with Goody in cuffs. He looked at me completely forlorn and I looked at him. My coppers slowly and cautiously stepped towards me as if expecting me to blow up or something, and beyond them the crowd pressed against every railing, walkway and window to see the free cop movie.

Against one window I saw Brian. He looked absolutely horrified at what was going on, and probably thought all this was down to the fact that he'd stowed us away. I expect he thought he was next and was probably wondering how he could've been so stupid as to get himself mixed up in something so dumb.

I knew how he felt.

'Turn around,' the policeman told me, so I did as he said and turned to face the sea.

It was a lovely clear evening. The sun was low on the horizon but there was still an hour or two of daylight left. Seagulls were squawking around in circles overhead and the ferry was still turning. We'd be in France in less than ten minutes at this rate, and that would be the last time I'd get to feel the free open air on my face for a couple of decades. It wasn't fair.

It just wasn't fair.

But then there's something about looking at an enormously long stretch that can inspire people to incredible feats of desperation and stupidity. I know this to be true because I read it in a book somewhere one time.

Two feet to my left, within easy reaching distance, was an orange emergency box. In this box was a rubber ring. And in this rubber ring was a tiny, slim, small, minuscule, laughable chance that I might not go to prison for a very, very, *very* long time. It was such a ridiculously feeble long shot that it was almost non-existent. Almost. But then tiny, slim, small, minuscule, laughable, ridiculously feeble long shots are better than no shots at all, at least that's what I always say.

The coppers were still ten yards away and preoccupied with holstering their guns and pulling out their cuffs when I made a grab for the box. I yanked open the door and grabbed the ring. It was heavier than I'd expected and for one daft moment I wondered if the bastard would float. But then, that's just me. A bit stupid, I guess.

Before the coppers could yell at me to stop, I'd clambered over the railing and was looking down trying to spot a soft bit of sea. I allowed myself half a second's glance over my shoulder but cut this short when I saw three pairs of hands closing in fast.

Then I jumped.

I launched myself off the back of the boat with one great kick and plunged fifty-odd feet into the sea. I went straight under and would probably have kept on going all the way down to Davy Crockett's locker had it not been for my rubber ring. I'd looped my arms through it on the way down and hung onto it with my last remaining strength as it took me back up to the surface.

The moment I reached air again, I let out a squeal and a scream at just how cold the water was before getting on with the business of gasping for breath.

The boat was already twenty yards away by the time I found it again, and showing few signs of slowing down. Up on deck all six coppers and Goody were all looking down at me as I bobbed about in the wake, but their expressions soon faded as the boat carried them away.

Once I finally managed to get my arms and legs moving again, I clambered through the ring and started kicking out in the direction of France.

I wasn't sure I fancied my chances all that much, but then I'd been saying this for the last half a dozen weeks or so and no one had actually managed to feel my collar yet. I may've been in the water, a mile from the coast, with every copper and lifeguard scrambling to their boats to pull me out, but they hadn't got me yet. Me or my soggy hundred grand.

They'd got Goody, they'd got Patsy, they'd got Bob, Jimbo, Jacko and Norris, but they didn't have me. Not yet at least, they didn't. I still had a little lead over them and this was all I needed. This was all I ever needed.

Because it meant I was still running.

It meant I was still free.

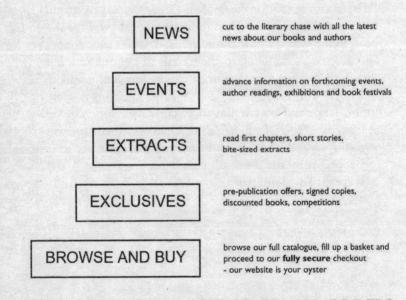